Found

Cinderella's Secret Witch Diaries

(Book 3)

Ron Vitale

Copyright © 2014 Ron Vitale

All rights reserved.

2nd Edition: February 2017

ISBN-13: 978-1544111537

ISBN-10: 1544111533

This book is a work of fiction. Names, characters, places and incidents are the product of the author's imagination or are used fictitiously. Any resemblance to actual events, locales or persons, living or dead, is coincidental.

Visit Ron Vitale's website at www.RonVitale.com

To Karen:

There are no guarantees.

Also by Ron Vitale

Lost: Cinderella's Secret Witch Diaries (Book 1)

Stolen: Cinderella's Secret Witch Diaries (Book 2)

Faith: The Jovian Gate Chronicles (Book 1)

The Jovian Gate Chronicles: Short Story Collection

Awakenings: A Witch's Coven (Book 1)

Betrayals: A Witch's Coven (Book 2)

Dorothea's Song

Dramatis Personae

Cinderella: Witch who has lost her powers and searches to find her daughter.
Charles Radley: American pioneer and husband to Virginia Radley.
Virginia Radley: American pioneer and wife to Charles Radley.
Martha Radley: Charles and Virginia Radley's ten-year-old daughter.
Ruth Radley: Charles and Virginia Radley's four-year-old daughter.
Sarah and Teresa Radley: Charles and Virginia Radley's eight-year-old twin daughters.
Jeremiah: Witch hunter who helps Cinderella to find her daughter.

Russia
Tsar Alexander I: Ruler of Russia who wishes to defeat Napoleon and save his country from Napoleon's invasion.
Veronika: Young Russian witch.
Mamochka Tatyana: Veronika's grandmother and powerful witch.
The Silver Fox: Faerie lord and Cinderella's mother's former lover.
Vladislav: An advisor to the Tsar and warlock.

France
Napoleon Bonaparte: France's emperor and powerful warlock.
Isabelle: Witch who helps Phoebe.
Phoebe: Cinderella's twelve-year-old daughter.

Otherside
Tristan: Faerie who guards Baba Yaga from entering our world.
Baba Yaga: Evil witch who is an old crone.

South America
Iara: Amazon witch.
Raga: Young tribal child.
Benjamin: An English officer.

Chapter 1

I stood at the edge of the hole and looked down. It was enormous, and with the waning light, I could not see how far down it went. My scarf blew in the wind and I pulled my coat tighter around me. Jeremiah walked over from the other side, more than several dozen feet away from me, and came to my side. "This is it, is it not?"

"Yes, it is."

He bent down to pick up a rock and then tossed it into the hole before us. The rock fell out of sight within seconds and we could not hear its hitting the ground. With the blowing wind, that did not surprise me.

"What would you like to do now?" He brushed the dirt off his hands and watched me closely.

I hid my feelings well from him, pushing them down deep. "I don't know yet. I need time to think."

"Maybe …"

"Don't say it." I cut him off and turned away from the hole in the ground.

"Cinder, please, listen." He approached me, but I would not hear any of what he had to say.

I went up to a tree and reached out to steady myself. Clenching my left fist out of habit, I focused and no magic remained. I could not sense Phoebe or even know if she still lived. I only had my mother's instinct to guide me and, so far, it had not served me well.

"Maybe it is time that we turn back?" There, he had said what was on his mind. He always did.

I clenched my left fist tighter and dug my nails into the palm of my hand. "No, I will not give up on Phoebe that easily. I can't do that."

"We have traveled across the ocean and spent months searching for this spot and now there's nothing here." He pointed out at the large hole in front of him. "Nothing has been here for a long time. The trail is cold. There is nothing for us here."

"I need some time to think." I turned away from the tree and walked back to the edge of the hole and, in frustration, I kicked some dirt into it.

"He is no longer here."

"But how is that possible? How could he have escaped?" I closed my eyes and took a deep breath. If I thought it would help, I would jump down into the hole and chase after him, but there were no guarantees. I remained quiet a moment or two more and then turned to him. His beard, thick and unkempt, had some gray in it and not just from the snow. "What do you think we should do?"

"We go back to Europe and face Bonaparte."

"I will not give up on her."

He edged closer to me and shook his head. "I did not say that. We go back and join the war and defeat the emperor."

"That is what he wants me to do. He wants me to come to him."

"But why stay here where there are no answers? The emperor is returned and his enemies need our help. If he's defeated, then we can make him tell us where Phoebe is. It is the only way."

I could see his point. "I don't disagree. Yet we've come so far only to see that the Silver Fox has escaped." I put my hands on my hips and glanced down into the hole. "I thought the Silver Fox was my best chance to find Phoebe quickly. I don't know how he could have escaped my prison spell."

He shook his head. "Quickly? We have traveled across the sea and through America until we found this spot. He is not here. It's time now to go back." He gestured at the hole. "I think he's left a clear sign that he's escaped the prison he was in. He is no longer here. We'll find nothing here."

"You think so much like a man." I turned away from him and then I knew. The answer came to me clear and simple. "Go back to Europe and face the emperor and he will defeat you. Victory cannot be had that way. His magic is too strong. Trust me, it is what he wants so desperately. He wants to meet us on the battlefield where he is invincible."

"Standing around here looking at a hole in the ground will not get us anywhere. We should go."

"Go back to Europe, if you must." I took a step forward, my mind made up. "Phoebe needs me and I will not give up on her."

Jeremiah stared at my feet and then looked back up at me. "What if she's dead?"

A thousand roiling emotions stirred up within me and I bit my tongue to hold back my tears. "She is not dead. I would know!"

He put his hand out to me. "It has been a long journey and we are both tired and cold. Come back and we can decide what to do in the morning."

I took all of him in and smiled. "Jeremiah, go back to Europe. Thank you for trusting me this far." I took another step forward and then went to jump into the hole before me. I closed my eyes and with a leap of faith, I willed myself to let go of all that I had known and to trust that this was the right path. For a split second, I could feel my body propelled forward, but then hands wrapped around my waist and I fell to the ground.

Jeremiah pushed me hard into the snow-covered earth. "Have you lost your wits?"

I struggled against him and tried to push him off. "I've lost my daughter," I cried out and rolled over, pulling him with me.

He forced his full weight on me and pinned my arms down. "This is not the way. We can find another path." His heavy breathing caused him to take a pause. "We can. Trust me."

I would not cry now in front of him. I willed it to be so. Instead I stopped fighting him. "Get off of me now."

"Do you swear that you will not do anything foolish?" He waited but held me firm.

What could I say to him? I looked away and broke eye contact with him.

"Swear it to me!" He held me down with all his force and his words washed over me and I ignored him still. "Why must you be so stubborn?"

I turned my gaze back to him. "Please, get off of me." My cold hard tone left no confusion in my intentions.

He pushed himself off the ground and stood between me and my goal. "Do not do this now. Please."

"I do not ask you to come with me." I pointed past him. "But that is where I must go."

He turned his face away from me and cursed at the ground. "Dammit, you are like a mule sometimes." Turning back to me, he clenched his jaw and I could see him settling his frame to prepare if I tried to run past him. "You do not know if the Fox is down there. He might have escaped and gone another way. Just because there's a hole in the ground does not mean that he went down there."

"I don't expect you to understand. I truly don't." I put my arms out to him, pleading. "But I have to go down there if it helps me to find Phoebe. I know that is where he went. I just know it."

"How are you so sure?" He eyed me up for a sign that I had not lost my mind.

"Because the Silver Fox left a big hole in the ground to gloat that he had escaped. He wants me to follow him. Trust me, I know him and this is his calling card."

"You don't know that for sure. Something else could have happened here."

I had one left card to play. "If you love me, then, please, let me go. This is something that I must do on my own."

I turned with quickness to my right and sprinted off. I ran as fast as I could, only needing a few moments to be ahead of him, and then I would jump into the hole in the ground and my fate would be sealed.

Jeremiah turned his body toward me and sprung to chase after me, but his left leg slipped out from beneath him. He stumbled for a moment, but that was all I needed. I ran past him and then jumped into the hole. If I were wrong, I would know sure enough. I heard him calling after me and for a second my body floated above the hole, the dark gaping wound in the ground, and then I fell. I knew I would have my answer soon. I closed my eyes and the rush of the wind surrounded me and a queasy feeling in my stomach consumed me as I fell. The fall had to be deep, deep into the Earth and then from there I would … My legs hit the water first and the shock came up all through me. The coldness of the water enveloped me and I heard nothing but the swirl of air bubbles around me. I closed my mouth and instinctively started to swim to the surface.

When I broke through to the surface, I could not stop my desperate grunt for air. I treaded water and could not see much in the near dark. The cold caused me to shiver and I could not see any passageway out. I floated on my back and could see the fading light as the sun continued to set. A feeling of stupidity washed over me and I swallowed my pride and yelled, "Help!"

I treaded water some more and tried again, "Jeremiah, can you hear me? I need help."

The sound of my voice echoed back to me and I could not see anyone at the top. The rush of excitement from my jump began to fade and the coldness of the water began to numb me. "Jeremiah, please, help! You were right and I was wrong."

I kept swimming, never a strong skill of mine, so I kept floating on my back and watching as the clouds drifted past the hole. I had no magic to escape, could not see a way out and the cold would soon have its way with me. Floating over to the portion of the wall where I had jumped, I tried to find purchase, but the smoothness of the rock left no handholds. I could not find anything to hold onto. Taking a deep breath, I dived back under the water and opened my eyes. I could only see the walls of the hole going downward with no cave or hidden passageway. Straight down below the drop continued and I could not see far into the darkness of the water. This would be my grave. I had not listened to Jeremiah and I would die here alone, in the water, where no one could hear me.

The sound of something hitting the water caught my attention and I came back up to the surface and on my right I could see Jeremiah had thrown rope down for me. An extra bit of the rope had hit the surface of the water and begun to unfurl, sinking into the deep.

"Thank you," I called up but could not see him or hear any response. That he had helped me was a good sign that he would still be talking to me. He probably had begun cursing me as he tied the rope to a tree so that he could pull me up. I shivered from the cold and took a deep breath and then swam over to the rope. My hands were numb and I found it difficult to wrap the rope around me, but I did my best. When I felt secure enough, I held the rope with both hands and tugged hard on it.

"I'm ready. Pull me up!" My voice echoed back to me and a few seconds later I felt a tug back.

I held on tightly with both my hands, having wrapped the rope around my waist as best I could, and positioned my legs against the side of the hole and waited. The first tug pulled my upper body out of the water and I braced my legs more firmly against the wall in front of me. I stopped moving and waited a few moments and then the rope moved upward again. Jeremiah must have made some sort of pulley system to gradually pull me up so that I would not slip back down and fall into the water. While I waited to be pulled to the top, I wondered if he would speak to me at all. I had pushed him too far this time and a man only has so much patience. He would not understand why I had needed to jump. He did not search for his daughter and continue to fail in finding her.

At around the halfway point, I looked back down and still could see nothing but water. My wishful thinking that the hole contained some secret appeared laughable now. A big tug on the rope broke me out of my daydreaming and I turned away, looking up. A few pulls later and I could almost see the top. The sky had turned gray from clouds moving in and it had begun to snow lightly. The sun had set and there was not much light left in the day. I would need to get out of my wet clothes and change into something dry. My body shivered uncontrollably and I hoped that Jeremiah could make a quick fire to help thaw me. Another big pull brought me within an arm's reach of the top and I held tightly to the rope. A few seconds later, another tug brought me over the lip of the hole and I rolled onto my side. I could hear the crackling of a fire nearby. I tried to roll over but could not. I could not stop shivering.

Arms wrapped around me and I was lifted up and placed gently next to the fire. Next a blanket covered me. Still I could not stop shivering. "Thank you."

"You're welcome, mon amie." The Silver Fox stood with his hands on his hips with a big smile on his face.

"Where's Jeremiah?" I tried to scramble up to my feet, but could not.

"Back in America, of course." He did not take the grin off his face. "Where do you think he would be?"

"Where am I?" I sat up and looked around. We appeared to be in a forest, but it was denser than what I had remembered. And the air smelled differently.

"You're not in America." I could see the enjoyment on his face and then I noticed his clothing. He wore a long coat and a strange hat with lots of fur. He held a bag in his hand and gave it to me. "I am going to get some more wood for the fire. Do you need help getting out of your clothes?"

I had imagined my facing the Silver Fox for many, many months and this conversation was not one I had ever expected. As hard as I tried to control my body, I could not stop shaking. I struggled and tried to take off my top, but could not.

He came behind me to help and I glanced back at him, being distrustful of him, but he had turned away as he pulled off my blouse and underclothes. The fire was so close to me on my right that I would have feared being burned if I didn't crave the heat so much. He wrapped my torso with a second blanket and then leaned me up against a rock. Pulling my boots off, he placed them by the fire so they would dry and then struggled to pull off my pants. He grabbed another blanket and threw it lightly over my legs and I tried as best I could to keep my dignity and take off the rest of my underclothes. The Silver Fox had turned away get me some more blankets. When I had finished undressing, I sat on a blanket and had wrapped myself tightly in two others.

The Silver Fox said not a word and went over to a pack and came back, handing me a small flask. "Take a sip."

I nodded and he helped me take the cap off and steadied my hand so that I could drink. The liquid, thick and warm, went down quickly. I expected it to be alcohol and for it to burn my throat, but it tasted like a beef broth. I swallowed more and my belly flooded with warmth. The fire crackled beside me and I watched the hot coals devouring the wood. This fire had been started a while ago. I turned to face him but he had gone back to his gear. Out of another pack he pulled out thick wool socks and another heavy blanket. He threw the blanket over me and then knelt before me, putting the socks on my feet. "You don't have any permanent damage. You'll be cold for a while, but I'll get you into some shelter as soon as you're dry."

"Thank you." I knew not what else to say. He had saved my life.

"Of course." He turned and put another log on the fire.

"I must admit that I'm a bit surprised." I looked at his white hair that peeked out from underneath the large hat he wore and he looked down, breaking eye contact with me.

"Twelve years is a long time to be trapped in the ground from the prison you put me in. For the first few years, I vowed to break out and kill you." He looked up and came in closer to me. "I wanted to tear you apart with my bare hands for what you did to me. But I could not stay angry all the time, and I realized that you had had no other choice. I had hurt you and my obsession in trying to bring your mother back had nearly ruined me. And then one day, a new memory suddenly popped into my head. Before you were born, your mother and I had a surprise visit from your future self. Napoleon came after you and we defended you."

"You remember all of that?" I had always wondered how my traveling through the dreamline would affect history. Now I knew.

"Yes, I remember seeing how scared you were and how I had come to your defense because I had always thought of you as my daughter. And when I saw how Napoleon wanted to hurt you, something in me broke and changed. I saw myself in him. I had that same anger and hatred and I came to accept that I had made great mistakes and hurt many people. I had lost control and nearly killed you. For many more years, I've been stuck in the ground, knowing that Napoleon still hunted you and I would have a choice to make one day."

I pulled the blanket closer around me and leaned even closer to the fire. Neither of us spoke for a while. I broke the silence finally and said, "How did you escape?"

He remained quiet for a moment and then said, "Two years ago, one side of the triangle prison you had put me in weakened. It took me a long time to gather my strength and break through the spell, but I did. Once free, I waited for you. I knew you would come."

I held his gaze and leaned in closer to him. "Why aren't you capturing me and bringing me to the emperor? He would reward you and you'd have your revenge against me."

"Yes, I've thought of that. I could do that if I wanted." He glanced away. "At times, I hated you more than I have ever hated anyone in my life. You could have brought your mother back for me. I could have had the happiness I so craved, but the natural order would have been broken and she didn't want to come back to me. She had moved on and I learned that I needed to as well. So I've made my choice. Crazy as I am with all my faults, I will help you—if you want me to."

I laughed. "I don't trust you." I pulled away from him. "You hurt me badly when we first met and broke a part of me."

"I cannot take back what I have done but only show you who I am now. But I understand your fear of me." He stood up and willed his left hand to light up with magic. "Though I am one of the last, I still have power where you have none." He tilted his head up and stared up at the dark, gray sky. The sun had fully set and darkness had begun to overtake what was left of the light. "Mab is gone as are most of my brothers and sisters. You have no power left and Napoleon looks to conquer the rest of the world. And I'll not stand for that. Before I fade away from this world, I will leave my mark. If you want me to or not, I'd rather throw my fate on your side than cast it with Napoleon."

"You could walk away and let us destroy each other and you'd be free of any mess."

He shook his head. "No, that's not my style. I would miss out on all the fun." A slow grin brought out a dimple in his right cheek. "I've changed, but not that much."

I smiled up at him. "I thought you'd say something like that. You do tend to like to be in the thick of things."

"Exactly." He bent back down and took a long stick to poke at the piece of wood he had thrown into the fire. He pushed it closer to the hot burning embers on the bottom and the wood caught up in a bright orange flame. "That is why I'm here. I'm going on a quest. It's been a long, long time since I've been on an adventure."

"You're on a quest?" I shivered and pulled the blankets tighter around me.

"And I want you to come with me on my journey."

I looked around and behind me I could see he had a small tent close by but I could not see anything besides the hole in the ground, trees and lots of snow. "Where are we now?"

The Silver Fox took a deep breath and then exhaled. "We are in the heart of Russia and I'd like for you to join me on my adventure." He picked up a pair of woman's boots and handed them to me.

"Tell me about this quest of yours." I accepted them and slipped them on.

"Get warm first and then we'll talk." He pointed over to the tent. "I set out some warm clothes for you."

"Thank you." I walked over and went inside the tent and changed into the clothes he had left out for me. "Where are you going?"

I heard no response from him. I finished dressing and then put back on the pair of boots he had given me. They fit perfectly. I brushed my long hair back, having dried it as best I could, and put on a hat he had left out for me. When I came back outside, I headed over to the fire.

The Silver Fox glanced over at me and nodded. "You look warmer. Good."

"You didn't answer me." I faced him with the fire between us. "Where are you headed?"

"I head to Moscow to see the Russian emperor and to convince him that he must help us defeat Napoleon."

I took in his response and asked, "Will you help me get my daughter back?"

"Yes, I will. Your coming with me to Moscow will be your best bet to get her back."

"Do you know where she is?" I wrapped my arms around me tight and leaned in to feel the fire's warmth.

"No, but Bonaparte has her. And if we convince the Tsar to join our side you will get your chance to get her back." He stared into the fire and said no more.

"And what about Jeremiah?"

"You mean the witch hunter?" He poked a log in the fire.

"Yes, where is he?" I listened but could not hear anyone calling from the hole in the ground. Only the fire crackled and the wind spoke with softness and light.

"He is where he is. I'm not keeping track of him. He is of no concern to me." He looked up from the fire and for a moment I could see a devilish glint in his eye. "But you matter to me and I have made an effort to help you." He stopped poking at the fire and said, "I need your help. Will you come with me?"

"But what about Jeremiah?" I leaned in closer to the fire.

"Forget about the witch hunter. He will be fine. Let him prove himself without you."

That did not sit well with me. "He has been faithful to me and has helped me on my journey."

"Then let him go and see what becomes of him. We have another journey to go on and he would only get in the way."

"Why do you not want him here with us?"

"It's simple, my dear. You love him and I want time alone with you. He would only muck things up and I'm not overly fond of him."

A gust of wind blew hard through the area and the fire flickered, but remained strong. "You have never met him."

"But I have watched him from afar and I know his kind. He and I would not do well together."

"I do not like this. I want him here with me. I don't trust you."

"It is good that you don't trust me." He came to my side and offered me the flask again that contained the warm broth. "He's still not coming here. Those are my terms."

"And if I disagree?"

He pointed to the hole. "You can always go back." He cracked a sly grin and paused a moment. "Though I'm not quite sure that the portal works both ways. I guess you would have to find out."

He held the flask out at me, shook it a bit and waited for me to respond. I thought a moment and knew what I must do. I took the flask from him rather roughly and then drank some. The broth did feel good, warming me up a bit. "I'll stay."

Taking the flask back, he smiled. "Good, I thought you might say that." He turned away from me and added, "I'll make us some dinner and then we'll get settled for the night. It'll be cold later and we'll need a good night's rest for the journey ahead. We've a long walk tomorrow."

I nodded and kept quiet, hoping that Jeremiah would forgive me. I didn't know what game the Silver Fox played, but it might be best to leave Jeremiah out of it. Whatever the Silver Fox's intentions, I would find out soon enough, and if it would get me closer to finding Phoebe, then I really did have no choice. It's what I had to do.

* * *

"Dammit!" Jeremiah pounded his fist into the ground and then scrambled over to the edge of the hole and looked down. "You couldn't wait and listen to me, could you?" He hung over the edge as much as he could, trying to see Cinderella but he could not see or hear anything from her descent.

A light snow started to fall and he lay there for a moment looking into the dark hole in the ground. He heard the breath that he took and the wind blowing around him, but nothing else. He pushed himself up and then ran hard, trying to not lose his footing and fall. After several minutes of hard running, he saw the wagon and the horses. Mr. Radley sat in the driver's seat, smoking a pipe. He heard Jeremiah running toward him and called out, "Is everything okay?"

"I need rope and lots of it."

Mr. Radley jumped into the back of the wagon and came out a few seconds later with a large amount of rope. "What happened?"

Jeremiah shook his head and said, "Sometimes I wonder what the hell is going through her head."

"Is she hurt?" Mr. Radley's expression turned into one of concern.

"We found a damn hole in the ground and she jumped in. I don't have time to explain now. Just come follow me." Jeremiah turned away and ran back the way he had come.

Mr. Radley slung the rope over his shoulder and then ran as fast as he could after Jeremiah. After a couple of minutes of hard running, Jeremiah stopped and helped Mr. Radley tie the rope around the nearest tree to the hole. He made a slipknot around the tree and gave the rest of the rope to Jeremiah. "Have you heard from her at all?"

"Charley, I wish I did. She ran around me, jumped in and I never heard her hit the ground." He shook his head and then said, "I think I'm half-crazy for following her around the world."

Mr. Radley laughed. "No, you are not crazy, you are simply in love."

Jeremiah laughed. "Is it that plain to see?"

Charley handed over the rest of the rope and smiled. "Just get down there and see if she's okay."

Jeremiah hefted the rope on his shoulder and allowed much of it to drag behind him. "I don't know if I'll yell at her or hug her when I find her." He stopped and searched for some good footing at the edge of the cliff. "You ready?"

Charley grabbed the extra rope around the tree and prepared to lower Jeremiah down the huge hole. "I am ready. Take it slow and you will be fine."

Testing the strength of the rope, Jeremiah nodded. "Here I go."

Charley gave a bit of rope to Jeremiah and he began to slowly climb down the cliff. At first his descent was a bit bumpy, but Charley steadied himself and continued to feed rope to Jeremiah. On the way down, Jeremiah used his legs against the cliff wall and climbed down cautiously to make certain that he would not fall. Minutes later he saw the ground below. The fall seemed a lot shallower than he had thought.

"I reached the bottom," Jeremiah called up and then after a few minutes he called up again. "Hey, Charley, I hit the bottom."

He walked around, looking for Cinderella and in the center he saw a woman's hat. Jeremiah ran over to it and stopped. He fell to his knees and brushed against the ground but it was solid. He saw no sign of Cinderella. No blood or any indication that she had been here. "Charley, I found her hat!"

He picked it up and beneath it he saw a large white envelope. In clear cursive, his name appeared across the front. He ripped open envelope and found a sheet of paper with a note on it that read:

Dear Jeremiah,

Cinderella has not been harmed and she is in my care. I know that you do not trust me, but I will protect her and help her to the best of my ability. Unfortunately, she is no longer in America but has decided to stay in Russia as we prepare to fight against the emperor.

I have seen how great your powers of tracking are. As a witch hunter, I challenge you to track a witch who's lost her powers. I wonder if you can. I guess we shall see, won't we? Good luck on your journey and to help you, I've given you a little head's start.

Yours with a twinkle in my eye,

The Silver Fox

Jeremiah ran over to where he had left the rope and stopped in disbelief. He could stand up on his toes and reach the top of the cliff. When he glanced up, he could see a dark sky filled with thousands of stars. "Charley, can you hear me?"

"Yeah, of course I can." Charley ran to the hole in the ground and stopped suddenly. "What the hell happened?"

He looked down and could see Jeremiah only a few feet down below. Jeremiah reached up and put his hands out. "I don't think we're in America any longer."

Charley squatted down and grabbed Jeremiah's hand and pulled him out of the hole. Jeremiah patted Charley on the back and then stood still and listened.

"Where do you think ..."

"Be quiet." Jeremiah waved Charley off and continued to listen. From off to his right, a loon flew down from the sky, lit by the light of the moon and landed in a river he could barely see ahead. The bird dipped his head into the water and then on coming out shook it with great vigor. Moonlight reflected off the water and as though it knew it was being watched, the loon turned toward them and then flew off again. Jeremiah watched the bird fly away. "I have never seen a species like that."

"Neither have I." Charley lost the bird in the darkness.

Jeremiah crouched down to the ground, closed his eyes and put his ear to the ground. He concentrated while Charley kept watch. "Jeremiah, I think ..."

Without speaking, Jeremiah again held up his arm to silence him. Keeping his eyes closed, he said, "I cannot sense her at all." He stood up and brushed the snow off of his coat. "I am not certain where we are."

Charley pointed at the moon. "I think we have traveled far. Look at the path of the moon. Minutes ago the sun had set and darkness began to fall, but the moon was not to come up for many hours yet."

Jeremiah looked up at the stars but the moonlight washed out much of what he could see. "I think you are right. We are a long way from America."

Charley walked past him and stared off into the dark forest. "Would I be right in guessing that our wagon and horses didn't make the trip?"

Jeremiah knelt in the snow and exhaled. "I found a letter from the Silver Fox down at the bottom." He handed the envelope over to Charley. "I doubt he left us our horses and wagon."

Charley opened the envelope and held the letter up to the moonlight. The spidery penmanship seemed to glitter in the light. He read the contents quickly and then put the letter away. He handed the envelope back to Jeremiah and took a few steps toward the river ahead. "How are we ever going to get home?"

Jeremiah followed his friend and said, "I'm sorry." He reached out to stop Charley from going any farther. "I did not mean to get you involved in all of this. With Ginny with child and the girls, I never meant for you to go on some crazy adventure with me."

Charley put both his hands in his pockets and stared up at the moon. "I know that. I do. I need to think about one thing right now and that's simply on how to get home."

"I understand. I do. Without much money or a sense of where we are, I think our best chances are trying to find the Silver Fox and Cinderella. If he could take us away from America so easily, he can get us home."

"What if it's all a trick and he just wants to have us chase after him and then we're trapped here? I have to get home as quickly as I can. My wife and children need me." Charley glanced up at the moon and put his hands in his coat's pockets.

"I need you to trust me." Jeremiah put his hand on Charley's shoulder. "I'll do everything I can to get us home quickly. But I've dealt with witches and faeries all my life, and I know that will be our best bet. What do you say?"

Charley kept quiet for a moment and then said, "The faster we find the Silver Fox and Cinderella, the better."

"Thank you." Jeremiah shook Charley's hand and smiled.

"Where do you think we should head?"

Jeremiah listened to the sound of the water flowing past them. He could see rocks ahead, and though cold, parts of the river had not frozen. He looked past the river and far off he spotted a thin column of smoke in the air. "Let's head there." He pointed and said, "Looks like a small house or hut."

Charley squinted and it took him a few seconds but he finally saw the smoke rising from the chimney as well. "You lead the way and I will keep an eye out from behind us."

Together they trudged through the snow and had to stop every few minutes when a strong gust of bitter wind blew at them. Charley pulled his hood over his head and turned away from the blowing snow. A few seconds later the wind stopped and Jeremiah turned around to him and asked, "You okay?"

"I just wish I would have packed heavier clothes." He shivered and then stopped, pointing to a light coming from the tiny house across the river. "Do you see that?"

"Yes, I do. That's good news for us. If we can convince the owner that we're not bandits, we might have a place to stay tonight." He sped up and in a few minutes came to the river's edge.

A few yards downstream Jeremiah saw an old rickety bridge that crossed the river. Charley led the way and Jeremiah followed, watching behind them to ensure that no one followed them. Another gust of wind caught them off guard and they huddled close together and watched the snow blow across the ice that stretched across a portion of the river. Together they finished the crossing and headed up the riverbank.

Jeremiah ran to the top and stood still. He threw off his hood and sniffed the night air. "Do you smell that?"

"I don't smell anything." Charley finished the climb and inhaled deeply. "Wait, what is that?" He scrunched up his nose and then coughed into his hand.

"Witch's brew." Jeremiah put his hood back up and headed toward the dilapidated house ahead. In the moonlight, he could see a broken fence surrounded the house along with chipped or missing shingles. "We should be careful."

"I'm not too fond of witches." Charley glanced around to make certain no one stood behind him. "Of course, I don't consider Cinderella a witch, but you know what I mean."

"You're lucky she isn't here. She would have had something to say about that." Jeremiah smiled and he turned back to the house. "Let's try to look inside before we knock on the front door."

Charley pointed at the broken fence. "If you think there's a witch in there, do you think we should hang back here and announce ourselves first?"

"We'll be fine." He took a few steps forward and stopped. He held up his hand and then knelt in the snow. "Look."

"What is it?" Charley put his hand into the footprint in the snow that Jeremiah had found.

Jeremiah moved his hand forward and pointed. The moonlight sparkled off of the snowy tracks. "An old woman lives here. Here is where her cane helped to balance her." He kept low and inched forward.

Charley came close behind him and whispered. "I think I hear something."

Jeremiah headed to the nearest window and tried to peek in behind the shutters. He pulled the shutter back a few inches and could see a wood stove inside. A large metal pot with a lid that jiggled and had begun to bubble over was all he could see. "Maybe it's not a good idea that we came here. We might want leave now."

He pushed the shutter back into place and backed away slowly. "Charley?"

No one answered him so he spun around with his pistol drawn. Charley had vanished. Jeremiah edged forward and made his way to the front of the house. Still he could not find his friend. He glanced down and could no longer see Charley's footprints in the snow.

The door to the small house suddenly opened slowly. It creaked as it opened and a warm and inviting light streamed forth from inside. "Hello?"

No one answered. Yet from behind a musket muzzle jabbed him in the back. He froze and heard a woman standing behind him speak quickly in a language he did not understand. She pulled the musket away from his back and then jammed it again against his back, pushing him forward. She took the pistol from his hand and pushed him forward again.

Jeremiah held his hands up and walked inside the house. "I get it. I get it. Ease off on the musket."

The woman shouted something incomprehensible and then laughed, following him inside. So far his luck today hadn't gone well and he hoped that tomorrow, if he lived to see it, would be a better day.

Chapter 2

I opened my eyes and saw the Silver Fox staring at me. Disoriented from just waking up, I recoiled back from him to the far side of the tent. He did not move, watching me in absolute stillness with his golden colored eyes. We had moved the tent closer to the fire before going to bed so flickering light cast odd shadows on the right-hand side of the tent. Still he did not move and as I came more to my senses, I struggled to wake and asked, "Why do you stare at me?"

He smiled and his teeth, perfect white, stood out in the semi-darkness. "I look at you, of course."

"You're frightening me. Please, stop." I pulled the blanket up around me, and even though fully clothed, I thought he looked through me into my soul.

He blinked and then relaxed a bit, leaning back against some pillows he had propped up into the corner of the tent. "I tried to escape that hole in the ground that you had put me in for years, but nothing I did ever made a difference. Do you know what made me not go insane that first year?"

I began to doubt my agreeing to stay with him. I scanned the tent, looking for a weapon, but my fists and legs would be my best options. "I'm not so certain that you're not a bit touched."

He laughed and put his head to the side and still stared at me with great intensity. Then he sprang forward and came quite close to me. "I remembered your mother and all the good times that she and I had. I remember how we would sing together and we would be in such a state of joy. But none of that mattered while I was in the ground trapped. Then it came to me, simple and clear. I could hear the birds above me and the wind with rain falling from the sky. I had found the answer and no one could teach it to me." He pointed at me and pointed his finger at my heart. "Have you found that answer yet?"

I brushed his finger away and sat up. "Back away." I clenched my fist and held it before me. "You do not want to test me."

He grinned again. "But I do. I truly, truly do. Where we go, you will need all of your wits about you. Are you ready for the journey?"

He backed away like an animal still keeping his eyes on me. "I wonder."

"I am not sorry for imprisoning you. You needed to be stopped." I came forward and put up my fists. "I will fight you again if I need to. I will not falter. I must go on. I must."

"You put up a good front, truly you do." He raised his left hand and turned it over as though he held a large goblet. His hand began to glow with an eerie blue light. "But you are afraid and that is good. Your fear will cleanse you."

I could feel my heart rate increasing and I prepared myself for what would come next. I had trusted in him, a half-crazed faerie, but in my desperation I had no one left to trust. Sometimes I had trouble thinking with clearness. "I must find my daughter. You can do whatever you want with me and I will help you on your quest, but I must find her. I had abandoned her and I will pay for my neglect."

I cannot describe the complex emotions that erupted on his face. He rushed at me and I swung my fists at him, but missed. He had somehow passed me and now leaned up against me from behind. He did not touch me but was close enough to whisper in my ear. "No, no. Don't beat yourself so. I will help you find Phoebe. I will."

I could not hold back my tears. I sobbed and put my hand over my mouth and allowed myself to cry.

"Shhh, it is all right. It is all part of my plan. We will go see the Russian emperor and that will be our first step to find your daughter. I promise."

"I miss her. I will do anything to find her." I sniffled and wiped my nose on the blanket.

"You will not need to. No matter what you think of me, I'm not a monster."

I turned and smiled through my tears. "No, you're just a half-crazed faerie."

He laughed and then waved his hands before him like a magician. "That I am."

The fire outside flickered low and I kept quiet a moment and we listened to the embers hissing as snow fell on them. "I can no longer sense her in the world. With my magic gone, I am useless and have no means to find her. You know why I've come to you for help. You do know, don't you?"

"You were pregnant when I captured and possessed you. You know that I spoke to her when she was in your womb so I know her intimately."

"She is my daughter and I am Mab. She is the first truly born half-faerie, half-human child conceived in love."

"When I first saw you, I was amazed at how much you looked like Queen Mab when she was young. But all of your mannerisms and turns of phrase are so uniquely yours. I don't know how she did it, but she created a copy of herself but all of your essence is separate and different. You, Phoebe and her children to come will be a new path for our kind. We will live on."

"If I find her."

"When you find her. When." The Silver Fox lit his hand with magic and outside the fire rose in intensity. He concentrated and then withdrew his magic. "I have one question to ask you and then I will leave you alone to get some sleep as we've a long journey ahead."

I faced him and asked, "What do you want to know?"

"How did you not go insane when Henri abandoned you with child and left you for your friend?"

He got to the core of me with that question. The secret that I had not shared with the world, but was so crucial for me. I thought a moment and then said, "Do you want the truth from me or the answer most people want to hear?"

"I want the truth. The whole truth. The truth that kept you up at night with worry and doubt. I want to know the real answer."

"Then I will tell you." In a way, he and I were family being faeries together, and we would need to trust each other on the journey ahead. "For ten years, I never let him go. I used my magic to travel back in the dreamline and relive my time with him. I hid in the past and even tried to recreate new moments with him disguised as other women. I gave all of myself to him and although he simply used me, I did not care. I felt love. I craved it. I was obsessed with it." I smiled then and ran my hand through my hair breaking eye contact with him. "When he and I met in the present, I saw him for what he truly was. And then I saw what I had become. I had built him up so big in my mind, my love for him could not be vanquished or destroyed. My love would climb mountains and I could overcome any challenge, but he did not truly love me. And I saw that. I realized it and saw the little thing that I had become. And I broke inside."

"Yes, yes, I know that feeling." He put his hands together. "What did you do then?"

"The simplest thing." For once, the warmth in my heart came true to me and I smiled with tears in my eyes. "I chose to let him go. I made the choice. I stopped chasing him and trying to make him be something that he wasn't. I let him go and accepted my mistake and how I had tried to use my love for him to complete me and solve all of my own problems. How messed up I was. How broken and alone. But that was okay. I would be okay. I simply let him go."

"Exactly." He clapped his hands and said, "Freud would be so proud of you!"

"Who?" I questioned his sanity again.

"Someone who isn't born yet. Do not fret." He leaned forward and pretended to pat me on the arm, but did not touch me still. "And may I ask one more question?"

"Yes, but I am tired."

"I will be brief." He leaned in close and turned his head up to look me in the eyes. "And why are you truly here now with me?"

And so there it was. He tested me. "I want to find my daughter."

"And?" He made a come hither motion with his hands. "Let me hear it. Come on."

"I want my magic back." I faced him and did not turn away, letting him see into me.

"Ah, that is what I wanted to hear. The truth. The full truth."

"Can you unlock my magic for me?" I waited and hoped beyond hope that he could.

He held my gaze and searched my face for an answer to a question I did not know and then said, "No, I cannot." He sat back up and then brushed his hands together. "But I know who can …"

* * *

Napoleon put his left hand inside his jacket and waited for Phoebe to wake. He leaned back in his chair and watched as the beam of sunlight nearly touched her face. He expected that when the light did shine on her cheek that she would wake. A minute passed and then another and Phoebe stirred and opened her eyes, looking a bit disoriented. She could not remember her surroundings, sat up in bed and turned toward the light. "Mama?"

"She is not here. You have been asleep for a long, long time so I want you to listen to what I have to say."

"How long have I been asleep?"

"Two years," Napoleon said.

"Where is my mother? Why do you have me here with you?" She rushed at him and held her left hand out before her and then stopped.

"My magic. It's gone." She stared at her hand and then closed her eyes, digging deep to awaken her magic and unleash it on him, but no energy came to her.

Napoleon laughed and then watched her recoil from him. He pointed with his right hand to a table next to him. "There is some breakfast for you. I've sustained you with my magic during your long sleep, but I would think you would be hungry."

Phoebe kept herself covered with the blanket and reached for a glass of water and drank a few sips. "Why am I here?"

"I have news that you will be glad to hear." He leaned forward and the chair creaked slightly from the readjustment of his weight. "My grand army and I head off to conquer Russia and now I have to decide what to do with you."

"Are you going to let me go? I'll head back to find my mother and I'll leave Europe. I just want to go home." She brushed her unkempt hair away from her face. "Please, let me go."

"If you would give me what I want, I could let you go. But in your sleep you resist me and are more resilient than I had expected. I overcame Mab sooner than you." He sighed and stared down at the marble floor. "I am a patient man and am not unkind, but I cannot let you go yet. First, I need you to give me your magic."

He stood and walked toward her with both hands in his pockets and leaned over her. She pulled back farther from him and crouched into the one corner of her bed. "I cannot give you my magic because I do not know how to do that."

"I have told you that I am patient. I will wait and so shall you." He sat down on the bed and turned away from her to look out the window. He could see a flurry of activity outside in the courtyard. Soldiers carried out his orders and had begun the preparations for the long journey ahead. "Do you wish to know why you cannot use your magic to escape?" He spoke the words slowly so that she could understand his French.

"You have some power over me." She showed her left hand and clenched it tight. "I cannot even feel my magic inside me. It is as though all my powers are asleep."

Napoleon leaned toward her and gently pushed her back with a finger. "That is correct. You are controlled here and your magic will not come to your aid. But if you were to surrender it to me, that would be a different story."

She brushed his hand away and began to sob. "But I don't know how."

"I will not harm you, but you will also not see your mother again until you give your power to me." He turned away and stared out the window at the activity outside. They could hear commands being given to the soldiers.

"How am I to do that if I cannot use my magic?"

Napoleon smiled and pulled away from her like a snake. "You will find a way. You will if you truly want to. But before I go, I want you to know of my plan. I have brought law and justice to the French empire and will strive to my last breath to champion my people. Your magic could help speed along my plans. With Mab gone and your mother without her powers, there is no one to resist me. And why should they? I do not rule like a tyrant. The people love me and I love them." He stood and walked to the window to get a better view of his troops outside, watching them load carts of supplies. "I wanted you to know that you will be watched and guarded day and night, but will not be harmed. You will never be able to escape and your magic will remain closed off to you until you will it to me. No matter how long and far your mother searches she will never find you. But if you surrender your magic to me, I will release you."

Phoebe clenched her jaw and fought hard to keep her emotions in check. She faced him and said, "But I already told you, I do not know how to give you my magic."

"Then learn how to do so. I will give you some time to consider, but my patience will only last so long." He clenched his fists and advanced a step, but then held back. "Do you understand?"

She nodded in silent agreement and watched the emperor turn away. But a small voice inside her, a vestige of her mother's influence, caused her to call after him. "Monsieur?"

He stopped to listen. "Oui?"

"You mentioned Mab. What happened to her?"

"She is gone and I am changed. Forever changed." He looked back over his shoulder and added, "But aren't we all?" He then turned away and walked out of the room and she heard the lock go in place on the door.

A few minutes later a maid brought in clean clothes and a towel and placed them at the bottom of her bed and left without speaking to her or making eye contact. Phoebe climbed out of bed and shivered from the cold floor. Surprisingly, her arms and legs did not ache or bother her from lack of use. She did feel tired, but the emperor's magic had kept her safe while she had been asleep. She sat down at the table and ate her breakfast in silence. When she finished, she waited a while to see if the maid would return and then rushed over to the spot where Napoleon had stood by the window. She leaned close to the glass and pressed against the bottom right-hand pane about the size of her hand. The pane of glass popped out and she moved it to the side.

In the courtyard below, men busied themselves with packing and preparing for the long march to Russia. Using caution, she glanced behind her and heard no one coming into the room. She put her left pointer finger out into the open air and closed her eyes. The March air still had a chill to it. She closed her eyes and concentrated, letting her mind wander into parts unknown. Energy coursed through her and she could see far into distant lands. A touch of cold came over her and she shivered. Snow. Definitely, lots of snow and wind. The tip of her finger lit up in the smallest of ways and she willed her magic to find release.

From lack of use, the magic flowed out of her in tiny wisps and sought flight like a baby bird. Invisible and cloaked in the upmost of secrecy, Phoebe's message flew high up into the air and then drifted off on its long journey. She pulled her finger back inside and replaced the glass pane. Walking over to her dresser, she sat in front of the mirror and brushed her unkempt hair. It would not do to look so bedraggled as though she had been caught out in the spring rain. She would need to work on her appearance and prepare for seeing her mother again. Soon the day would come and they would be together. With methodical intent, she brushed her long hair out, over and over, untangling the worst parts. She smiled into the mirror and knew that soon she would be free.

Outside in the hallway, Napoleon had taken his glove off his right hand and watched it glow in a pinkish light. Hope was a powerful tool and he knew that without hope there would be no reward. As Phoebe's magic faded off, the light surrounding his hand vanished and he smiled. His plan was taking much longer than he had anticipated, but, in the end, he would succeed. No one would be hurt and the prize would be there for the taking. He put his glove back on and signaled to the maid. She bowed to him and he walked over, knowing that all went according to his plan. His empire stretched throughout most of Europe and soon Russia would be his as well. Order would reign and the world would be in a better state. He could not keep a smile off of his face as he walked away. He loved the springtime.

* * *

  Jeremiah kept his hands up in the air and walked through the doorway into the house. A large black pot boiled over and the smell in the room reminded him of sauerkraut. He saw no sign of Charley, but a large elderly woman stood before him with a long wooden spoon in her hand. He was shoved again from behind by the young girl with the musket. He took a few more steps into the room and said to the old woman, "I do not mean you harm. My friend and I are lost and need your help."
  The old woman turned away from him and went to stir the foul smelling ingredients in the large pot. The young woman behind him spoke a flurry of words in a language he thought Russian and the old woman ignored her, but continued to stir. When finished, she put the spoon down and faced Jeremiah.
  "Sit." Her thick Russian accent confirmed their whereabouts.
  The young woman behind him pushed him toward a chair at the table and he sat down.
  "You want dinner?" The old woman wiped her hands on a towel she had thrown over her shoulder.
  "Yes, please." Jeremiah folded his hands and felt the young woman behind him take his other pistol from off his back holster. She walked around him and he saw her put his guns down on a counter. She then stood next to the old woman and kept the musket pointed at him. Her dark hair was tied up in a bun and she wore plain clothes, wearing a coat over her dress. Seeing her in the light for the first time, Jeremiah was struck with how beautiful she was and young.
  The old woman dished out a bowl of stew for him and placed it in front of him. She handed him a spoon and asked, "Would your friend like some, too?"
  Jeremiah glanced around the room. "What friend?"

"The one who stands at the back window and looks in on us." The old woman pointed and Jeremiah could see Charley's profile by the back window.

"Charley, she sees you. Come to the front door." Jeremiah folded his hands on the table and remained calm. "We're both lost and mean you no harm."

Charley walked into the small house and the young woman aimed her musket at him and motioned for him to sit down at the table net to Jeremiah.

"Thanks for coming to rescue me," Jeremiah said as Charley sat down.

"Looks like my attempt at stealth needs some work." He leaned back in his chair and asked, "May I have some of the stew?"

Jeremiah rolled his eyes at his friend and smiled. "Truly, we're not here to cause any trouble."

The young woman leaned over to the elderly one and they spoke to each other quickly. The old woman pointed at Jeremiah and asked, "My granddaughter thinks you are here to steal from our land. Is that true?" Her thick accent made her English difficult to understand.

"I have told you the truth. We are lost and need help." Jeremiah saw that she did not seem convinced so he continued. "We were in America and looked for a friend of ours who had fallen into a deep hole. When we went to rescue her, we came out here."

The young woman asked a question and the old woman held up her hand. "You speak of magic?"

"Yes, I do." He put his hands out to her and said, "You are a witch and we ask for your help."

The old woman stared at him and tried to read his face. "Are you a hunter?"

Jeremiah glanced at Charley and then back at the women. "Yes, I am, but I am not here for you. I look my friend. She is lost and we search for her. Have you seen her?"

"No, we see no one but you two." She came forward and placed another bowl of stew before Charley. "I am Mamochka Tatyana and my granddaughter is Veronika." She pushed down Veronika's musket and said, "Welcome to our home."

Charley looked to take Jeremiah's lead in answering. They exchanged a glance and Jeremiah nodded at his friend. "My name is Jeremiah. Charley and I do not wish to intrude on you and your granddaughter but could we stay the night? If you have a barn, we would be happy enough to just find a place out of the cold."

Tatyana tapped Veronika on the shoulder and she put the musket down in a corner of the room. When she returned, she went over to the stove and poured some tea from a black kettle into several cups. Putting the four cups on a tray, she brought the drinks over and served everyone. Tatyana sat down and put her one leg out and started massaging it. "I detected no magic from your journey. You have come far if you are from America."

Charley leaned forward on the table and chanced to ask, "What country are we in?"

Veronika sat down across from Jeremiah and answered in perfect English, "You are in Russia."

"You speak English?" Charley asked with interest and crossed his arms over his chest.

"Of course I do."

"Why did you pretend you didn't?"

"I wanted to make certain you weren't here for any trouble." She sipped some tea from her cup. "Treasure hunters have sought us out over the years and we have had to be careful."

Jeremiah put his tea down and asked, "Why do you trust us?"

Veronika glanced at her grandmother. "She trusts you, I do not."

Tatyana made a scolding sound. "Be kind. They are not here to harm us."

"How do you know that? He has admitted that he's a hunter." Veronika put her hands around her cup of tea and took another small sip. She did not look down but held her gaze, waiting to see if Jeremiah or Charley would make a move against them.

"Neither of us have come here to cause you trouble. We are lost and will be on our way in the morning." Charley nodded in agreement.

"I simply want to find our friend and then get home to my wife and daughters." He took a sip of the tea and relished in its warmth. "We did not choose to come here."

Mamochka Tatyana banged the table and nearly knocked over her cup of tea. "They are the ones that I have foreseen. You must go with them."

Veronika spoke in her native tongue and Mamochka Tatyana shook her head. "No, you must decide if you are ready and what path you will take. Will you stay here with me or head on the adventure laid out before you?"

Jeremiah glanced over to Charley and warned him to stay quiet with a look.

"They are men." Veronika's thick accent added a twisted and dark implied threat to her words.

"And you are a young woman who is a witch. The world calls you on this journey. My time for adventures is done. Yours is yet to begin." She sipped her tea and turned to Jeremiah. "We have some supplies here for you both to take. I will help you both and in the morning you will go."

"But where are we to go?" Charley looked around the room, hoping one of them had a compelling answer. When no one spoke, he said, "We don't know which way to go or where we are."

Mamochka Tatyana asked, "Is the friend you search for a witch who has lost her magic?"

Jeremiah could find no reason not to admit the truth. "Yes, we search for my friend Cinderella. Do you know of her?"

Mamochka Tatyana closed her eyes and then shook her head. "No, I do not." She sipped her tea and then nodded. "Yes, yes, I know where she would be taken to though."

"Where?" Jeremiah tried to hide his enthusiasm but did so poorly. He leaned forward in his chair and waited for the answer.

"To see Baba Iaga kostianaia noga in the north."

Veronika shook her head. "Mamochka, you jest with us. Baba Yaga is just a tale for children to be told when you want them to listen to you."

Jeremiah kept quiet and did not speak. He ran his hand through his beard and kept his thoughts to himself. Butchering the name, Charley asked, "Who or what is Baba Yaga?"

"She is an old woman who lives alone in the forest and likes to eat children. Some say she's a goddess with great magic powers. She lives alone deep in a forest far away in a hut that stands on giant chicken legs." Veronika rolled her eyes.

"Legs of a chicken?" Charley made his fingers walk on the table in front of him. When Veronika did not correct herself, he asked again, "Did you say chicken?"

She ignored him and went on. "And she flies around in her magical mortar with her broom, looking to sweep up little children. It is all nonsense."

"No, it could be possible. I have seen things in this world that defied explanation. An old witch who harms little children isn't hard for me to imagine." Jeremiah spoke low and with serious intent. He held Mamochka Tatyana's gaze. "Are you certain Cinderella will go to Baba Yaga?"

"That is where she will head. Go what way you will, but all your paths will lead to her." Mamochka Tatyana stood up and hobbled over to the far corner of the hut. "I will help you as best I can, but you will need more than I can give you to prepare for this journey."

Veronika's look of disdain for her future travelling companions stood plain on her face. She folded her arms across her chest and sat back in her chair.

"We thank you for all of your help and assistance, but I have one more favor to ask of you." Jeremiah looked at Charley and asked Mamochka Tatyana, "Can you send a message to my friend's wife to let her know he is safe?"

Charley perked up in his chair and folded his hands together. "I would be so grateful for your help."

"Come here and I will help you. Your heart is strong and I can see you wish to ease your wife's fears." Mamochka Tatyana slowly pushed herself up from her chair and held on to the table for balance. "We will send the message at the stove. Come."

Charley rushed up out of his chair and then followed Mamochka Tatyana to the stove. Veronika kept her cross look on her face and Jeremiah watched her, wondering what type of travelling companion she would turn out to be. Mamochka Tatyana opened the oven and threw another log into the burning fire. "Look inside and tell me what you see."

Charley crouched down before the fire and said, "I see burning embers of white and orange."

"She wants to know if there is room for another log." Veronika pursed her lips and glanced over to Jeremiah to eye him up.

"Oh, I thought she wanted me to see something magical." Charley took a small log and added it to the stove. He used the poker to better position it in the fire and then shut the door.

Mamochka Tatyana had filled the teapot with water and put it on the stove. She positioned the pot over the hottest spot and waited with her hands on her hips. "Tell me about your wife. What is her name?"

"Ginny." Charley corrected himself. "Her full name is Virginia. We met when we were older. She came out to Ohio with me to start a family and we have been blessed with five girls." He lowered his voice and said, "Until we lost Mary back in 1810."

Veronika's expression changed and she watched as Charley looked away. Mamochka Tatyana saw the beginnings of steam coming out of the teapot and asked, "What is your wife's favorite smell?"

Without thinking, his answered rolled off his tongue. "Chocolate."

Jeremiah laughed and Veronika smiled. Mamochka Tatyana raised her arms and reached for some spices in tiny glass jars. She held one up and shook a pinch into her hand. Speaking in a low voice in Russian, she blew the cocoa through the steam emanating from the teapot. Her left hand began to glow in a soft orange glow that mimicked the fire. She closed her eyes and said, "Think of her and where she would be. Think of your home, of the land, the smell there and the trees." She closed her eyes, concentrated and then commanded, "Tell me when you see her."

The steam wafted in the corner of the room and they all could see a picture form there. The steam solidified and Charley could see his home. Ginny carried a bucket of water and she stopped and turned back around to glance up at the sky.

"Charles?" She put down the bucket and scanned the sky. "Is that you?"

Charley rushed up to the cloud of steam and reached out to touch it. His finger went through the steam and the picture blurred a bit and he pulled his finger away with quickness. "Ginny, can you hear me?"

"Yes, yes, I can." She smiled and asked, "Where are you?"

"Ginny, it's a long story. Jeremiah and I are in Russia."

Mixed emotions crossed her face. "What are you doing there?" She did not let him answer and asked, "Is Cinderella with you? Have you all found Phoebe?"

"We were separated and are no longer with Cinderella." He heard a voice coming through the steam and for a moment the vision dispersed.

Ginny saw four-year-old Ruth run through the image of her husband before her. "Daddy, Daddy!" The cloud disappeared as she ran through it, but reappeared once she had cleared the cloud. "That tickled!"

Charley called over to Mamochka Tatyana. "Can they still hear me?"

She ignored him and Veronika unfolded her arms and walked over to add another log to the stove. Mamochka Tatyana kept her eyes closed and she only nodded at Charley's question.

Veronika came over to Charley and she said, "Focus on your family. Your strength will feed Mamochka Tatyana and she will bring them back."

Charley closed his eyes and for a moment he pretended that no one else could see him. "Ginny, please come back."

With intense clarity, the steam condensed into an image of Ginny's face. "I am here still and I can see you again. Ruth, come say hello to your father."

Charley opened his eyes and reached out to Ruth. "I love you, honey. Tell your sisters that I will be back as soon as I can."

"Daddy, we love you." Ruth blew kisses at him and he pretended to catch them.

"Ginny, send a letter to my brother and he will help you while I'm away. You shouldn't be alone now." He swallowed hard and then continued, "If I could be there, I would. I'm sorry." He could see the steam fading again.

"I will contact your brother Sam. Do not worry about us. We will be fine." She crossed her hands over her pregnant belly. "Just come back to us safely." Ruth had wrapped herself around Ginny's leg and she put her arm around her. They were as close to the steam cloud as they could get without touching it. "May God watch over you and bring you home to us safe and sound." She had closed her eyes and stretched out her hand to her husband. "Please God, bless him. Keep him safe."

Charley saw the steam dissipate and he reached out to touch his wife, but her visage had already faded. "I will be safe. I love you."

"I love you always." The steam disappeared and everyone in the room could hear the echo of Ginny's voice.

Mamochka Tatyana dropped her hands and sat down with great weariness on a chair beside the stove. Veronika came to her side and whispered to her in Russian. Jeremiah stood by his friend and said, "I would understand if you want to leave tomorrow for your home. You do not have to come with me."

Charley remained quiet a moment and then brushed a tear from his eye. "No, I will see this through with you. Travelling alone from

Russia back to America would not be easy and we have no money. I would not have an easy journey home." He put his hand on Jeremiah's shoulder. "Plus, you will need my help and I will not desert you."

Jeremiah thought to question him and to send him away, but he held back his words and hugged his friend. "I will need your help."

Charley returned the hug and said, "We will find her and Phoebe. Trust me, we will."

Jeremiah patted his friend on the back. "Thank you."

Chapter 3

I could not find Phoebe, but I knew that she ran around an extensive yard and in front of the large, white house stood an old cherry blossom tree. Thick limbed and stable, the tree took up most of the front yard. Renée turned to me and asked me a question and I glanced away from the tree and we talked. How good it felt to see her again and to hear her voice. A noise from outside attracted my attention and I turned to see Phoebe slide down one of the large branches and bound, almost unnatural, like a cat on all fours to the ground. She smiled at her skill and then from above a tremendous amount of leaves and dried flowers fell on top of her.

Panic filled me inside as I saw the largest tree branch fall and crash against another part of the tree. The first branch fell and hit the ground with a thunderous crash and I sprung out of my chair and ran outside. I had lost sight of Phoebe under the pile of leaves and dried flowers yet I ran faster knowing what would come. And it did. The second branch fell forward toward Phoebe and I cried out in fear. Phoebe, who had flattened herself onto her stomach, popped her head up out of the leaves and the second branch fell perpendicularly toward her. She flattened herself back down onto the ground and the branch crashed against the trunk of the tree, leaving so little space for Phoebe. I heard her cry out in pain and I kept running and a stranger pulled her out. She was crying and people came from all sides and I wanted to settle down and simply see if she were injured.

Someone, I do not remember who, held her and her crying frightened me. I pulled her dress up and on the left side of her chest to her shoulder she had a brush mark from scrapping her body against a branch. Tiny droplets of blood pooled there and I saw blood in the bottom of her dress and by her hip but I could not see any other injuries. I had feared that her heart had been crushed.

"Are you okay?" I held her in my arms, but she kept crying with such franticness that I could not tell if she cried from pain or from fear of nearly being crushed by the tree.

Renée appeared at my side and she pushed away some of the house maids and gardeners who had come to see what had caused all the commotion.

"I want to take her to a physician to make sure that she's all right." I held her close to me and rushed inside the large, white house, but I could not avoid all the people there. Children played in the sitting area, chasing after marbles that they played with, friends whom I had not seen in years came up to me and asked, "Is she okay? Let us see. Let us see."

Still I held Phoebe tight against me and more people came up asking about her. I put Phoebe down and willed for some space to form around us and kept us secluded from everyone. I looked down and saw my hand shaking and realized that I had nearly seen my daughter die. "I need space. I need some space. Please, leave me alone."

I imagined a tiny bubble of energy around me, like when I had my magic, and I pushed that sphere outward to protect myself, but no magic came. I had none. People did back away from me and then Phoebe ran forward. She had stopped crying and something caught her attention. I chased after her and she ran faster than I, able to navigate easily through the people in our way. She climbed through a tight spot in the kitchen and out through the back door and I could not catch up with her. My slowness held me back. "Phoebe, wait for me. Please!"

She kept on running and I watched her and could see the blood on her white dress. I simply wanted a physician to listen to her heart to make certain that she did not bleed inside and that she would be okay. I simply wanted her to be safe in my arms, hold her and to protect her. But she ran off and I could not catch her. The constant prattle of society talk surrounded me and I ignored everyone. I only wanted to catch up with Phoebe and to see her and know that she was okay. Couldn't everyone understand that?

I opened my eyes and the Silver Fox eyed me with concern. "Are you well?"

My hands clenched the blankets on both sides and my heart pounded with fierceness. "I had a dream."

"I know. I heard you calling out and I did not know if I should wake you or not." He pulled back from me and folded his arms across his chest. "Often I think we dream to work through what we avoid in our waking life. The dream world is a magical place."

"I saw Phoebe and she was in danger." The memory of it all came back to me and I desperately held onto the images in my mind before they faded. "I saw Renée there and a tree fell and nearly crushed Phoebe, but she was spared." I sat up and could see that the sun had not risen yet. "I'm sorry if I disturbed you."

"Are you better now?" He held out some water for me.

I accepted and took a few sips to settle myself. I could hear the wind blowing outside and the cold bit deep. "I don't know. I truly don't know."

"I remember one day that your mother and I swam in the lake. The sun shone enough for us to be warm but not uncomfortable. Your mother wanted to jump off some rocks into the lake and she wouldn't listen to me. I thought it unsafe. She ignored me and climbed up the rocks and then went to dive off, but slipped on some moss. I saw her fall head first and I could do nothing to save her. She hit the water belly first and I swam over to her to see if she were hurt. I can still hear the smack her body made against the water.

"When I reached her, I saw that she had taken a big gulp of water and had started choking. I dragged her to the side of the lake and helped her cough out the rest of the water and felt useless. I have such magic and power, but cannot change the simplest of things. Afterward I held Justine and took her back to our cabin. I realized then that one day she would pass on and I could do nothing to stop that. I have no power over death." He leaned back against his pillow and looked away.

"I miss Phoebe. I often don't pray, but for her, I do." I pulled my blankets tighter around me and listened to the blowing wind outside. Neither of us spoke for a time and yet we could not fall asleep. After several minutes of listening to the blowing snow, I asked, "How much farther do we have to go and where exactly are you taking me? I have remained quiet for more than a week now and still you haven't told me your plan."

"It is not that I distrust you, but I fear that the emperor can reach inside your mind and pluck out your thoughts. With you and he being cloned from Queen Mab, I worry. Yet I sense a change in him since he has returned from his battle with Mab."

"I doubt that he can harm me so far away. I've not a drop of magic in me for him to sense." I held my left hand out and instead of magic I saw only chapped skin from the cold.

"That is good that you do not sense him. His powers are different now. Maybe he is not quite as powerful or his empire has grown too large and he cannot control everyone with his thoughts." The Silver Fox reached over to his coat and pulled out a rose from his lapel. He held it in his hands and lit it up with magic. Red and still vibrant, the rose did not seem to be affected by the cold. He had worn it on his coat through the past week and still the rose stayed protected from the cold by his magic.

"Will you at least tell me if we are almost at our destination? It would be helpful to give me some hope that we'll be out of this cold soon."

He adjusted the rose again on his lapel and smiled. "We are almost to the city. A few more days of travel and you will then be able to sleep in a bed and to take a bath."

"I would welcome that."

A twinkle came into the Silver Fox's eye. "I would welcome that as well. You could desperately use a bath."

"Do not joke with me. I am in no mood." I fell back into my blankets and tried to go back to sleep, but sleep would not come. "Is there a reason why you do not use your magic to hasten our journey?"

He rolled onto his back and he stared up at the roof of the tent. "Yes, there is a reason. There is a reason for everything I do. You must trust me that I have your best interests at heart. Without trust, what is there?"

I thought of a witty answer but the moment passed and one came too late to me. Instead I closed my eyes and pretended to sleep, imagining that I could send my thoughts out to Phoebe, letting her know I was safe. I concentrated and imagined sending my spirit out across the land, searching high and low for her until I came to the spot where she could be found and I poured my love out to her. She needed to know that I would not give up on her and that I would find her. Yet without a clue on where to begin, I searched the globe in vain. She could be behind me or before me and I would not know. If she were disguised in a crowd, I could not sense her. I would only be able to see her if I crossed her path and found her to be by me.

When doubt crept up on me, I closed my eyes tighter against the voices I heard inside. What if I never found her? What if the emperor had already killed her? What if? I took a deep breath and instead chose to think of a happy memory of her. I blocked out the dream and the Silver Fox's cryptic responses to me and focused on what I knew. I loved my daughter and would not give up on her. I had failed often enough, but on this, I would not. No matter if it cost me my last breath.

* * *

Phoebe opened her eyes and stared up at the ceiling. More than a week had passed since she had released her first magic message out into the wild and she had no way of knowing if her message had been received. The room that she had been locked in had plenty of sunlight and was large enough for her to exercise or read the books the emperor had given her. But she had not been outside in a long time. Her food arrived at set times along with teachers who helped her learn French and to practice her writing. For all his faults, Napoleon did not torture her or use her badly. He simply kept her imprisoned.

Nighttime had come and she held close the doll that she had been given and tried to go to sleep. From across the room, the door opened and she could see a lit candle headed toward her in the dark. Napoleon came to the desk near her bed and sat down. He still wore his military uniform but had no weapon that she could see.

"I have come to check on you myself. Are you well?" He placed the candle holder on the desk across from her bed and sat in the chair by her bed with arms crossed.

Phoebe took a moment to think before she answered. Sleep had nearly come to her and her thoughts were fuzzy and unclear. His coming to her so late at night was unusual.

"I miss my mother." She regretted her words and sat up watching him to see what he would say next.

"When I have been away, I have missed my family as well. The distance is too great and I tire more easily now. I cannot control everything and everyone as I once thought. Even I am not that great." Out of habit he slipped his right hand into his vest and looked off to the window and kept silent a moment and then said, "I come to tell you that I have had a change of heart."

Phoebe leaned forward and asked, "Will you be sending me back to my mother?"

Napoleon's slow sly smile grew on his face and he shook his head. "I cannot do that. Your mother is too dangerous and she must be contained. By keeping you, I will help to keep her safe." He put his finger on the candle and touched a piece of dripping wax. "You will come with me and Marie Louise on a little journey. I think the sunlight will do you well rather than to keep you locked up here. Would you like that?"

"Yes, yes, I would." Phoebe had difficulty containing her excitement. "I could use to see the outside and enjoy the fresh air."

Napoleon tapped the table with his hand and the room's door opened. A woman of slender build and long, dark, curly hair came in. Phoebe had never seen her before. "Isabelle will be your travelling companion and will be responsible for your safety on the journey. I would like you to meet her."

Isabelle stood before Phoebe and bowed. "Enchanté."

Phoebe tilted her head down in a small bow but kept her hands folded in her lap. "Nice to meet you."

"Isabelle will take care of you and will also be responsible for your well-being. I would also advise that you not try to escape." He glanced over at Isabelle and smiled. "I would make her a member of my officers if I could." Napoleon stood up and clapped his hands. "Good, I am happy that all is settled. We will leave in the morning so I suggest that you get some sleep and prepare yourself for the journey. Bonne nuit."

He turned without another word and left the room. The door shut and was locked behind him. Isabelle stood still, looking around the room. "I will sleep in the cot off to the side of the room. I hope that we will get along well."

Phoebe stood up and walked over to the cot and asked, "Are you my governess?"

"I am that and more." Isabelle turned and went to sit on the cot. "We can talk more in the morning and will have plenty of time on the journey tomorrow."

"Will we be going far?"

"Now is not the time. It is late and we will need to get ready before the sun rises so we will not have much sleep tonight." Standing back up, Isabelle came over to Phoebe and tucked her into bed. "I do not have many rules that I will want you to follow, but the most important one is that you listen to me when I ask you to do something. I will not be harsh with you or cruel. That is not my way. But I will be obeyed. Do you understand?"

"Yes, madame."

"Please, call me Isabelle." She smiled. "Go to sleep and we will talk more in the morning."

"But why can I not know where we are going?"

Isabelle held up her hand to silence Phoebe. "Enough. Go to sleep. I am going as well. You have nothing to fear from me and I promise we will talk in the morning."

"Can you tell me a little more about yourself?" Phoebe allowed herself to be tucked into bed.

"Can you keep a secret?" Isabelle asked.

"Yes, I can."

Isabelle raised her left hand and concentrated. Her hand began to glow in a soft, bluish light. "I received your message that you sent out from that very window." She pointed at the pane of glass across the room.

"You are a witch, like me!" Phoebe sat up in bed and tried to use her own magic but still something blocked her.

"Yes, I am and we will talk more in the morning. I am in the emperor's employ as a witch and he thinks me a loyal servant and what he thinks will remain that way. Do you understand?" Isabelle pointed at Phoebe and said, "I will help you escape and find your mother, but it will take time to devise a plan. You will need to keep my secret, but I wanted you to know that you are truly safe with me. I am here to help you."

Tears filled Phoebe's eyes and she reached out to grab Isabelle in a strong hug. She tried to speak, but her voice came out as a tiny squeak. Phoebe clung to Isabelle and would not let her go. And for the first time, in a long, long while, she allowed herself to cry.

* * *

Mamochka Tatyana opened the shutter and the sun's morning light streamed into the tiny house. She then passed a bowl of porridge to Jeremiah and said, "If you wish to find your friend, you will need to go north and find Baba Yaga's hut."

Veronika put down her spoon and laughed. "What you ask of him to do is impossible. Even if Baba Yaga exists, how would he find her?"

Charley poured some goat's milk into the thick porridge and remained quiet. Jeremiah put down his spoon and asked, "Will you tell us how to find Baba Yaga?"

"No, I cannot do that, but she will." Mamochka Tatyana pointed at Veronika with her spoon and then looked down to continue eating.

"How can I help?" A scowl crossed Veronika's face.

"I have dreamed that you would do so." She stopped talking and took a few moments to chew. "Do you doubt me?"

Veronika began to speak, but Mamochka Tatyana interrupted her. "I have cared for you for many years and helped you when you needed it. Now it is time for you to leave the nest for good and to help these men. Another witch needs your help and you must do so."

"But I do not want to go with these men up north looking for a fairy tale." She crossed her arms over her chest.

"When you came into my care, did I turn you away?" Mamochka Tatyana glanced up from eating and Veronika turned away.

"But you are my family and these men are strangers!"

Charley put down his spoon. "We do not wish to cause an argument between you two. We can go on our own. Right, Jeremiah?"

Jeremiah remained silent.

"She must decide for herself, but the journey that awaits her is for her to choose." Mamochka Tatyana softened her look at her granddaughter. "Though you might not believe me, your future lies with them."

"But I do not wish to go." She put her spoon down and stared into the lumpy porridge.

"You cannot hide here much longer. You are old enough to be on your own. If I were younger, I would go, but my hip aches and my time on grand adventures is done."

Jeremiah stopped eating and said, "If you do not wish to go, we will leave after the meal. Charley and I do not wish to cause you any problems. We will be fine."

He stood up and nodded to Charley to come with him. "We're going to pack the wagon you gave us and tend to the horses. When we're back, let us know what you decide."

Charley wiped his mouth on the back of his hand and headed outside with Jeremiah without a word.

Mamochka Tatyana reached into a pocket and pulled out a necklace and placed it on the table in front of her. "Do you know what this is?" She touched the large topaz in the necklace and then pushed it toward her granddaughter.

"It's my mother's necklace." She reached for it and took it in her hands. In the morning light, the topaz appeared to be filled with a magical glow. "I thought it lost after she died."

Mamochka Tatyana shook her head and folded her hands in front of her and took a deep breath and then sighed. "Your mother wanted you to have this when you were old enough."

"I cannot go. I'm afraid." Veronika let the words roll out. "What if it happens again?"

"Your mother was also afraid at your age. But you will need to make a choice, live always in fear or face your fears." She put her hand on Veronika's and said, "These two men are the ones I have had dreams about. Do not pass up this chance. Your mother would have wanted you to do this."

Veronika looked down at the necklace and remained quiet for a few moments. She clenched the necklace tightly in her hand and looked up. "I will go. You have never led me wrong. If you dreamt that I would go on the journey, then I will trust you and go." She put the necklace in her pocket. "But I'm afraid. What if I can't ..."

Mamochka Tatyana grabbed her hand and shook her head. "Do not worry yourself. Being afraid is normal. Yet it is not me you should trust, but yourself. Learn that lesson and you will be well."

They finished their meal in silence and then heard Jeremiah and Charley arrive with the wagon and horses. Jeremiah knocked on the door and Veronika opened it, letting him in.

"I have decided to go with you." She said nothing else and Jeremiah did not push the point. He nodded and smiled over at Mamochka Tatyana. Together they began to fill the wagon with supplies and extra food and water. Charley came in to help and in a short while they had completed packing and were ready to depart. Mamochka Tatyana glanced outside and smiled. "The sun has come out and begun to melt the snow. You must be on your way."

Mamochka Tatyana led Veronika out of the hut and gave her a hug.

Jeremiah stood by his horse and adjusted the saddle and then patted the horse's side. He climbed up into the saddle and settled himself. "Thank you for all of your help."

Mamochka Tatyana leaned heavily on her cane and smiled up at him. "Take care of my Veronika and may you have luck on your journey."

Veronika hugged her for a good while and said not a word. Mamochka Tatyana put her hand on Veronika's forehead and whispered some prayers over her in Russian. Kissing her on the head, she pulled back and pushed Veronika away. Charley sat in the wagon and had the reins in his hand waiting to head off. The sun had come out and had already begun to melt much of the snow. Travelling might be difficult with the wagon, but they would need the supplies and the extra food and water. Veronika mounted her white mare and took a moment to take in the small house and Mamochka Tatyana one last time. She turned away, thinking she might never see either again and urged her horse onward.

Jeremiah matched his horse's stride with Veronika's and they travelled on in silence for several hours. Charley whistled a tune to keep happy and by midday they had journeyed far to the north of Mamochka Tatyana's tiny house. Jeremiah raised his hand to signal that they should stop and he took some time to walk his horse to a stream and allowed the animal to drink.

Charley glanced back on the dirt road and could not see anyone coming behind or before them. "I expected to see more people on the roads. Where is everyone?"

Veronika took a swig of water and pointed over to the right. "They're all in Church. It's a Sunday and all of the locals are there."

"I can't see anything through the forest. How far away is it?"

"Not too far, but the town is not on our route."

Jeremiah walked up to both of them and asked, "Do you think me crazy for agreeing to go find Baba Yaga?"

"Yes." She did not even hesitate with her answer. "I have seen great magic in the world, but I don't believe that Baba Yaga exists. But maybe I'm wrong."

Charley exhaled and steam came out of his mouth from the cold. "I believe she exists. My family and I have seen some things that I wish we had not and I lost a daughter to a spirit that dripped death from the sky. My not wanting to believe it existed didn't stop it from killing my daughter."

Veronika watched Charley walk back to the wagon and Jeremiah passed her and said, "He didn't falter that day. He and his wife never stopped fighting and together they survived. There is no other man I'd rather have as a companion at my side than he." He stopped a moment and turned back. "Baba Yaga does exist. I need to know what you'll do when we face her. That's the important thing. Think on that."

Jeremiah walked away and left Veronika to her thoughts.

* * *

We entered the city of Vilna and the Silver Fox led the way through a busy street filled with merchants and their carts and lots of people. He had sold our winter gear in a smaller town a few days before and the spring temperatures had helped brighten my spirits. Seeing signs of civilization helped improve my mood as well.

"Where are you headed?" I would be happy to stop walking and get off my feet for some time. A nice bath would also do me wonders.

"Straight to see the Tsar himself." He walked onward with exaggerated purpose and whistled as he strode down the street.

"You're just going to walk in on the emperor of Russia and pay him a visit?" I shook my head in disbelief. "You amaze me sometimes with how you have survived this long."

He laughed and shook his head. "No, you're going to walk in to the emperor's spring home and demand to see him. I'll be right behind you all the way."

I started to protest but he turned away and pointed at a big building and said, "We have arrived."

"You have forgotten that I don't speak Russian. What am I to say?"

"We are here on a mission of diplomatic emergency. You will speak French, of course. All the royals throughout Europe speak French. Even the people from your stogy England."

We arrived at the iron gates and two guards blocked our path. I led the way and right before the guards saw us, the Silver Fox handed me an envelope with a seal on it. I glanced down and smiled. I slipped into French and said, "I have an urgent letter from the King of England. I ask to have an audience with the emperor."

The two guards looked at each other in confusion and the Silver Fox stood in front of me and spoke quickly in Russian and then showed them the letter I held. He pointed at me and spoke loudly, waving them off. He crossed his arms over his chest and we watched as one of the guards ran off inside.

Leaning close to me, he whispered. "It appears that the common guards do not speak French. I had forgotten that."

I smiled at the remaining guard and a few minutes later several people came to meet us. A tall man with a long beard streaked with gray ushered us through the gates and in passable French said, "Welcome, I am Vladislav. We are happy to accept emissaries from

King George. We will bring you to see the emperor in a few moments. May I see the document you bring with you?"

I handed him the envelope and he nodded to the guards. They pointed their muskets at us and Vladislav said, "We will take all precautions against spies and troublemakers. You will be held until we have had time to read through the document and decide if your story is false. Hand over your papers."

I glanced over at the Silver Fox and saw that he had no magic up his sleeve. "We have no papers and have come in secret. We are here to speak against Bonaparte and to warn the Tsar against him."

Vladislav kept his thoughts to himself and did not express any surprise or judgment. "Guards, take them to the waiting room and watch them there."

The Silver Fox allowed himself to be led away and I followed his lead. Once inside the gates, we were led through the courtyard to the large white building, strewn with columns in the front. The building's façade had many windows and reminded me of some of the Parisian governmental palaces I had seen years ago. The guards brought us to a large sitting room filled with several sofas and tables and huge paintings on the wall.

Once inside, they left and locked us in the room. I went to the window and looked outside and said, "That did not go as well as I had expected."

"No, but we are inside, are we not?" He threw himself down on the sofa and put his feet up on the table. "Do you want to wait around or should we go directly to see the Tsar?" He had bridged his hands together and squinted at me waiting for my reply.

"I doubt they would take to us kindly if you started using magic to get us past the guards." I paced back and forth in a straight line, thinking.

"It would be fun though." He stared up at the paintings on the ceiling and sighed. "A long time has passed since I have had any fun. Why don't we make a grand entry and show some style?"

"I'm afraid to ask what you have in mind." I changed the topic and asked, "What should we say to them once they come back? We should have a plan."

"That is up to you. I have brought you to the Tsar's residence and now you need to use your brain to get us to him and have him believe us."

"But I don't know how we can help him. Without my magic, I don't know what I can do."

"Hopefully, you'll think of something." His grinned at me mischievously. "Or you can agree with my using some magic to spice things up around here. I think there needs to be a lot more feathers. Have you noticed there aren't any feathers in here?"

Before I could respond, the door opened and Vladislav walked in still holding the envelope I had given him. "Who are you both?"

I glanced at the Silver Fox for guidance and he shrugged. He would be of no help in these sorts of matters. Maybe it would be best for me to tell the truth. "I am Cinderella, former princess of England, and half-sister to Bonaparte. My friend and I have come to offer our assistance to the Tsar."

Vladislav stroked his beard and said not a word. He turned around and spoke firmly in Russian to a guard who came up to us and searched to see if we had any weapons. Finding none, he left the room and Vladislav said, "I will take you to see the Tsar. Any treachery on your part and you will be killed on the spot and we will ship your bodies back to England as a message to the king there. Do you understand?"

Although his French lacked clarity, I did understand him well enough and nodded. The Silver Fox jumped up from the sofa and said, "Let's go."

On the way out, I bumped into the Silver Fox and nearly hissed at him under my breath. "Act normal or the Tsar will have our heads."

He rolled his eyes at me, but did keep quiet.

Vladislav led the way out of the room and four guards followed behind us with two in front. We were taken to a large audience room that had a throne at the far end. A man in military uniform paced before the throne. When we entered, he turned to us and I bowed and pulled at the Silver Fox's coat, suggesting he do the same. Following my lead, the Silver Fox tilted his head lightly and smiled at the Tsar.

He walked over to his throne and waved us closer. The guards brought us before him and Vladislav said, "They claim to be from England and have information regarding Bonaparte and his plans."

I glanced over nervously at the Silver Fox. I had not actually read the envelope he had given me and had no idea of its contents. Tsar Alexander waved at us and commanded, "Speak and tell me quickly why you are here." His fluent French flowed off his tongue with pure melody. Slim of build and fair of skin, his hair had receded, but he wore a fine figure for an emperor.

The Silver Fox looked at me and whispered, "You're on. This is your time to shine."

I wondered for a moment on what I should say and took a chance to look up from my curtsy and to see the Tsar's face. I would need him to trust me. "Your Imperial Majesty, my name is Cinderella and I have come from afar to warn you against Bonaparte."

"You have not hailed from England because we would have received notice of your coming."

"That is correct. Although I am originally of England, I now live in America." I stumbled on what to say and thought it best to be truthful. "Bonaparte is my half-brother. We are related through magic and I wish to help you stop him."

Vladislav leaned over to the Tsar and whispered into his ear. Alexander waved him away and folded his hands together and asked, "What proof do you have of your claims?"

"I have none. Only my word." Cinderella stepped forward. "Bonaparte is not to be trusted."

The Silver Fox edged closer to Cinderella and stood by her side. "He has professed his alliance to you, has he not? But there still has been conflict between your great empires. He gathers a grand army and will march on your beloved Russia and there will be great destruction and death."

Alexander turned his attention to the Silver Fox for the first time and asked, "How are you certain on this?"

"Because I am the Silver Fox." He threw his coat to the ground and came forward. "I've seen the sun rise far in the future and have looked back. The French emperor will bring great death to your people if you do not act."

Vladislav edged closer to the emperor but did not say a word.

The Tsar pointed at his guards and said, "Remove him from this chamber. I wish to speak with Cinderella alone."

Four men dressed in military uniforms rushed forward and pointed their muskets at the Silver Fox. He turned to Cinderella and offered a quick glance of apology and then a crazed look came into his eyes. He threw his head back and laughed and said, "Oh, how I love to revel in such joy. Approach me farther and I will turn each of you inside out." He raised his hands in front of him in a defensive posture and they began to glow white with pure magic.

"Your Excellency, please do not hurt him." Cinderella rushed forward but was grabbed from behind by a guard.

"Let them come and I will melt their faces off like the last spring snow before the warmth comes." The Silver Fox licked his lips and pretended to rush at the guards and then pulled himself back. The men stood their ground and did not flinch.

Vladislav left the Tsar's side and pointed at the Silver Fox and yelled, "Stop." He then slipped into his native Russian and barked a command.

The Silver Fox's hands stopped glowing and the guards grabbed him and began to pull him to the ground.

"Wait, please. Stop!" Cinderella pulled away from the man who held her and knelt before the Tsar. "Please, do not hurt him. He will not harm anyone. I promise."

Vladislav kept pointing at the Silver Fox and had an intense look of concentration on his face. "You are correct in that he will harm no one. He is powerless here."

So far our makeshift plan had failed miserably. I only hoped the guards wouldn't come for me next.

The Silver Fox struggled and tried to escape but the guards wrestled him to the ground and he caught my eye and mouthed. "I'm sorry."

Chapter 4

Phoebe kept her hands folded in her lap and waited. It would be any minute now. For too long she had been locked up in this house without being let outside. She had saved her energy and would be ready. The flood of her magic would sing again through her veins, but she would not be a fool and give herself away. No, she would play along and pretend that all would be the same.

The door opened to her room and Isabelle entered wearing her travelling clothes and a bright smile on her face. "Bon matin, mademoiselle!" She bounded over to Phoebe and patted her on the knee. "Are you ready for your journey? Today will be the first big step to your escaping."

"Yes, I am ready." Phoebe smiled and hugged Isabelle. The morning had been filled with many last minute preparations.

Holding her finger up, Isabelle said, "Lentement, lentement." She held Phoebe's hand and pointed outside. "You must go slowly and trust me. Do not try to rush off and fly away. The emperor would be after you like a fly to honey. Do you understand?"

Phoebe nodded and heard footsteps in the hall. Her heart beat faster and several soldiers came into the room. Isabelle stood up and pulled Phoebe off of her bed, eyeing up her long, blond hair that had been neatly coifed and braided for the occasion. The emperor had spared no expense. Phoebe smoothed down her dress and allowed a small smile to break forth on her face at the touch of its silky feel. The soldiers led them out into the hall and then down the stairs. After another hallway, two of the guards went out first and Isabelle followed, holding tightly onto Phoebe's hand. And then, she felt it. The warm spring sun beamed down on Phoebe and warmed her face. She closed her eyes and took a moment to bathe in the light and the beautiful weather outside. Several more steps and she and Isabelle entered the courtyard. Phoebe reached out with her senses and took a timid breath. She glanced down at her new shoes and focused on the pink bows on her dress.

Isabelle held her hand firmly and asked, "Are you okay? Would you like to stop for a moment?"

Phoebe shook her head and walked on faster and bottled up her emotions. The rush of magic had not returned. She willed magic to surge through her left hand, pouring her strength and will into it, but nothing happened. The soldiers marched them to a carriage, one of many in a long line, and Isabelle stopped and started to help Phoebe in.

"Please, can I have a moment. It has been so long since I could feel the sun and a breeze on my face." She closed her eyes and tilted her head up, hiding well her disappointment. Her magic had not reawakened. The little burst of energy she had experienced several weeks ago to send her message of help out did not reappear. Empty and depleted, she thought of her mother and hoped that tomorrow would be a better day. All her hopes had been hinged on getting outside. She would pull forth the wind, the warmth and the freedom of being outside and then burn inside like the sun. She had planned on breaking away and then dropping through the dreamline, away and to another place where she would be free.

She had focused on her mother's face, her hands and smile. The exact moment in the past had been clear and secure. Before she had left America, the two of them had spent a morning waking up early. Just the two of them, looking out over the plains, seeing the lazy clouds drift across the sky and how they changed to a brilliant orange and pink as the sun rose. Her mother had pulled her close and kissed her on the forehead. But there would be no travel through the dreamline today, Phoebe could feel no inner spark. Taking a step up on the ladder to climb into the carriage, Phoebe smiled at Isabelle and resigned herself to still being a prisoner.

"Give yourself time." Isabelle climbed up after her. "You have been a prisoner for a long time. Allow yourself the time to just be happy that you are outside. We will have a long journey to Dresden and we will have much time to enjoy the road together. Doucement, doucement."

Phoebe turned away from her and hid her face. She would not allow anyone to see her cry. Not even Isabelle who had been so kind to her. Isabelle put her hand on Phoebe's. "Gently, mademoiselle. Go gently. Trust me and you will be fine in a few days. All will be well."

Phoebe nodded quickly and turned away to look out the carriage's window. Tears streamed down her face and she used a handkerchief to dry away the tears. A few minutes later, she had settled herself and saw a big, fluffy cloud stretched over the sky, blocking out the sun. She heard a whistle and a call in response and the carriage jolted forward. The long caravan had begun to head eastward, leaving Saint Cloud for Dresden. Phoebe glanced out the window at the city and she watched the people doing their chores and saw a few children playing with a ball.

When would she have her day to play? When would she be able to see her mother again and be free? She did not know why, but no magic had opened up within her. The call and pull of her power remained silent. She leaned her cheek against the window and stared out at the people they passed and hoped that her day would come soon.

* * *

Tsar Alexander stood up and said to Vladislav, "Enough. Do not hurt him."

Vladislav lowered his arm and the Silver Fox slumped to the ground. Two guards held him down and he could not get up.

"Tell us true, who are you and what do you want?" The Tsar sat back down on his throne and folded his hands together listening intently.

"I am Cinderella and am born from Queen Mab, queen of all the faeries. Bonaparte is my half-brother and took my daughter from me in hopes of using her magic to control all the empires of the world." She pointed to the Silver Fox and said, "He is my companion who travels with me to help me find my daughter. I need help to find her."

"What is so special with your daughter that Bonaparte would covet her so much and take her from you?"

"She is how I used to be. She will grow up to be a great Chronicler and will be able to walk through the dreamline."

Vladislav reacted visibly from her words and said, "How can she be a mistress of time? Such powers have not been seen for hundreds of years."

The Tsar held up his hand to silence Vladislav. "The way you used to be. What do you mean by that?"

Cinderella opened up her hands and showed them to him. "I am a witch who has given up my powers to help stem the tide of Bonaparte's reign. Both Queen Mab and I have fought him and resisted him. Now he tries to take my daughter's magic to help him conquer the rest of the world."

"He is coming for your Russia. I have seen it." The Silver Fox tried to pull himself back up to his feet but a guard pushed him back down to the ground.

A troubled look crossed the Tsar's face. "An uneasy alliance exists between France and us. But to say that Bonaparte raises a grand army to march on Russia is another thing."

The Silver Fox shook his head. "His court is headed to Dresden and he will celebrate there for a time and then leave his empress and turn his attention to you. He has already fortified the surrounding countries with tens of thousands of soldiers. Can you deny this?"

Vladislav pointed at the Silver Fox and he fell silent to the ground no longer able to speak.

Cinderella rushed forward and grabbed Vladislav's arm, pulling it down. "Please, stop hurting him."

Vladislav pointed at her and his face strained with concentration, but his face only reddened and Cinderella succeeded in moving his hand down. She appeared unaffected by his powers. The nearest guard grabbed her from behind and held her still. She addressed the Tsar and tried to show him her hands, but the guard held her still. "I have no weapons or power to harm you. I need your help. If it is true that Bonaparte will march on Russia, can we not work together to help each other?"

"How can you help us if you have no powers?" the Tsar asked.

"I have fought with Bonaparte and I know how his mind works. He will try to sway you to his side with words and his powerful persuasion."

Vladislav nodded. "I have and will continue to protect the Tsar from the French bastard's magic. He will not win."

"Vladislav, enough. I trust you will not allow me to be harmed by him. You have proven yourself well, but a grand army of hundreds of thousands of men marching to our lands is another matter. We would not be able to stand against such force."

"May I speak?" The Silver Fox struggled to pull himself to his knees.

"Let him up." The Tsar waved his hand and two soldiers pulled the Silver Fox to his feet.

"Thank you." He dusted himself off and said, "You do not have to fight him. You can do something even better. Something that will infuriate him and drain him of his power."

"And what would that be?" asked the Tsar.

"When he invades, pull back your troops. Let him take your city and as you retreat you will burn the crops, the lands, houses and all around you. Pull back deeper into the heart of Russia and draw him in."

Vladislav shook his head. "You suggest that his Excellency allow his own cities and lands to be burned? Are you insane?"

"Sometimes I admit that I have lost my wits and I'm not the most stable of folks, but in this I'm certain. Draw Bonaparte in, pull back, draw him in farther and as you retreat burn the land. Burn the towns. Goad him to come after you by holding the carrot up and walking farther into mother Russia. And then …"

Tsar Alexander looked to me. "Where do you come in to all of this? What will your role be?"

I did not know how to answer, but I suspected that the Silver Fox had planned this all from the start.

The Silver Fox scratched his head and then spun in a circle and pointed at me. "You will come with me to the north. We will go visit her and ask her for her help."

I tried to hide my bewilderment, but did a poor job. "Who will we go visit?"

Vladislav answered for me. "He speaks of Baba Yaga."

The Tsar laughed out loud. "Children stories? You go to hunt down an old witch from a fairy tale?"

The Silver Fox leaned forward and said, "No, we go to see the real Baba Yaga and ask her for her help."

Vladislav crossed himself. "You are mad."

"I am not angry today and will forgive you for your treatment of me on this fine day." He crossed his arms and glared at Vladislav. "She will come for us if we call for her up north. I know she will."

"And how can an old witch help us against the French emperor and his grand army?" the Tsar asked. I watched the guards around me and made certain that I kept my distance from the Tsar. "What do you know about her that can help us?"

The Silver Fox smiled. "She is the mother of winter and of solitude. She will descend from the north on our enemy and decimate him and his so-called grand army. Cold, starvation, sickness and fear will be our weapons." He turned toward the Tsar. "You will need to move your people from the cities where Bonaparte advances and many of your soldiers will lose their lives, but you will not be defeated. You will grow stronger and survive."

The Tsar paced back and forth before the throne and said, "The French emperor will need to be cut down to size and be taught a lesson. He was once a brother, but now he and I are on opposite sides. I will try diplomacy with him if he does choose to invade my empire, but if that fails, then I will lead my armies and fight. I do not fear him."

"He will cut your forces down in size and you will not be able to defeat him with military force." The Silver Fox pointed at Vladislav. "You are a warlock. Have you not seen the signs? Tell your emperor the truth."

Vladislav looked troubled, but kept quiet.

"Do I speak a lie? Can Bonaparte be defeated on the field of battle?" The Silver Fox shook his finger at Vladislav. "No, that is not the way. But drawing him in and cutting off his supply lines and then having the Russian winter from Baba Yaga become his lover and freeze him to his bones. Well, that will do the trick."

"But where is Phoebe? How will I find her?" I doubted that this grand plan would help me in the end.

"Your daughter will be where the emperor is. He will use her to find you. And we will use that to be his downfall. He needs Phoebe's powers, but I don't know why. But if we resist him, then his rule will end soon. I have foreseen it."

I kept my finger on my lips and wanted to speak, but feared to say the truth. But I spoke anyway. "I do not trust you."

The Silver Fox put his hands on his hips and said, "I do not ask any of you to trust me. I am simply telling you and the Tsar how Bonaparte can be defeated." He pointed again at Vladislav. "He's a seer. Tell him to contradict me. He knows who I am and what I bring to the Tsar. I can help him defeat the French emperor."

"But that still doesn't help me find Phoebe."

Tsar Alexander stopped pacing and turned to Vladislav. "Speak the truth. What do you think of this plan of his?"

Vladislav began to speak, then stopped and chose his words with care. "I cannot find fault in his plan." The Silver Fox pointed at him and smiled, giving him a big wink. "But I would caution going north to confront Baba Yaga. She is lost in obscurity and is best left alone. Waking her might cause other challenges."

I stepped forward and asked, "Other challenges?"

Vladislav ignored me and spoke to the Tsar. "She will not want to come out of hiding unless for a good reason."

I spun and turned to the Silver Fox. "And that is my role. She'll be drawn to me. Why?"

He did not deny my accusation and walked up to Vladislav. "Try your magic on her again."

He kept his arms crossed over his chest and did not move.

"Do it and you will see." The Silver Fox looked at the Tsar and asked, "What harm would it cause?"

I stepped back and held up my hands. "What is he going to do to me?"

The Silver Fox shrugged. "Not much. You will not be harmed at all."

The Tsar nodded at Vladislav. "Compel her to kneel."

The guards stepped far back away from me and I kept my hands up.

Vladislav raised his right arm and then pointed at me. I could see a vein bulging in the center of his forehead from his concentration and I simply stood still and felt nothing. The Silver Fox ran up to me and pretended to wrap his arms around me. Vladislav grunted with frustration and yet I stood unharmed. "Do you see?"

Vladislav continued to concentrate but I walked freely and did not feel any force compelling me to do anything. The Silver Fox lit up his left hand with light and tried to take my hand in his but could not do so. A force propelled his hand away from mine. He glanced over at Vladislav and saw him lower his hand and shake his head in defeat. Vladislav breathed deeply and tried to recapture his breath. "I cannot touch her with my magic."

The Silver Fox nodded. "Nor can I." He also gave up and put his hand at his side.

"Why am I like this?" I closed my eyes and opened my heart. I thought of Phoebe and could feel no power within me. "I feel no magic."

The Silver Fox said, "There is no magic in you. You are a void in which no magic can touch. I do not know why you are like this, but no one with magic can harm or influence you."

Tsar Alexander looked at me with new admiration and asked, "Would even Bonaparte's magic fail to affect her?"

"Because they are related, I do not know. But she could still be harmed by guns." The Silver Fox stood before Vladislav. "She and I can travel north and be out of your way. We will awaken Baba Yaga and draw her down south. She will bring winter and Bonaparte will lose and scurry back to France like a rat in the night. I don't often think I have a good plan, but I think this one will work."

Vladislav interrupted him from continuing. "This plan of yours will take time. Months of time to travel far north, find Baba Yaga and convince her to come back. Our soldiers would need to be deployed to pull Bonaparte in. The planning will take much work."

The Silver Fox nodded. "And that is why we are here in April. By October, we will have the French emperor on the run. It can work. It will not be easy, but with Your Excellency's help, we can defeat him."

I thought for a moment about Phoebe, my two years of searching for a way to find her and realized that the Silver Fox's plan would be the best bet I had in finding her. "I will go with you." But I faced him and added, "But I do not trust you. You play another game here and I do not know what it is. All of this is too well planned out for my taste. I will keep my eye on you."

"I have told you that you need not trust me, but I will help free Phoebe and defeat Bonaparte. I promised that and I will deliver." He put his hands behind his back and turned to the Tsar. "Your Excellency, what is your will?"

Tsar Alexander thought for a moment and said, "I need time to think and speak to my advisors. While I do that, you both will be my guests here in the palace."

The Silver Fox turned to me and mumbled, "Looks like he trusts me even less than you do." He bowed to the Tsar and I curtsied. Two guards walked up to us and led us out of the room. How long the Tsar would need to be convinced, I did not know, but I knew that I would do anything I could to find Phoebe. And even this plan, so outrageous and unbelievable, would be better than roaming the world aimlessly without a means to find Phoebe. I would grasp at any chance, even one as risky as the Silver Fox's.

* * *

Jeremiah knelt on the ground and studied the tracks. Charley had taken the horses to graze and Veronika searched the local area for some herbs and berries. The mud, thick and wet, left a clear track of footprints. Standing up, Jeremiah wiped his hand on his pants. Charley noticed him stand and called over to him. "What do you think?"

"I think it might be soldiers marching in formation. Not a large company of men, but they're headed east." He put his hand on his forehead to shield his eyes from the sun but saw no sign of people ahead.

"I expected that we would have encountered more people on the road. The traffic has been light over the last few weeks." Charley glanced over at the horses and saw that they grazed lazily on a patch of grass.

"With the weather holding, I suspect that people are starting to prepare their farms for planting." Jeremiah glanced around and could see no patches of snow left. The spring weather had warmed the countryside.

"I have had enough of snow for this season. Let us hope that the warmth continues." Charley took a swig of water from a skin he carried on his shoulder and offered it to Jeremiah.

Jeremiah declined and asked, "Do you see Veronika?"

"I just saw her over there." Charley pointed up ahead and neither of them could see her.

"Veronika!" Jeremiah cupped his hands over his mouth and called loudly.

His voice echoed across the land and came back to him but they saw no sign of her. Charley started to walked ahead to look for her and asked, "Why would she run away?"

"I do not think she has left us but was taken." Jeremiah pulled out one of his pistols strapped to his back and spun around looking for any sign of her. "There is no place to hide. No trees or rocks. Where could she have gone?"

Charley ran over to the wagon, climbed inside and came out again with his musket loaded and at the ready. He stood on the wagon and glanced ahead, thinking the higher view would help him see farther, but he only saw grass and some shrubs far off to the horizon. Climbing back down, he saw the horses ignoring them, resting in the sun. They continued to graze without any concern for their missing companion.

Jeremiah headed away from the wagon in the direction that Veronika had gone. He searched the ground for any dropped berries or crushed shrubs, but he could see no signs of where she had been.

Charley ran up behind him and together they slowly walked on, searching the ground for a sign of a disturbance.

"Do you see anything?" Charley scanned ahead and could only see yellow grass with several green patches growing from the warmth.

"No, I don't." Jeremiah stopped and listened, but could hear no sound except that of a light wind.

"Maybe a soldier deserted from his company and he has been hiding near us?"

"He would have to be a master at deception for us not to see him. No one could hide himself and her so well. We would have heard her struggle and call out."

Charley stopped and scanned the surrounding area. "True, I just thought that …"

He stopped talking and just stared back the way they had come.

"What is wrong?" Jeremiah stopped and turned back around. One of their horses had disappeared. Only one remained, grazing on a patch of grass not too far from the wagon.

"What could have done that? I heard nothing. Neither horse made a sound." He squinted and held his musket in the firing position prepared to shoot at anything that moved. "We never heard either of the horses in trouble. Whatever it is, they are not afraid."

"Maybe they do not have any time to be afraid." Jeremiah pulled his second pistol out and held both weapons at the ready and started walking back to the wagon. "We should be extremely careful."

Charley nodded and said, "Do not worry about me, I will be."

From the corner of his eye, Jeremiah thought he saw movement. He turned and aimed his pistols and prepared to fire them, but he could see nothing unusual or different. Charley turned along with him and asked, "What did you see?"

"Nothing." He stood still and did not move, wanting to make certain. "I thought I saw movement but nothing is there." The sun shone above, bright and steady, and for as far as he could see the land appeared clear of anything unusual.

"Why are we standing here if you didn't see anything?" Charley refused to blink and kept steady and still. He glanced down at his feet and saw no tracks in the grass, and in looking back up did not notice anything different than the beautiful look of the landscape before him. Filled with patches of yellow grass that slowly had begun to turn back to green with spring having arrived, he could see no animals or people in his field of vision.

"Let's turn back." Jeremiah lowered his guns and slowly turned back around and froze.

Charley followed his lead and asked, "Where did it go?"

The other horse by the wagon had disappeared. Jeremiah dropped to the ground and put his ear to the dirt. He closed his eyes and concentrated.

"How could it have disappeared so quickly and without our hearing?" Charley held his musket out and continued to the wagon.

"Shh, be quiet. Let me concentrate." Jeremiah remained on the ground, listening.

Charley crept up toward the wagon and once there he peeked inside. He could see their supplies and his rolled up blanket. Nothing appeared unusual. He stopped and looked at the ground and took a tentative step forward to the other side of the wagon. Again, nothing appeared unusual. He kept walking and, chancing fate, jogged around the back of the wagon. Still he could not see anything out of the ordinary.

Charley turned back toward Jeremiah and could not find him. "Jeremiah?"

The spot where he had been was empty. Charley climbed up on the wagon and looked out across the land. Holding the musket at the ready, he kept staring, willing to see some movement, but did not. Everything appeared normal and he detected nothing out of the ordinary.

"Jeremiah? Can you hear me?" His call echoed out throughout the lonely landscape. He heard no birds, animals or any sign of life. He could only hear the wind.

A large white, puffy cloud passed in front of the sun and shadows fell across the landscape. He stood still and waited for the cloud to pass. Each breath he took, he waited for something to happen to him.

"I will not run. I will not run. Ginny, send me some luck, darling." He tightened his grip on his gun. He kept talking to himself slow and sure, climbing down the back steps of the wagon. When he touched the ground, he noticed a flicker from the corner of his eye and he turned but could see nothing different. "I know I saw something. I do not know what it was, but I did see something. Steady and easy. Relax, relax, relax." He edged forward and the cloud above fully passed the sun and bright light filled the area. To his left, he thought he saw a shimmer in the air and a shadow on the ground. He headed in that direction and again glanced down at his feet, expecting to be swallowed up by the ground.

"What are you?" Charley edged closer and focused on the shadow on the ground. He remained steady in his gait and the wind picked up and when it did, the shadow he headed toward disappeared. It had moved and he did not know how or where to. The wind blew stronger for a few moments and Charley froze. "Where did you go?" He kept facing in the same direction and after the wind stopped decided to chance a few more steps forward.

He kept calm but could feel his heart racing. "Okay, okay. Nothing is wrong. I just need to think this through."

Moving closer to the spot where he had seen the shadow, he reached it and a quick burst of wind blew him a step forward. He braced himself from the wind and held his ground.

"What was that?" He spoke to no one and then a strange sensation washed over him. He saw the land around him washed in the beautiful midday sun and then as though he had walked through a doorway to the outside, the scenery changed. Day became night and the grass disappeared, replaced by a blanket of fresh, untouched snow. Above, the moon had replaced the sun. Nearly full and showing an eerie ring around it, the moon shone down on the land. All had changed. His light jacket helped protect him from the cold, but he would need to find shelter quickly.

When he glanced down, the snow appeared to sparkle in the moonlight like tiny diamonds scattered throughout. The land around him appeared magical and bright. To his left, he saw several trees and that confirmed that he had been moved to another place. He took a cautious step forward.

"Charley, are you okay?"

He spun around with his musket at the ready and saw Jeremiah coming toward him. "I'm fine." Charley lowered his musket and took Jeremiah's hand and embraced him. "I thought you had died. Have you seen Veronika?"

Jeremiah shook his head. "I have not. I started looking but I am not quite certain where we are."

"You are where you are meant to be." Both Charley and Jeremiah spun around and saw a thin man standing right behind them. He wore all white clothes and his hair, spiky and long, was white as well. "Don't be afraid."

He raised his hands and smiled. "My name is Tristan." When Jeremiah and Charley did not lower their guns, he said, "You are safe and I can take you to your friend."

"Who are you?" Jeremiah kept his pistols trained on Tristan.

"I truly mean you no harm." Tristan blinked and disappeared. He reappeared next to Charley and had removed the musket from his hands. Tristan pointed the musket up at the sky and his smile, almost goofy, remained plastered on his face. "But I don't like having guns pointed at me. It's not friendly like."

Jeremiah lowered his pistols and put them away slowly. "Where are we?"

"These questions do get tiring to answer time and time again by your kind." He held a finger up to his temple while still holding the musket. "I have it. Let me try this. You are on the Otherside in Winter. I'm a faerie and I'll bring you to your friend. Does that fit the niceties for what your kind looks for?"

Charley put his hand out and asked, "If I agree to put my musket away, might I have it back?"

"Of course." Tristan tossed the weapon to Charley, who caught it and put it on his back strap. "I am quite surprised though that you came here first. I fully expected to see our cousin get here first with that glass slipper girl."

"Have you seen Cinderella?" Charley asked.

Tristan shook his head. "Is it polite by your people to ask so many questions? Is it? You know how annoying that is, don't you?"

Jeremiah walked toward Tristan with his hands opened up and said, "We are not quite used to the customs of faeries from Russia."

"From Russia?" Tristan laughed and then shook his head. "I wouldn't have a name like Tristan if we were still in Russia. I'd probably have some long name with more syllables than could be pronounced. No, you're not in Russia any longer. We're on the Otherside in the province of Winter. Did you not hear that I had just said that a few moments ago?"

Charley turned to Jeremiah and started to ask a question and stopped. Jeremiah put his hand on his friend's shoulder. "We'd like to go onward now with you to find our friend Veronika."

Tristan began to walk and as he did so he left no footprints in the snow. "I must say that the two of you coming to face Baba Yaga alone brings a little bit of Spring to my jaded heart."

Charley could not help himself. "Do you know about Baba Yaga?"

Tristan glanced back at Jeremiah and asked, "How do you put up with him?" He turned back around and remained silent a few moments and then said, "We will talk more of her later. Let us enjoy the moonlight walk and I'll take you to Veronika. She will be happy to see you both."

Charley nodded and Jeremiah came up to his friend. "Patience. We will be fine. If he wanted to harm us, we would be dead already."

Tristan turned back and flashed his brilliant, white smile and tapped his right ear. "What your friend says is correct. I don't play around like that fox of a cousin of mine. I just kill my prey good and dead with quickness. It makes things easier that way. For both me and them."

Charley pulled his light coat tighter around him. "I guess that is good to know. Might as well know where we stand up front."

Tristan replied, "Of course, it's so much more civilized that way." He bounded off through the snow humming a little tune, still not leaving any footprints, and Charley and Jeremiah trudged through the snow after him.

Chapter 5

I stared out the window and tapped my fingers on the windowpane. "How long will they keep us here?"

"I suspect the Tsar doesn't quite trust us and we might be here for a very long time." The Silver Fox lay on a couch with his feet propped up on a table, eating grapes. He finished the grape and then scratched the back of his neck.

"You don't look too disturbed being held captive here."

The Silver Fox turned to look at the bowl of grapes he had beside him and shrugged. "I don't necessarily call this imprisonment." He thought for a moment and said, "Though being trapped underground for nearly a decade, that's a different story."

I ignored his attempt to engage me in an argument. "I'm leaving tonight if we don't get to see the Tsar again. We're wasting time here." I had had enough of waiting.

"And where would you go without me?" He again scratched the back of his neck with great vigor.

"I would make do and find a way. I always do." I turned away from him and stared out the window. It had begun to rain.

"Hmph." He kept quiet but I could still hear him scratching.

"Do you have fleas or something?" I walked over to him and took pity on him.

He sat up and rubbed the back of his neck. "I'll be fine."

"Let me see." I went to look at the back of his neck but he pulled away.

"Please, leave me be. I'll be fine." He tried not to scratch his neck but after a few moments he gave in again.

I grabbed his shoulder and then moved away his collar from his neck. He fought me and pulled away. "I said I'll be fine."

But I had already seen. "Your neck, it's turned to the color of gold. Why is that?"

"It's embarrassing." He rushed across the room and positioned his back toward the window. "I'd rather not talk about it."

"Maybe the Tsar's men could get you a salve to help with the itching?"

I moved toward him but he crossed his arms over his chest. "Thank you, but I'll be fine."

The door opened to the room and we both turned to see Vladislav glide into the room wearing his long, black robe flanked by two guards. He came right up to both of us and said, "His Excellency would like to see you now."

I spoke not a word and followed him out of the room. The Silver Fox waited for me to go first and appeared distracted. I knew not what ailment he had or how Vladislav had power over him, but I did like seeing the Silver Fox a bit rattled.

Vladislav led us to a smaller room in which the Tsar sat at breakfast. He ate while reading a newspaper. We stood away from the table with the guards flanking us and Vladislav standing behind. Looking up from his breakfast, the Tsar said, "I have decided to trust you both."

"What changed your mind?" I had had enough of being a pawn, so spoke out.

"We have received news that Bonaparte is nearly at Dresden and troops are mobilizing in Poland and several other countries. A grand army is being formed as he foretold."

The Silver Fox took a step forward but made no threatening move. "And of my plan? What have your advisors thought of it?"

The Tsar wiped his mouth with a napkin. "I do not wish to allow Bonaparte to soil my country."

"Do you not remember your loss at Austerlitz?" I came forward and pressed onward. "Do you wish to repeat it?" I could see that the Silver Fox approved of my line of questioning.

Tsar Alexander put his napkin down on the table. "Leave me alone with them."

Vladislav began to protest, but the Tsar banged his fist on the table and the silverware by his plate clinked. "Leave us, now."

The guards needed no further encouragement and left with a disgruntled Vladislav behind them. I had been before royalty before and knew enough to never underestimate them. I looked to the Silver Fox and took the lead. "Even in America, we came across the news in the papers of your great defeat at the hands of the French emperor."

Tsar Alexander kept his composure and said, "I could have both of you killed and no one would miss you. And yet, you stand before me with such defiance." He took a sip from a crystal glass. "Maybe I need more of your spirit in my armies." He put the glass down and held my gaze level and steady. "Hear me now and understand. We will not allow Bonaparte to advance. I will meet him in battle and lead my troops to victory."

The Silver Fox shook his head. "You would lose and that is what he wants desperately for you to do."

I chanced to risk my audience with the Tsar, but I had no choice. "Would you not learn from your mistake? You have already been defeated by him once. You and all the armies of Europe are not a match for him."

The Tsar's face turned several shades of red and he smashed his fist down on the table, knocking his fork and knife to the floor. "No! I will rise up and raise an army that will crush him and send him back home to his people in fear of us. We will not falter."

"Or you can listen to our advice and actually defeat him." I came closer and leaned down on the table facing Tsar Alexander off squarely. "Do you know why you would lose?"

The Tsar regained control of his anger and asked, "What secret do you know that my spies and all at my command do not?"

"He is a warlock." I kept staring at his face and leaned in so close that I could see his vein pulse in his neck. "There is magic in him that makes him invulnerable. He can control men's minds and cast out a wide swath of his power, bringing the multitudes to his command. Maybe you felt it on the battlefield when you last met him? Though you were enemies, still you thought it wise to be his friend. Am I not right?"

The Tsar looked away and I could see him remembering the day of the battle back at Austerlitz. "Yes, you are right. Even then, I wanted us to be friends. I remember when we sued for peace that he came up to me and implored that we remain friends and he spoke of friendship and how we both were destined to rule the world."

The Silver Fox came by my side. "If you face him on the battlefield again, you would suffer the same fate as before."

"But Vladislav said that he could help." The Tsar turned back to us. "We would use his powers to win."

The Silver Fox shook his head. "Vladislav's magic would not be enough. Bonaparte would crush him and you would lose all that you ever fought for. Your people would be enslaved and next he would march on to India and amass most of the world under his command. All would be his and none would be left to fight him."

"There is still England. The English king wishes for me to join him and together our forces will win." Tsar Alexander pushed back his chair to stand up and put his hand to his head. "I want to do what is right for my people, but your plan seems like madness. How can I let him into mother Russia and destroy our cities?"

The Silver Fox lowered his voice. "Lead the spider into a trap. Pull him in, drag him in. His ego and thirst for victory will be his downfall. Drag the war out and then he will be cut off next fall. When you do engage him, do so only to taunt him and then retreat. Burn all in your path. Burn the crops, the towns, everything. He will be incensed with your madness but it will not sway his course. He will keep coming for you until it's too late."

"How can I allow my armies to do this? People's homes would be destroyed. Would I fall back burning all the cities until even Moscow itself burned in flames?" The Tsar paced back and forth, ignoring us as he thought. "Madness. Absolute madness."

I saw the Silver Fox's plan and aided him. "Yes, it is madness. And that would enrage Bonaparte and cause him to keep coming onward. His supply lines would dwindle and become thin and inefficient and then winter would come. Winter and your victory."

"You talk of winter as though it is a person." He turned to face us and then realization came to him. He turned to the Silver Fox. "You plan on bringing winter here early, do you not? That is why you came to see me."

The Silver Fox smiled and bowed. "Yes, you see through to my plan now."

I had missed an important point in the conversation. "What does he mean?"

The Tsar came forward and said, "Your friend is either brilliant or crazy. I do not know which." When I did not grasp his meaning, he continued. "He will bring Baba Yaga down from her hiding and winter along with her."

The Silver Fox turned to me and said, "Winter is a place on the Otherside where Baba Yaga dwells, my dear, and I plan to incite the craziest and strongest witch in this part of the world to bring her whole domain to Russia. Winter will come early this year and Bonaparte will be forced to retreat back to France with sickness and Winter on his heels. He will be crushed and all his magic will do naught for him. He will not be able to stop the cold."

"But how do you plan to bring Baba Yaga here?" I knew the answer, but I wanted him to say it. I needed to hear him say the words.

"That's where you come in, of course. You will face Baba Yaga and cause her to leave her domain that she's been happy to live in for the last hundred years."

"And how will I do that?" I had no ideas, magic and not much hope left.

The Silver Fox flashed his brilliant smile at me and simply said, "I don't know, but you'll need to find a way."

* * *

Phoebe left the ball feeling tired. She had had enough of dancing and needed to get some sleep. Since arriving in Dresden, the Emperor Napoleon had celebrated his grand army with parties, large dinners and even a street parade. Phoebe leaned against a wall and took off her shoes. Isabelle followed her out of the ball and asked, "Are you ready for bed?"

"I could fall into a sleep and stay there straight through past morning." She massaged her toes and then took her other shoe off. The dress she wore flowed down to the ground and she did not care that her white stockings would get dirty. "When will the army leave?"

"I know you become impatient, but you must trust me. Once the emperor leaves, we will do so as well." Isabelle led her to their room on the other side of the palace. Ever since they had left Saint Cloud, Phoebe had been inundated with people, places and events. The emperor no longer kept her locked in a room, but Isabelle was her constant guide. And, no matter where they went, guards kept an eye on them.

"Let us go to our room and we can talk more." Phoebe led the way and from behind them they could hear laughter coming still from the great ball. She knew that Napoleon would be up late as he had the last several nights celebrating in advance of the launch of his grand army.

Isabelle opened the door to their room and Phoebe went inside, hoping to throw herself on her bed, but stopped. Napoleon sat alone in a chair in their room. "Do I disturb you both?"

He sat alone with no guards, dressed in his best finery but still had his right hand tucked into his vest. He had put on some weight since the last time she had seen him as though he knew that the road to Russia would be long and he needed to fatten up for the journey.

Isabelle recovered first and said, "No, Phoebe and I wished to retire for the evening. Both of us thoroughly enjoyed the ball, but all the dancing has made us tired."

Phoebe kept quiet and sat down on her bed with her hands folded in her lap. No matter how much she had tried, she had no magic and could not summon any to her. She knew not his intentions and thought it best to play tired and remain quiet.

Napoleon crossed his leg over his other and leaned back in the chair. "Have you enjoyed yourself since we left Saint Cloud?" He directed the question to Phoebe.

"Oui." She thought if she responded in French he would be in a more forgiving mood. She still did not fully understand the extent of his powers. He seemed to know all she thought and even now she feared that he could peel away her defenses and know of their plan to escape his grasp.

"Did I ever tell you what happened between Queen Mab and me after Mab pulled us from this world when your mother tried to stop me?" He stretched his hand to the desk in front of him and drummed his fingers there.

"Non." Phoebe almost squeaked her response like a mouse.

"Well, let me share it with you." He stopped drumming and leaned forward out of his chair. "Mab thought to take me from this world and keep me trapped in the dreamline, hoping that I could do no more harm here. We fought and I struggled against her until I pulled myself from her and defeated her." He banged his fist on the table for emphasis. "I defeated her and cast her off in the dreamline so that she can never come back here again. I have defeated her and she cannot save you. Her sacrifice has meant nothing in the long run. I am still emperor and now I will stretch my long arm out across Europe and fold Russia into my empire."

"But you are different and, I see how you act now." Phoebe spoke up and a bit of courage seeped into her blood.

"You are perceptive." He stood up and came over to her, ignoring Isabelle and standing in front of Phoebe. "I paid a price in defeating Mab. She can no longer come back here and I can no longer use the dreamline. Not even for small trips. It's all lost to me. But ..." He brushed Phoebe's hair away from the side of her face. "You have an abundance of magic within you. You can give me some of your magic and I will once again be able to travel through the dreamline."

Isabelle inserted herself in the conversation. "Your Excellency, she is tired and only a child. Let her go to sleep and she can talk in the morning. It is late."

"A child?" He laughed. "She looks at me with murderous rage and would strike me down in my sleep if she could. Oh, I can read her fine. Trust me, I can." He turned to Isabelle and said, "She will go to sleep when I say she can. Leave us."

"But she's tired," Isabelle pleaded.

"Leave us alone before I lose my patience." Napoleon turned away from her and she bowed. She stared at Phoebe for a few seconds to make eye contact with her and nodded once she knew that Phoebe would be okay. Without another word, she left the room.

"What do you want from me?" Phoebe stared Napoleon in the eyes and held out her hands. "I have no magic. I have tried to call forth my powers, but there is nothing."

"Maybe you only need the proper motivation and then you will find your magic." He sat back down and pulled his right hand from his jacket. His hand glowed red with power and he pointed at the wall. "Watch what I can show you."

The wall flickered and a picture began to take shape. They could hear no sound, but could see Cinderella and a man talking.

Phoebe ran to the wall and put her hand on her mother's face. "My mother. She is safe!"

"Yes, she is." Napoleon waved his hand and focused on the man with her mother.

"Who is that?" Phoebe pointed at the elegant looking man in the image.

"That is the Silver Fox. Your mother has taken up with him in the hopes of defeating me. It seems that I am such a formidable enemy that she has decided to work with a half-crazed faerie."

Phoebe watched her mother talk, but could not hear any of the words she spoke. She closed her eyes and willed her magic to blossom within her, but still no spark answered within. She moved her hand to touch her mother's head and stayed quiet for a moment.

"I will ask you again. Will you commit yourself to me and give me your magic?" He held up his hand at seeing her start to interrupt him. "Let me finish. If you could have access to your magic again, would you freely give it to me?"

Phoebe glanced back over her shoulder but the vision of her mother and the Silver Fox had disappeared. "I cannot reach my own magic and I do not know why."

"But if I were to help you rediscover your magic, would you give me some of it? I do not need it all. And you would have so much to spare. Then you could be reunited with your mother and help her."

"Why does she need help? Is she in danger?" Phoebe turned back to the wall and pleaded, "Please, bring her back. Let me see if she is in trouble."

Napoleon shook his head in an exaggerated motion. "I no longer have magic within me to keep the vision going for long. I would need your magic to help me. Maybe another day I can bring the vision back, but tonight I am also too tired. My magic is not as great as it once was."

"But is my mother in danger? Why would she need my help?"

"Your mother has given up her powers to protect you from me." Napoleon walked over to the chair and sat down.

"What?" The full truth of what Napoleon revealed to her washed over her. Without thinking, she said, "But how is she going to be able to rescue me?"

"Precisely. How can she come and save you from my evil clutches?" He shook his head. "I have been patient and kind with you. You are not mistreated and I have made certain that your lessons are kept up and that your development remains consistent."

"But you have not let me outside much and I have had no companions to play with. I am like a trapped bird in a cage."

Napoleon gestured at her. "The ball you went to tonight was not to your liking? Or the gown you wear? I do not have you locked inside the Bastille but have allowed you to be out with me. It is late and do not test me. I am also tired." He gathered himself for a moment and asked again, "If I could help you regain your power, would you share it with me? I only ask that you give me some and the rest could be for your mother."

"I have no magic to give anyone. I cannot call it to my aid. Do you think I have not tried? I have prayed and tried to open the gate within me, but I feel no magic. I do not know why it has left me but it has. I am alone." Phoebe began to cry and covered her face with her hands.

Napoleon quieted his voice and spoke low. "I am not good with children. My own son is only a little more than a year old. I can rule countries and set rules to govern the lives of many, but in these matters I am weak." He put his head in his hands. "I am no monster who will force you to give me your magic. I have an empire to rule and a son to raise and I wish to have your power to help me travel the dreamline again. I could make certain France's future and ensure her people are safe from harm."

Phoebe wiped the tears away from her eyes and replied, "How can I give you what you want? What you ask is not for me to give. I have no magic and, if I did find it again, I fear what you would do."

"You fear me?" He leaned back in his chair and waited for her response.

"You are the emperor and when people do not obey you then you force them to do your will. I am afraid of what you will do to me if I continue to disobey." Tears filled her eyes again. "I miss my mother. Please, send me to her. I am but a child. I only want to be sent to her."

She began to cry and Napoleon watched her for a moment and then said, "Maybe you do have magic in you still, for you have moved me." He stood up and began to leave. "I might regret this, but you and Isabelle can go and head back to find your mother. I know she is in Russia, but not exactly where."

Phoebe watched him leave and hugged herself, trying to stop her tears. A wave of joy washed over her and she called after him. "Your Excellency!"

He stopped and in the candlelight he looked older and tired. He turned back and listened.

"Thank you." She went up to him and took his hand.

He nodded to her and pulled away. "I am no monster. Go find your mother and remember what I did for you." He left the room quickly and Phoebe ran to the window and glanced outside. She could hear people leaving the ball, spreading out into the gardens. Soon she would be free and could go search for her mother.

* * *

Jeremiah followed Tristan and Charley walked next to him. The night remained cold but the pace they kept would keep them both warm enough. "How much farther?"

Tristan stopped and said, "You ruined a good thing. For a good while, there were no more questions. I really detest questions." He abruptly turned and started walking away at a fast pace.

Charley reached for the musket on his back but Jeremiah held his arm and only shook his head. "I forgot about questions." He resumed walking and changed his line of reasoning. "You have a beautiful landscape here."

"It is beautiful. I take pride in my work." Tristan slowed down a bit and pointed ahead. "Ah, the long striders are right ahead. They're sleeping now so we'll have to be careful not to wake them."

Charley kept his voice low. "I do not see anything."

"Of course you don't. They're invisible to you." Tristan crept forward and turned back. "That's how you came to be here. The long striders stepped over you and brought you here." Seeing the confusion on their faces, he took an exasperated breath and exhaled slowly. "You two really need to get out more if you don't know what a long strider is."

Tristan reached his hands out to both of them. "Quickly, grab my hand."

Jeremiah and Charley did as they were told and when they touched his skin a shock went through their bodies. They both blinked in awe as they could now see deeper shades of black and blue that stretched into the ultraviolet. Charley took a few steps forward and kept his hand firmly on Tristan's. "Those huge shapes there that are bent over like an enormous giant's legs. That's it, I can see them!"

Jeremiah glanced down the slope in front of him and marveled at the moonlight reflecting off the snowflakes on the ground. And up ahead, he could see the huge, lumbering shapes. "I see two of them. They appear to be holding each other and end up in the clouds." He looked up and the moon hung high in the sky to his right and in front of them a stationary cloud with the two giants' torsos entwined together like taffy. Their legs, solid and wide, covered a tremendous amount of space. Their shape resembled somewhat of a human frame, but they appeared to have no feet. And as far up as he could see, the torso never ended into a head. The clouds obscured the uppermost portion of their bodies.

Tristan pulled his hands away from them. "Enough staring. I'm hungry and would like a drink. Let's go onward." He took two fingers to his mouth and went to whistle but no sound came out. He waited a few moments and then blew again. From out of the clouds, a rope ladder magically appeared in front of them. "There we go."

Charley looked up but could not see anything through the clouds. Jeremiah jogged forward and grabbed the ladder and held it still. Tristan saluted him and said, "Thank you, sir." He climbed up so quickly and with such grace that he resembled a cat.

In seconds, he was out of earshot. Charley grabbed hold of the ladder and asked, "Do you think it's safe to follow?"

"He appears harmless enough. He might be the closest we'll find to a friend here."

Charley started climbing the ladder and then stopped. "You know, I wish I had a way of showing all of this to the girls. It is truly amazing."

Jeremiah held the ladder still as Charley continued to climb up and then called up after him. "Just think of the great stories you will have once you get home."

Charley laughed and kept climbing up. After a while, Jeremiah started climbing up himself and as he moved up the ladder the temperature began to change. Warmth entered his tired limbs and after a few minutes of climbing he passed through the clouds and began going through a tunnel. He kept climbing and he could see the moonlight a dozen or so rungs away. The tunnel ended and he appeared to be climbing out of a well. Charley helped pull him out and he expected to be standing on the clouds, but solid earth existed under his feet. Before them loomed a castle of unusual design. The walls appeared curved and ended in spires of craggy points. The top spires resembled the ones children made in the sand by grabbing a fist full of wet sand and squeezing out the water, allowing the grains of sand to build towers of unusual beauty.

Tristan bounded up to Jeremiah and said, "Home sweet home. Let's go inside and relax a bit."

He led the way through the front gate and they followed in awe. Charley turned to Jeremiah and said, "Do you think he lives here all alone? I haven't seen anyone else around."

A large white cat suddenly ran from behind and passed right between them. They moved out of her way and the cat took her spot right in front of Tristan and he stopped for a moment to allow the cat to jump up into his arms. He petted her fur and kissed her on the head. Ignoring that Jeremiah and Charley still followed him along, he addressed the cat. "Yes, I've missed you, too. I'm back after my long stay and I'll not be leaving for a while." He paused as if listening and then looked up at Jeremiah and Charley. "Yes, yes, I brought them home with me. They're harmless enough. But they've come here to find their friend."

Charley went to ask a question, but Jeremiah tugged on his shirt to keep him quiet. He walked past Charley and approached Tristan. "You have a beautiful home. I have never seen anything like it in my life."

"Thank you." Tristan looked down to the cat and offered her paw to Jeremiah. "Misty here would like to say hello."

With exaggerated gentleness, Jeremiah took the cat's paw between his thumb and forefinger and shook it. Misty purred in response.

"My, my. It's not often that she takes so quickly to someone. I'm rather impressed."

Charley came up next to Jeremiah and Misty turned away from him, jumping into Tristan's arms. He looked down at his clothes and said, "She probably smells my dog on my clothes. I've not washed in a long time."

"I can tell." Tristan turned away and said, "Follow me. We'll go inside, get something to drink and look out at the scenery."

He walked on without looking back at them and kept stroking Misty as he went. Together they seemed to be having an intense conversation and Jeremiah and Charley simply followed along. Once inside the castle, Tristan led them up a narrow set of stairs to a large room that looked out of the rock cloud they floated on in the sky. He put Misty down and she ran off out of the room. On the table, glasses had been set along with plates of cheese and some fruit.

"Please, sit down and let us relax a bit." Tristan offered them each a chair.

Jeremiah and Charley took seats and waited. Tristan picked up a glass, had a sip and scrounged his face up and shook his head quickly a few times. "Ah, there's nothing like apple juice." Having another tiny sip, he put the glass down and savored the flavor. "I don't know how you humans can deal with so much sweetness."

Charley picked up one of the glasses and had a long drink. "Tastes fine to me."

Jeremiah followed and tried a few pieces of cheese, but remained quiet and waited.

When Tristan had finished his drink, he placed his glass down on the table and then palm down smashed his hand down on the table. The plates jumped a bit and the silverware clattered. "There we go. No one has asked a question for more than a few minutes. And I like it that way. Now here's how this game will go. I'll ask a question and then you both can." He didn't wait for them to respond and asked, "So why are you truly here?"

Charley glanced over at Jeremiah, wondering what to say. Jeremiah put his hand on the arm of his friend and leaned closer to Tristan. "We have come to find our companion Veronika and we seek Baba Yaga."

"Veronika will be back soon. She went out to go exploring and I expect her within the hour." Popping a grape into his mouth, he started chewing and continued talking, "As for Baba Yaga, well, that's another story. Why do you seek her?"

Jeremiah shook his head. "No, we get our question first."

Tristan stopped talking and smiled. "You do listen well. Go ahead then. Ask your question."

"What do you know about Baba Yaga?"

Charley reached for a piece of cheese and decided to take two. Tristan pushed the plate closer to him and leaned back into his chair and fully faced Jeremiah. "That's a complicated question, but I will answer as best I can. She is an old witch who lives here on the Otherside." Tristan waited a bit and then said, "My turn. Why do you want to see Baba Yaga so much?"

"We also search for Cinderella and were told that if we headed to see Baba Yaga that we would find that she searched for her as well."

"Do you love Cinderella?" Tristan asked his next question with quickness, trying to catch Jeremiah off his guard.

Jeremiah started to respond, but said instead, "Two questions in a row isn't fair."

"Yes, it's not fair, but I'm changing the rules of the game. So I ask again, do you love Cinderella?"

"Yes. Yes, I do." Jeremiah sat up straighter.

"You do, don't you?" Tristan hummed to himself and then pointed out the window. "You would brave the dark woods to find Baba Yaga's hut and the crazy witch herself to find this love of yours. Would you now?"

"Yes, I would."

"Even if she doesn't love you? Because what if she doesn't? What if you've chased the globe for her and she finds you lacking?" Tristan folded his hands in from of him. "What then?"

"That is not for you to worry about." Jeremiah remained calm.

"I do not worry. I simply ask and as guardian of Baba Yaga I need to make certain that those who get to see her are well-prepared for what awaits them."

"We are prepared." Jeremiah looked at Charley who continued to eat a plate full of cheese and fruit.

"You have no idea of what you say. You chase the world for a woman you do not know if she loves you back and now you ask to be let in to see Baba Yaga. You are both crazy."

Charley chanced a question. "Where is Veronika truly?"

"She came like you asking many questions and having much need for answers." Tristan's smile turned wicked. "And I let her in."

Jeremiah and Charley both reached for their guns and pulled them out at the ready. Jeremiah leaned across the table, pointing his two pistols at Tristan's face. "What did you do with Veronika?"

"I fed her to Baba Yaga of course. Everyone needs to eat you know."

Charley jumped up out of his chair. "You what?"

"Fed is a bit too strong of a word. I offered her the chance to go meet Baba Yaga." Tristan paused and scratched his head and thought a moment. "Maybe 'offered' isn't quite the correct term. I forced her to go into Baba Yaga's domain."

Charley swung his musket like a club at Tristan but the faerie moved like lightning and had backed off from the attack. "Tsk, tsk. You have a temper and I don't quite like that." Tristan stayed far enough away and said, "My turn to ask a question."

Jeremiah played along. "Go ahead. Ask."

"Why do you love Cinderella?" He walked closer to Jeremiah. "Why her? Why are you traveling the world for her and spend your life with her? I want to know. I truly want to know why she is so special to you." He held up his hand to hold off Jeremiah's response. "I have seen many who have come here and many quest for power, wishes, revenge, but love is unique. Don't mistake me. People have come to make people love them but not to save someone they love. Tell me true."

Jeremiah lowered his pistols and put them away. He walked step by step closer to Tristan and said, "I have seen her at her weakest and still I love her. She has such good in her and I want to see that good grow. I have followed her far and we are now friends. If she loves me not in return, then I would be happy just to have her friendship.

The love I offer her, I give freely and ask for none in return. If she were to accept it and be happy, then I would build my life with her."

Tristan shook his head. "Words, words, words. You tell me how you love her." He rushed forward and shouted at the two of them. "Now show me!"

Charley raised his hands to protect his face, but a spray of frost shot out of Tristan's hands and the world shifted. Jeremiah turned away to shield his body from the attack, but Charley and Jeremiah found themselves in a dark and dense forest. The castle had vanished and Tristan stood before them still all in white against the dark trees that surrounded him. He held up his hand and pointed at the two of them. "Welcome to the dark land of the Otherside." He held his hands up like a circus ringmaster. "Here you will find Baba Yaga or she will find you. All of your answers can be had here if you can survive."

Charley stood firm and asked, "Why are you doing this to us? What harm have we ever done to you?"

Tristan dropped his showmanship for a moment and replied, "It is not anything that you have done, but I have been tasked to keep Baba Yaga trapped here. She must not escape. It is my job to keep her safe here in the Otherside." He turned to Jeremiah and said, "Behind you near the closest trees you will find some packs with supplies. You will be able to live well enough here if you learn to survive. Your Cinderella will be coming soon. If you are patient, you might find each other. But both of you will never escape here alive. No one ever has and no one ever will. Not as long as I remain guardian."

Jeremiah grabbed Charley by the arm and pushed him toward Tristan. "Please, take him from here and leave me. He has a wife and a family who need him. Take him home."

Tristan shook his head. "I cannot do that. Good-bye."

"Wait!" Jeremiah ran forward, but Tristan had already vanished.

Charley came up to Jeremiah. "Thank you for trying. You did not have to do that."

"You do not deserve to be here."

"And you do? Let us stick together and we will both find a way out."

Jeremiah looked up at the gray sky. "I would be lying if I said I wasn't worried. Getting out may not be possible."

"If you don't believe, then you will never succeed. I am getting home. I am going to see Ginny and the kids. There is no doubt in my mind that I am going home." Charley turned away from his friend and walked toward the trees. "So let's go get these packs and start looking for Veronika. I think that would be a good place to start."

Jeremiah followed and asked, "You always impress me. Just when I think I understand you, I see another side of you and am amazed. How do you not doubt and give up hope?"

Charley stopped but did not turn around. "I'm a man who lives in a household with four children and one on the way." He waited until Jeremiah caught up to him and then faced him. "I'm not missing the birth of my next child. Nothing and no one is going to stop me from missing that."

"And I will do everything I can to help you get home to your family. Thank you for sticking with me." Jeremiah shook Charley's hand and then patted him on the back.

"Neither of us knew that we'd be sent through a hole in the ground to another part of the world. And there's no point in being upset about it. Best thing I can do is remain positive, stay strong and smart and do everything I can to get home to my girls. They need me and I won't disappoint them."

Charley walked away and picked up one of the packs that rested against the trunk of a tree. He slung it on his back, adjusted his musket and tossed the other pack to Jeremiah. "He could have left us with no supplies so it could be worse."

Jeremiah put his pack on and laughed. "You're right."

Charley tightened the straps on his pack and asked, "Ready?"

Jeremiah nodded. "Ready."

Charley saw a path ahead and said, "Good, let's head out. Time's a wasting." He started off on the trail and Jeremiah followed.

Chapter 6

Phoebe woke up to beams of brilliant light from the rising sun streaming through her window. She had a few moments of disorientation and then stretched her arms over her head and yawned. Napoleon had said that he would let her go. He had said it. She had not dreamed it.

She sat up out of bed and saw that across the room Isabelle still slept. A look of worry danced across her face and she mumbled a few words in French deep in a dream. Phoebe snuck to the corner of the room without waking Isabelle up and used the chamber pot. When finished, she washed her hands and face. The cold water woke her up fully and she came back to her bed to see that Isabelle had awakened.

"Bon matin." She sat up in bed and rubbed her eyes.

"Good morning to you as well." Phoebe bounded over to Isabelle's bed and threw herself on it. "You were asleep when Napoleon returned me to our room last night."

"I tried to stay awake but I fell asleep." Isabelle put her hand on Phoebe's hand. "Is everything all right?"

Phoebe could not contain her excitement. "He told me that he would release me and that I could go find my mother. I am free!"

Isabelle appeared shocked and did not know what to say. Phoebe grabbed her hand and pulled her out of bed. "Come on. We have lots to do today. We'll be leaving here and I am free!"

"I do not understand. What did he tell you?" Isabelle sat on a chair in the room and listened.

"He told me that I could go free. That I could go find my mother and that he would not stop me. Will you come with me?" Phoebe ran to the window and looked outside. "I so need your help. Please, will you help me?"

Isabelle glanced back at the door and noticed it opened. No guards stood outside their door. "I don't know if I can do that."

"But why? We are free. He told me I could leave!" Phoebe spun around in a circle and her nightgown twirled around her.

"Of course he said you could leave. He is trying to prove a point." Isabelle pointed around the room. "Look at us. We have nothing. No money, supplies and just a few change of clothes. We could leave here, but where would we go?"

"Can we not find other witches to take us in? We need to leave. We can't stay here. This is the chance that I was waiting for. Please, you have to help me." Phoebe grabbed her arm and implored. "Please, please you must come with me!"

"I am trying to help you." Isabelle put her arm around Phoebe. "I need time to think this through. We would be safe enough to find some local help and to maybe even get back to Paris, but we would not be any closer to finding your mother."

"I know I could find her. I could use my magic and …" Phoebe glanced down at her hand and then stopped. She jumped off the bed and turned to face Isabelle. "I have no magic now, but maybe it would come back to me. Maybe in time I would be able to reclaim it."

"And maybe not." Isabelle folded her hands in her lap. "What if we leave and we cannot find your mother?"

"Then at least I would be free. I can find help elsewhere. Other witches would help me. You must know some we could go to, right?" Phoebe went to their window and stared out at the city. "We can leave this place and I can be truly free."

Isabelle shook her head. "Napoleon does not make plans lightly. He offered you your freedom and if you take it he will probably find a way to track you. There must be a reason for why he would let you go. He is a calculating man and would not make this choice lightly."

"What if he truly just wants me to be free?" Phoebe stopped twirling and sat down on her bed. "Would that be so strange?"

Isabelle shook her head. "He is the emperor of Europe. He does not make a decision like this lightly." She got up off her chair and stood before Phoebe with her hands on her hips. "I will go with you to help you, but we should be cautious."

Phoebe squealed with delight and threw her arms around Isabelle. "Thank you, thank you, thank you."

Isabelle disentangled herself from Phoebe's hug and said, "I worry for you and think that he has a plan to put into action that we cannot see. We will need to take caution."

Phoebe turned away and went back to the windows. The sun had risen above the buildings and she could see it behind the clouds in the sky. "Yes, you are right. We should be cautious. You are probably right in that he would find a way to track me, but I have to risk that. And once I find my mother, all will be well."

"Then it is decided and we will leave later today. We will pack light and head out later this morning." Isabelle stretched and reached toward the ceiling. "But first, I need to wash my face and dress. Why don't you head downstairs and get some breakfast and I will meet you soon."

Phoebe bounded over to Isabelle and kissed her on the cheek. "This is the best day of my life!" She hugged Isabelle again and then skipped out of the room singing a little ditty in French.

Isabelle watched her go and smiled. She turned to head to the basin and saw Napoleon standing before her. Where he had come from, she did not know. Immediately, she took to her knees and bowed her head to the floor. "Your Excellency, I did not hear you enter."

"I did not wish you to." He did not motion for her to rise and came closer to her. "As you have heard, my plans have changed. I head out on my grand adventure to take Russia and I have no desire to torture the girl. She has proved more resilient than I would have thought. She locks away her magic with great skill and my power cannot touch her. I have decided to let her go. And I will also allow you to go. You will be her guide and together you will find Cinderella. She will not be easy to locate. Without her magic, I have no means to trace her and my spies cannot find her either. But maybe Phoebe and you can find a way."

"We will do our best to find her. And if we do, what do you want me to do?" Isabelle spoke with hesitation and appeared to want to say more but remained quiet.

"All you need to do is to let me know where she is and I will do the rest. It will be an easy task for you. The hardest part is trying to find her. I will provide you both with all you need for the journey." He approached her and put his hand on her shoulder. "If you do find her, then all will be well."

"But what about my family?" Isabelle could not hold back the question. She put her hands together in prayer. "Please, do not harm them."

Napoleon smiled. "I will take great care to make certain that your mother and children are well provided for while you are gone. I have already explained to them of your departure and they wish you well." His hand lingered on her shoulder and he caressed it. "I told them that you love them and that you will be reunited with them soon. If you find Cinderella, all will be fine."

Isabelle began to sob and she took a few moments to control herself. "Yes, I will do my best and find Cinderella. I will do it for you. I will do anything for you if you do not harm my family."

Napoleon patted her shoulder lightly and then tilted her head up to him so that he could look into her eyes. "Exactly. Now we understand each other."

* * *

I had tired of riding on horseback. I stopped and stretched my legs and saw that the Silver Fox followed suit.

"I need to take a break. We have been riding for hours and I feel sore."

He nodded and came down off of his gray stallion. "You have been quiet. Is all well with you?"

I had not much companionship so I wondered if I should trust him or hold back. "I miss my daughter and my friends."

"There is much I could say to you now, but I doubt that you would like any of it." He patted the side of his horse and then walked away so that it could graze. The surrounding countryside had begun to bloom with a myriad of purple spring flowers.

"What do you mean?" I came up to walk next to him and watched as my horse followed his.

"I can sense that Phoebe has used magic again." He closed his eyes and took a slow and deliberate breath. He opened his eyes and looked off to the west. "She has left Bonaparte."

"Do you know where she is so that I can go to her?"

"Yes, I do know." He kept quiet and walked away from me.

"But you're not going to tell me where she is. Are you?" I did not know what game he played but I would find out soon enough.

"That is correct."

I clenched my fist at my side, but no magic came to me. The silence inside remained. "Why tell me this but not help me?"

"I am helping you. I thought you would want to know about Phoebe."

"But you're withholding information from me." I came up to him and confronted him. "I have been searching for two years and cannot find her and now you're telling me that you know where she is but won't tell me? Can you not understand why I am angry?"

"I told you that you would not like what I had to say." He stood his ground but turned away to look west.

"Please, tell me where she is. If you don't wish to come with me, I will go on my own to find her."

"I know you would and that is why I cannot tell you where Phoebe is."

I clenched my left hand tightly as I could by my side and took a deep breath. I rushed forward and dug deep within me, searching for the spark that I once had. I dug and dug and willed my essence to flare up and willed my power to return. With my right hand, I had grabbed his shirt and with my left I released my power at him. And nothing happened. He took a step back and allowed me to push him another step and did not resist me.

I let out a scream and clenched my hand tighter. I would not be defeated and would find a way to regain my magic. Here and now I would be done with all of this. Nothing could stop me.

He reached up and grabbed my hand. "Had enough?"

"Tell me where she is." I struggled with him and pulled my hand away. "I need to know."

"If I do that, then you will go to find her and would be doing exactly what Bonaparte wants. He wants you to do that. Do you want to play his game and lose?"

"Tell me!" I shook him and then bit down on my tongue and willed my magic to come to life.

He shook his head and then scratched the back of his neck where I knew he still hid a gold patch of skin. "I will not do that. You have to go see Baba Yaga. That is where I am taking you."

"No, I want to go to my daughter. I need to go find her. I need her to know that I haven't abandoned her." I pushed him away and let the tears come. "Are you so heartless that you choose to not help me? Have I not suffered enough?"

"You choose to suffer because it makes you feel something. All the mistakes you have made in the past cannot be simply undone. Phoebe knows you love her and she will come to you. If you go to her, then you risk being captured by the emperor. Is that what you want?"

I cried and covered my face with my hands. "I am so tired."

"I know, but now is not the time to falter. I have seen that Baba Yaga can help turn the tide against Bonaparte. He and his grand army will not be able to withstand the winter that she will bring with her." He turned away from me and looked to the north. "We are almost to her lands. We are so close. I simply wanted you to know that your daughter lives. I thought you would want to know that."

I started walking and ignored him. If I walked and closed my eyes, I might be able to find a way to meet with Phoebe again. Maybe I could get a signal from what direction I needed to go. Maybe I could rediscover what I had lost.

"If you leave here, you will die at Napoleon's hands and Phoebe will lose her mother. Is that what you want?" he called after me and something in his voice angered me.

I imagined hellfire emanating from my fingertips and burning him alive. "No, that is not what I want. I want to go to my daughter and to rescue her. I am tired of searching the world and going in circles. You have given me the first real news on her whereabouts in two years. I want to go to her." He stood calmly behind me with his arms folded over his chest and not burned by the imaginary magic I had thrown at him.

"That hate you feel, bottle it up and use it to keep you true. Phoebe will be fine without you. Your destiny lies north. Would you rather I had lied and not told you about your daughter? I have given you hope and now you cast me aside." His voice softened and he came up to me. "I know that you have not had many people to trust and that I have been full of tricks in the past, but I swear to you that Baba Yaga is the key to the emperor's downfall. Please, you're so close. Don't give up now."

The fight left me and I saw the world stretch out in front of me and wondered what Jeremiah would do. He had much more calm than I. I wondered where he was right now and wished I could have his guidance and his love. I froze as the thought had come to me unhindered and free.

"What is it?" The Silver Fox stood by me and waited.

I took a moment to calm myself and then faced him and said, "You are right. I will go with you. It is the sensible thing to do, and though I tire of being sensible and wish for Bonaparte to burn for all he has done, that day will come soon. But it is not today. Let us go."

He thought he hid his sly smile from me, but I caught it. He believed he had won and defeated me. I only needed a way to win. And, God help me, I would do that and more.

* * *

Charley walked through the forest and followed Jeremiah. "I guess there will never be a sunrise here. Do you think that's right?"

"I think we're too far north for a true sunrise or maybe the magic here is too strong. I don't truly know." Jeremiah led the way and moved a tree limb from in front of him. The branch bent back easily enough and he held it so that Charley could follow.

"What exactly is our plan?"

Jeremiah thought for a moment and said, "Honestly, I don't have one."

"Do you know what I want to do when I get back?" Charley ducked underneath the tree branch and kept up the pace. "I'm going to never leave my land again and stay with my wife and kids."

Jeremiah stopped. "I should never have allowed you to come with me. I'm sorry. I truly am."

Charley ignored him and went on, saying, "I'm going to sit with the girls and take part in that tea party that they always want me to join them in."

Jeremiah laughed. "Do they still dress Hunter up as a princess with ribbons in his fur?"

"Yes and it is the funniest sight."

"We'll get you home. I will do everything I can to make certain that you're home in time for the baby's birth."

"I know you will. I have no doubt …"

A call from their left caused them both to stop in their tracks. Jeremiah listened and heard a woman's voice calling. "Do you hear that?"

"I do." Charley walked a few steps to the sound of the voice and said, "I think it might be Veronika."

"Can you make out what she's saying?"

They both heard the voice again and Charley replied, "I think she's calling our names. Should we respond?"

Jeremiah held up his hand. "No, no. Let's take it slow and find her. I don't know who else might be listening or if it's truly her. It could be some sort of a trick."

Charley nodded and continued moving forward. The gray clouds hung low and Veronika's voice echoed throughout the area. They kept quiet, moving with purpose toward her. Ahead Jeremiah could see her wearing a pack on her back and calling their names. She looked to be in good health. Jeremiah waved Charley back and whispered, "Stay here. Let me see her first and if all is okay then you can come out."

"Sure." Charley stood behind a tree and hid himself from view.

Jeremiah cupped his hands over his mouth and called, "Veronika, is that you?"

At the sound of his voice, she turned to his direction. "Jeremiah, yes, I am here. Where is Charley?"

"Are you okay?" He jogged up to her and saw no signs that she was hurt.

"I am fine. Do you know where we are? I met a strange faerie and he tricked me into coming here." Her thick accent made some of what she said difficult to understand.

"He tricked us too." Jeremiah turned back around and called, "It's fine to come on out."

Charley jogged up to the two of them and he greeted Veronika with a warm smile. "Glad to see that you are okay. We were starting to worry that something had happened to you."

"No, I am fine. One minute I walked on the plains and the next I found myself with that faerie. He brought me here and then abandoned me. I did not think that I would ever find either of you again." She hugged Jeremiah and then put her hand on Charley's arm.

"I'm glad to see that you're safe." Jeremiah returned the hug and then pulled away.

Veronika put her hands on her hips and looked out at the trail in front of them and asked, "What should we do now?"

"We head north and hope we somehow find Baba Yaga." Jeremiah slung his pack on his shoulder and headed off through the woods.

Veronika called after him. "What are we going to do once we find Baba Yaga? I think we should have a plan."

Charley stood by Veronika and heard a noise off to his right. "Shhh."

Jeremiah called back to them. "Our plan is to stay alive and get Charley home as quickly as we can."

Veronika heard the noise too and whispered after Jeremiah. "Wait, we heard something."

Jeremiah kept walking off as though he had not heard them talking and soon was out of sight. Veronika pulled out a long knife from her belt and held it at the ready. Charley checked that his musket was loaded and aimed it in front of him. They heard the noise again and turned toward it. The leaves rustled to their right and it sounded much louder.

"I cannot see anything. Can you?" Charley came closer to Veronika to protect her.

"I see nothing as well ..." Veronika edged forward toward the trees and then stopped.

In front of them, the trees parted as though they bent to the side from a command and three gaunt looking men, dressed in tattered clothes, shambled toward them. Their skin was pale and deathly white and they stared at Veronika with an intense hunger.

"Stop!" Charley shouted at them and aimed at the first man. The trio still shambled forward and Charley fired. His shot pierced through the man's chest and a burst of red broke through the man's clothes. His expression changed and he stopped walking and appeared to wake from a dream. "Thank you." He mouthed the words and then fell dead to the ground.

The other two quickened their pace and Veronika backed away, holding her knife in front of her. Charley pushed Veronika behind him and yelled, "Jeremiah, we need some help!"

Another shot rang through the air and the second man fell into a tree and hit the ground never to rise again. Veronika spun around and saw Jeremiah running at them with both his pistols out. An additional shot hit the third man in the head. He stumbled toward them a few more steps and then fell backward. Charley quickly loaded his musket again and asked, "What in hell were they?"

Jeremiah came up to them and said, "I'm sorry. There is some powerful magic here. I didn't hear that you both had stopped and needed my help. The musket shot broke the spell."

Veronika kept her knife out and walked over to one of the dead men. "What was wrong with them? They appeared possessed."

Jeremiah went to her and pulled her away. "I don't think we should stay here. We should keep moving."

From the north a sudden loud keening could be heard. The noise echoed through the area and they all froze in place, afraid to move. The keening went on for a full minute and then ended suddenly. The forest remained still and the trees had come back together again, but the dead men had vanished. No traces of them or their blood remained.

Jeremiah listened intently and then pushed Veronika and Charley forward. "Run!"

They did not question him and headed off the path to the north, running at their fastest speed. From behind them, the trees creaked and stretched, pulling themselves back once again. Charley glanced back over his shoulder and yelled, "Just run, don't look back. Trust me, just keep on running!"

Veronika thought to turn back, but stayed as close behind Jeremiah as she could. They ran through the forest, and from behind them the rustling sound became louder and louder with the creaking of the trees announcing the coming of something wicked and cold. Charley kept running and carried his musket in his hands, careful not to trip on any tree roots. Behind them, they could hear groaning and then a voice. "Veronika, please stay. Stay with us. Please."

Veronika stopped and turned around. Charley nearly ran into her but avoided her at the last second and stopped against a tree. He pulled at her arm and said, "Come on, let's go. Don't stop!"

She resisted him and refused to move. "That voice. I recognize it." She called out in Russian, yelling a greeting.

Charley grabbed both her arms and called to Jeremiah. "I need some help."

Jeremiah stopped and turned around to run back and help them. The trees behind them had all moved as if by magic and dozens of shambling men in all walks of life came toward them. They walked with purpose and did not run, but appeared to need no rest or sustenance. Their eyes glazed and askance, they all stared at Veronika with an unholy lust. One of the men came forward and answered her in Russia.

Charley shook Veronika. "Whoever you think he is, it's not him. It's a ghost or a trick. Please, come on."

A young man, who stood out among the rest, reached out to Veronika. "I have missed you. Come back with me."

Veronika held her hand over her mouth. "It's a boy from the village. A boy who liked me last year, but disappeared. We all thought he had run away or had been captured and forced into serving the army."

"No, I have searched for you. Only for you and I have found you. Now we can be together." He stumbled forward and in the pale light they could see his skin covered in sores. "She promised me that she would give me magic to find you and she did. Now we can be together."

Veronika allowed Charley to pull her away. "I am sorry, but I must go."

Jeremiah arrived and did not think twice. He fired a shot at the young man and he fell back against the dozens of men behind him. The young man stumbled and cried out, reached for Veronika but in moments the horde of possessed men pushed him to the ground and then crushed him. He disappeared from sight and the men kept onward.

"We have to find a way out of here. Come on, let's go. There is nothing you can do to save them. They are already lost." Jeremiah pushed Veronika ahead and tried to fire his second pistol into the crowd of men and realized he had not had time to reload. He holstered his pistols and ran.

Charley pulled Veronika along and said, "Just run. We can talk later. Keep on running."

Veronika followed them and glanced back one last time. Jeremiah took up the rear and he gently pushed her forward. "It is not your fault. There is dark magic at work here. We need to keep going."

She stared up into his face and saw compassion there. "But it's not right. They were tricked."

Jeremiah put his arm on hers. "Please, just go." He nudged her onward and she took off at her fastest pace with him right behind.

They ran onward for a long while and after a time the horde could not keep up with them. At a small creek, they jogged through the water for a while and then crossed over to the other bank. The noises behind them had fallen away a long time ago and they could not see or hear any evidence of the cursed men. They picked up a path to the north and crossed on that, heading onward without stopping for fear that they would be found again.

Jeremiah had reloaded his pistols and secured them on his back, preparing for another attack. Though hours had passed, the sky remained the same shade of gray and the light remained consistent. "We need to keep going."

Veronika called after him. "I will need to rest soon. I am tired. Can we not take a short break?"

Charley glanced over his shoulder and heard no sounds behind them. "I think it would be safe to stop."

Jeremiah had them run on for a few more minutes and he put his ear to the ground and listened. Hearing nothing, he stood up and said, "I think it's safe to stop now. I do not hear anything coming. But we shouldn't rest long and need to keep on moving."

Charley leaned against a tree stump and took a drink from his water skin. "Do I want to know what those things were?"

Veronika chose a patch of ground to sit down on and said, "Those creatures looked to be from the fairy tales Mamochka Tatyana told me as a child."

"I do not know what type of magic rules here, but I think we should head to find Baba Yaga and leave here as quickly as we can." Charley rubbed his hands together and shivered.

"But how are we going to find her?" Veronika asked.

Charley heard a scratching sound coming from behind him and he spun around with his musket at the ready. He froze and asked, "Does everyone see what I am seeing?"

Jeremiah grabbed for his pistols and stared in disbelief. Veronika stood up and looked at the small hut behind Charley. The hut stood a good twelve feet off the ground, balanced on two giant chicken legs. The legs moved forward and the hut, attached to the legs, moved closer to them. She stared up at the hut. "By the Blessed Mother, it's right out of the stories."

Charley backed away and asked, "What is that?"

The hut stood still and balanced on one giant chicken leg as the right leg scratched the left. Jeremiah looked to Veronika for an answer and she said, "That is Baba Yaga's hut. It looks like it has found us."

Chapter 7

Phoebe turned her face into the wind and smiled. The sun, warm and inviting, rose high in the sky and the possibilities stretched out before her. She wore a backpack with some clothes, a bit of food and some water. "I wish we were back in the great plains of America. My mother, Renée and I used to look out across the land and see grass as far as we could see."

Isabelle led the way in the center of Dresden and neither of them had looked back. Most people in the town had turned out to see Napoleon's grand army leaving. No one paid them much attention. She walked at a steady pace and replied, "I have never been to America. I wonder if its plains are similar to the sunflower fields in France."

"I doubt it. The plains stretched out for miles upon miles upon miles." Phoebe twirled and stopped abruptly and looked down at her dress as it still spun around her. She ran a few steps to catch up to Isabelle and changed the subject. "Do you think my magic will come back now that we have left?"

"I hope so. It might take some time with having been in captivity for so long." She pointed up at the sky. "But with some fresh air and the warm sun, I expect you'll have your powers back soon."

"Good. I miss it. It's like I've lost an old friend." Phoebe fell in stride next to Isabelle and asked, "Where are we going?"

"I need to find a place where other witches can be found. I thought we would leave the city and talk to a local farmer." When Isabelle saw Phoebe's confused look, she went on. "Witches often help heal the sick and are midwives for those outside a city."

"I have only been around a few witches so I don't have much experience."

"If we are lucky, we can find a coven that will take us in and help us." Isabelle slowed down a bit. In front of them, the large square held merchants with their stalls selling their wares. People milled about going about their business. Up ahead, sitting beside a fountain, an old man played a lute and sang a song.

Phoebe paused to listen to the music and she thought of her father. She had heard him sing a few times and his voice had always held steady but had never held the emotion she had expected. She lost herself in the old man's song and closed her eyes taking in the music.

"Are you not feeling well?" Isabelle came beside Phoebe and put her arm around her. "You do not look well."

"The singer reminds me of my father. I haven't seen him in more than two years. I have often wondered if he would he take me in if I went to him."

"Why would he not do so?" Isabelle turned toward the old man and watched his expert hands strum the strings of the lute.

"He is married into royalty now and has another daughter. He and my mother did not marry. I doubt he would want me in his life now. I would complicate things." Phoebe turned toward Isabelle with tears in her eyes. "I just want to find a safe place to live and to be given a chance to learn and have fun. I want to find my mother and to have time to rest with her. If I cannot find her, I truly do not wish to go to my father."

"Did he treat you badly?" Isabelle asked.

"He seemed distracted the time we were together and more interested in himself than in getting to know me. I doubt he would even care that I've gone missing." Phoebe wiped tears from her eyes.

"Come here. You will be all right." Isabelle embraced her but appeared distracted, looking off to the right.

Isabelle noticed and asked, "What's wrong?"

"Trust me and do not turn around." She hugged Phoebe tighter and in the crowd that formed to listen to the old man play Phoebe felt someone bumped into her from behind.

Isabelle reacted with intense speed and snatched the hand of a young boy who had tried to steal from Phoebe's backpack. "Hey, stop that!"

The young boy said not a word, but twisted from her hold and tore away, pushing through the crowd. Phoebe caught a glimpse of his blond hair and darted after him, running hard. She imagined she was back on the plains of America and chased after the buffalo or the wild horses. She could run and fast. The boy knew the area better than she and had snuck between two carts, thinking he could get away, but Phoebe kept on following him. Behind her she could hear Isabelle calling her name, lost in the crowd.

The boy ran to the end of the block and made a quick right, ducking into an alley. Phoebe followed right along and saw him ahead. He had turned into another alley and had doubled back around headed past the square toward an old church. Phoebe continued to chase after him until she saw him run up the church's steps and then into the building. Catching her breath, she slowed down and followed him up the stairs. She turned around but could not see Isabelle and knew that if she did not hurry that the boy would sneak out a window or a back door and he would be gone without a trace. She had to act fast.

Once inside, she ran past the doors into the main part of the church and heard a noise up ahead. She saw the boy push past two side doors and disappear into the back of the church. But the moment she walked down the main aisle, she stopped and stared up at the stained glass windows. Sunlight streamed in and she stared in awe at all the beauty.

"May I help you, child?" A deep voice coming from behind startled her.

She spun around and took in the middle-aged priest. "The boy. Where did he go?" She stumbled over the words and turned back to point where he had been.

"I saw no boy, but I appear to have found a lost girl." He kept his hands folded in front of him and appeared calm. "Would you like to join me for a late lunch?"

"But the boy, I need to find him. He tried to steal from me."

His face expressed no concern at her words. "If he has harmed no one, let him go. He will either learn his lesson or be caught next time. Instead, come with me and let us sit down a bit." He walked up to the nearest pew and sat. "Is your mother looking for you?"

"You know my mother?" Phoebe sat down next to him. "Do you know where she is?"

"I might know your mother. There are many people in my parish and I can help you find her if you would like." He thought a moment and asked, "Have you lost your mother?"

"Yes, but I don't think you can help me." Phoebe turned away and she fought back tears. "I thought you knew my mother, but how could you? I just misunderstood. I am sorry, Father." She bowed her head to him and went silent.

"You know, I come here at this time of day to look at the light coming through the stained glass." He pointed up at the figures in glorious red, yellow and blue. The colored light filled the church with warmth. "It gives me hope that I am not alone and that if I could relax for a moment that I would realize that the world is a good place and that there are good people. Help comes to those who have helped others. Don't you agree?"

Phoebe had begun to cry and she hid her face in her hands. "I'm sorry." The words came up mumbled and raw.

"It is quite all right. If I had lost my mother and a boy had tried to steal from me, I would be upset as well." He pulled a handkerchief from a pocket and handed it to her. "Take this and dry your eyes. You will be well and I know that soon you and your mother will be reunited. You will need to go find her in Russia and I will help you."

A moment passed in which Phoebe blew her nose into his handkerchief and then she paused and turned to him in bewilderment. "Who are you?"

He smiled and rubbed his hands through his graying beard. "I am Father Karl and you are Cinderella's daughter."

Phoebe perked up and asked, "How do you know that? Do you know my mother? Is she near here?" Her string of questions rolled off her tongue and she waited for his answer.

"When I pray, I have seen your mother and knew that you would be coming to see me today." He remained calm and did not move.

"You're a warlock!" Phoebe shouted in delight and then covered her mouth embarrassed at her outburst.

"I am Father Karl." He offered his hand to her and when she took it she was amazed at how smooth it was. "I will help you find your mother."

The front door to the church slammed shut and the noise startled both of them. Phoebe saw Isabelle run toward them at full tilt, brandishing a broom in her hands. "Get away from her. Now!"

Father Karl remained calm and took his hand from Phoebe and stood up slowly. He only had his black cassock and white collar to protect him and Phoebe doubted that would be enough, so she rushed out of the pew with her arms up and yelled, "Stop, he's not harming me! Please, stop!"

Isabelle ignored Phoebe and pulled her behind her and protected her like a mother hen. "Stay where we can see you. We're leaving now and I don't want you to follow us. Do you understand?"

Father Karl put his hands up. "I can help you."

Isabelle turned back to Phoebe and asked, "Did you find the boy? Did he take anything from you?" She then spun back around and flicked the broom at Father Karl as he tried to leave the pew. "I said stay!"

Phoebe grabbed Isabelle's arm. "He's one of us. It's okay. Please."

Father Karl remained silent and did not move.

"I think he's a warlock." Phoebe convinced Isabelle to put the broom down.

"He's a priest and they're not to be trusted." She took a step forward and held tightly onto the broom and asked, "Who are you?"

Father Karl answered, "It is true that I am a warlock, but I am also a priest." He took a step forward and asked, "Can I lower my hands now?"

Phoebe pulled the broom from Isabelle and said, "Certainly. Tell me more about how you can help us find my mother."

Isabelle still resisted and said, "But he's a priest and they're never to be trusted."

"The priests here in this church are different. We hide our powers but she guessed right in that I am a warlock." He walked into the aisle and kept his voice low. "I have the gift of sight. I can help you if you will come with me."

Isabelle pulled Phoebe close. "In France, the priests have tortured and killed many of us witches over the years. I do not trust him. We should go."

Phoebe raised her left hand and tried to use her magic but still none came to her call. "I think we should trust him. We are going to need assistance and he has offered to help us. I think we should hear what he has to say."

Father Karl started to walk away. "Follow me and I will help you. If not, then I send God's blessing on you both and wish you well." He did not pause and headed off through a door to the back of the church.

Phoebe started to follow him but Isabelle hesitated. "I don't think we should go. I don't like priests and have never trusted them. It is best if we move on."

"Let us just hear what he has to say. What if he could help us?" Phoebe pulled at Isabelle's hand. "Meeting him is a great omen. We should not just walk away."

Isabelle hesitated but still did not move.

Phoebe folded her hands together and asked, "Please?"

Isabelle thought a moment longer and then gave in and allowed herself to be pulled along by Phoebe. Once through the door, they went down some stairs and came to a tiny room. Father Karl sat at a table and had poured some water for them. He had also put out some bread and cheese for them to share.

"Please, take a seat and let us talk." He pushed the tray of food at them. "Have a bite to eat."

Phoebe nibbled on a piece of cheese and asked, "Do you know that boy who tried to steal from me?"

"He is the baker's son. I will deal with him when I see him next. He will not be trying to steal with anyone again after I talk to his father." Father Karl spread some cheese on a small piece of bread and took a bite. He chewed with a singular purpose and enjoyed the silence while they ate.

Isabelle took some bread and cheese, but did not eat at first. "I apologize for not trusting you. The priests in Paris are the servants to the emperor and I have seen them take men and women from their homes to imprison them for heresy." She played with the piece of bread in her hand. "I simply wanted to ensure that Phoebe was safe."

Father Karl shook his head. "No, that is not what you thought." He brushed the crumbs off of his hands and onto the floor. "You feared that Phoebe would be taken from you as others have been taken."

Startled, Isabelle asked, "How do you know that?"

"Because I am a seer and know why you are truly here." He picked up his glass and sipped some water but said no more.

Phoebe turned toward Isabelle. "What does he mean?"

Torn and unsure how to answer, Isabelle faced Phoebe and said, "He simply plays with us now. We should go."

Phoebe knew not what to say but Father Karl leaned in closer to both of them. "If you go, you will walk along, trying to find Cinderella. But if you stay, I can send you both on your way to finding her. I know where she is. The choice is yours."

Isabelle pulled at Phoebe's arm to go, but Phoebe resisted and said, "I think we should trust him."

Father Karl leaned back in his chair and smiled.

* * *

Days had passed with us on the plains, heading north to find Baba Yaga. We had times of not talking and my being lost in regret, but I did my best to hold onto my hope. I envisioned seeing Phoebe again like a diamond that lived in the center of my heart. I imagined its brilliance and hardness and then wrapped that power around me so that nothing could get through. I would remain strong. We slept in our tent and I watched the Silver Fox sleep. He had curled himself on his side and had begun to mumble in his sleep. The day would start soon and I had not much time left of such solace.

I watched the Silver Fox and with great stillness and practice I left the tent and walked outside. I stretched my arms up at the sky and took a deep breath, held it and then exhaled slowly. I glanced down at my left hand and saw that my skin had begun to crack a bit around my knuckles. The weather, so raw and forceful, had been hard for us to go against. First we fought against snow, then wind, sometimes rain and, other days, just lots of sun. The days had teased us, building in warmth, until I worried that the summer heat would be too great for us without proper protection. But the deep summer was months yet away. I stood alone and more tired than I had ever found myself. I missed Phoebe and often dreamed of her, imagining her in different situations, trapped and unable to escape. I would awake from the recurring dream knowing that I was not one step closer to finding her.

If I could not find Baba Yaga and somehow convince her to fight against the emperor, then I knew my last move. It would be desperate, but I had nothing left to give. I would go directly to the emperor, confront him and throw my chances there. I had no other ideas. What would Jeremiah think of my plan? I often wondered. He had such a sense of sureness about him. I had never seen him truly crack and fall to pieces as I had often done in my younger days. I wondered how he was and if he searched for me. He would be furious with me for not listening to him and I could not blame him, but he wasn't a parent. He did not understand that some risks were worth taking.

I heard the Silver Fox call out in his sleep and I went back inside the tent to watch him. He tossed in his slumber and spoke in a language that I did not understand. He kept rubbing at the back of his neck with his hand and then rolled back over on his side. He bolted awake and sat up, staring through me, seeing what I did not know. I just watched him and after a few minutes said, "Good morning."

He swallowed and then rubbed the sleep out of his eyes before answering me. "We're here."

I pointed outside and said, "I've been out there and didn't see anything."

"Come with me." He crawled past me to get outside.

I followed him and he stood a few yards away from the tent and pointed to a spot right in front of him. "This is the place. This is where we need to go."

"Are you sure?" I walked around the spot and didn't see anything different or unusual.

"Use your imagination. Just because you can't see anything there doesn't mean that there isn't." He put his hand out and he concentrated and then put his hand through the spot and ... nothing happened.

"I'm fine at using my imagination. But it seems that you're not having much success either."

He huffed at me and tried again, but his hand went right through the spot again without anything unusual happening. "Strange." He ignored me and stared at a spot before him that I could not see.

"What am I supposed to be seeing?" I came beside him and crouched down to try and see something that wasn't there.

Distracted, he scratched at his neck and said, "Damn, damn, damn." He backed off and rubbed furiously at the spot on his neck.

"Everything fine?" He kept his hand on the back of his neck.

"No, it's not. I'm having a bit of a problem." He moved his hand away and turned to show me.

At first, I couldn't see anything different and I said, "Do you have fleas?"

He did not laugh and ignored my attempt at a joke. "What do you see?"

I came closer and moved his shirt away from his neck and stopped. "Does it hurt?"

"What do you see?" He pulled away from me and turned around to see my face. "Tell me."

I spun him back around and took a second look. "It's grown larger."

"Describe it to me."

I took a chance and put my finger on his skin and touched the back of his neck and felt nothing strange. "The gold spot has spread to all of you neck and part of your back."

"Damn." He pulled away from me and pulled the back of his shirt up.

"Does it hurt you?"

He ran his hand over the spot again and shook his head. "No, it just itches a lot."

"Why is it happening?"

He tucked his shirt back in. "If I tell you, do you promise not to laugh at me?"

"Why would I laugh?" I didn't understand.

"I'm changing." He sat down on a rock and looked away. "I'm maturing."

"What do you mean by maturing?" I stood before him with my hands on my hips.

"If I were human, you would say that I was becoming an adolescent." He glanced back at me quickly to gauge my response.

"You mean you're going through puberty?"

He jumped up off the rock and stomped away like a little child.

I found it hard to contain my laughter. "Wait, don't go. You didn't answer my question! Is that what's happening to you? You're going through puberty?"

He turned back around and a mix of emotions crossed his face. "Yes." He wrapped his arms around himself and lowered his head and I realized I had pushed him too far.

I remember how I had felt when I had become a woman. My mother had already been dead and my stepmother had not shared with me any information about womanhood. I had thought that I had been injured when I first bled. My stepsisters played along and had me convinced that I would die. I cleared away the laughter from my mind and approached the Silver Fox slowly. "I am sorry for mocking you."

He tried to turn around and see the back where his skin had turned golden but could not do so. "I'm changing into a new me and I don't know who I will become." He held his hands up and pointed around. "And we're trying to get to the Otherside and find Baba Yaga. This couldn't happen at a worse time."

"Come here." He hesitated a moment and then came over to me. I gave him a warm hug and he pulled away.

"Why would you do that to me? After all I've done to you."

He tried to find the answer on my face but I grabbed him and pulled him into a full embrace. "More than twelve years have passed since we first met and a lot has happened since then. If we don't begin to trust each other, then we will never get anywhere." I released him and held his gaze. "There have been many nights that I can't stay awake and you have not tried to harm me. I believe you have changed.

You have served your prison sentence and now it's time that we move on. There will be times that we might distrust each other, but we have to get over that. I want to find Phoebe. Nothing will stop me. Do you understand?"

He scratched the back of his neck where his skin had turned gold and replied, "I do. Thank you. And you are right in that if we work together, we can overcome anything. Distrust will tear us apart and Bonaparte will win. I can't let that happen."

I went around him and looked at his discolored skin. "Does it still itch?"

"Yes, it does." He went to scratch again but then lowered his hand. "I wish I had a salve to put on it. Or some honey. Honey works well."

"Maybe we'll find some honey on the Otherside?" I looked out over the land and saw nothing unusual.

"It's possible but I doubt it." He walked back over to the rock and asked, "Are you ready to cross over to the Otherside?" He pointed over to a spot in front of him that was several feet above the ground. "Let's head on over."

"Are you serious? I thought you had been joking with me earlier. Are we really there?"

"Yes, we are. Come with me." He grabbed my hand and kept pointing to a spot right in front of us.

I humored him and allowed him to pull me a few feet forward. "What do I need to do?"

"Just put your hand through this spot in the air." He pointed and asked, "Are you ready?"

I nodded and held my hand out. He guided me and then pushed my hand through the air and nothing happened.

"Damn, I missed."

"Missed what? I didn't feel anything." I leaned forward and tried to see whatever it was he tried to do.

He stared at the invisible spot in the air, thought a moment and then put his hands in his pocket. "Okay, let's try again, but I'll guide you through how to unlock the portal."

I held my left hand up in front of me and he grabbed my hand and squeezed the fingers together.

"No, like this." He cupped his hand and made his fingers be a point. "I want you to put your hand through the spot like you're threading a needle. Got it?"

"But where is the hole? I can't see anything. I need to see where I'm threading my hand." I really tried to see the hole but could not. The sun had begun to come up and I heard several birds calling to each other.

He took my hand and bent it slightly and held it before me. Shaking his head, he said, "No, that's not the right angle. He came around me and then guided my hand more easily from behind. "I will guide your hand like the needle and thread it on through. Are you ready?"

I glanced back over my shoulder and asked, "What's going to happen if this works?"

"We'll be on the Otherside." He stared right at me and asked, "Do you really trust me?"

"Yes. Yes, I do." Before I could say anything else, he took my hand and then threaded it through the spot that I could not see. I could feel it when my hand went into the hole and then caught in the slot. The temperature there was colder and my hand appeared to be stuck on something in midair. I could still not see it, but it had caught on a metal frame. "I can feel the doorframe. Now what?"

He backed away from me and said, "Unlock it. Turn your hand and wrist to the left."

"Is it going to hurt?" I wasn't happy that he kept backing away from me like something might explode.

"No, it won't hurt." He still backed away.

"Then why are you leaving me alone here. What's going to happen?"

"We'll find out once you open the portal. Just slowly turn your hand to the left." He covered his face with his hands. "Hurry now."

I turned away from him, took a deep breath and then turned my hand to the left. I felt something move, but then my hand fell back down. It was as though I needed to push over a metal bar with my hand. The bar was solid and heavy. I tried to turn it again, but couldn't. It was too heavy for my wrist.

"Come on, go ahead and move it!" The Silver Fox peeked out through the slits of space between his fingers. "Really, it's not going to hurt … much."

I turned my hand to the left and then put my right hand around my wrist and twisted. I could feel the invisible piece of metal move and I grunted and put my legs and back into it and heard a click. My hand fell free and I stumbled back. A door suddenly appeared in front of us and it opened inward. Nothing else happened. I turned back to the Silver Fox to see a huge grin on his face. "Funny, real funny."

"Well, I had to make things a bit more suspenseful. It was a lot more fun that way."

"Maybe more fun for you, but I thought something was going to explode in my face."

He came over to me and pretended to put his arm around my shoulders. "You ready to enter?"

"Where exactly are we going?" I glanced through the doorway but couldn't see much.

"To the Otherside." He made some eerie noises and moved his hands around like he was a bedtime monster trying to come and get a child in the middle of the night.

"Is Baba Yaga over in there?" I took a step forward and peeked in.

"Oh, yes, she's waiting for you right now. It won't be long now. We're nearly there."

"And what are we going to say to her when we meet her? Do I just ask her to come on a journey with us to defeat Bonaparte?" I pulled back from the doorway and looked at him.

"I'm not going to tell her anything. It's all up to you. She won't listen to me. Trust me."

"And why is that?"

"She's not really a big fan of men." He walked forward and made way for me to go through the doorway first. "Ladies first."

"Thank you." I had a difficult time holding back my sarcasm and then decided that I could not stall any longer. Phoebe waited for me somewhere. The sooner I made it through this part of the journey, the sooner I would see her. I clenched my fists at my side and walked through the doorway. I expected there to be a shift and dropping through space like how I used to travel through the dreamline, but the journey took place instantaneously. One moment we stood on the plains of Russia and the next I stood in a forest. Above, thick, gray clouds stretched across the sky and I could not see the sun. It was daylight but I couldn't place where the sun was in the sky.

I turned around and the Silver Fox followed after me. He passed through the doorway and it vanished without a trace. We would not be getting home that way.

"Where do we go now?"

He shook his head. "I don't fully know. I was hoping you might help in that department." He walked past me and looked around for a bit. "Any instincts telling you which way we might want to go?"

"How should I know where we're headed? I've never been here before." I went up to the nearest tree and looked up. I couldn't see anything unusual.

"I was just asking." He put his finger in his mouth and then held it up and tried to figure out which direction the wind blew. He stood still for a few moments and then said, "West is best. Let's go."

I followed him for a bit and I could see no animals or insects. We saw no sign of life outside the trees all around us. "Can you tell me more of what I'm meant to do or what exactly we're looking for?"

He ignored me for a moment, lost in concentration and then said, "Baba Yaga isn't easy to find. She likes to be a bit elusive so I'm trying to follow the signs to get us to her as quickly as we can. You could help, you know."

"I don't know how to help." I turned back and then stopped to look all around. "I just see a bunch of trees."

"Well, use your instincts and see what you can find. Reach out a bit and see if you sense anything unusual."

"You're the one with the magic. I can't sense anything." I held my hands out in front of me and gave up in trying to call the magic to me. It was an old habit that I still had a hard time letting go. But then I had an idea. I stopped walking and closed my eyes. Jeremiah had often done this and I thought that maybe I could try it. I crouched down to the ground and put my ear to the forest floor. The Silver Fox saw me and stopped. He held his breath, kept still and I simply listened.

For a few seconds, I heard the sound of my own beating heart in my ears and then nothing. I heard nothing unusual for a good bit of time. I kept my eyes closed and then I heard it. Movement right behind us. I couldn't tell what it was but it sounded big and it came from behind.

"Do you hear anything?" The Silver Fox came over to me and knelt down.

"Yes, I do." I tried to focus and concentrate but he walked away and the sound of crunching leaves distracted me.

"What is it that you hear?" He searched off the trail we followed but couldn't see anything.

"It's loud and headed our way." I pulled away from the ground and then stood back up. "Do you think we should head away from it or go toward it?"

"I think that we should …"

He was cut off by a loud crashing sound from behind us. Both of us jumped and turned in that direction. "Let's go. Now!" I headed off at a fast run following the trail that led west.

The Silver Fox ran behind me and we heard a second crash louder and closer than the last one. A tree had fallen right behind us and we heard the breaking of wood as it cracked and shattered into pieces. "Run, faster. Come on."

He overtook the lead and I could see how dexterous he was, avoiding twigs on the ground and uneven parts in the path. He ran faster than I could because he appeared to have a natural way of avoiding obstacles or broken tree limbs. I followed after him as quickly as I could, running but careful not to trip on anything. Ahead, the ground sloped down and we ran down a dirt hill, filled with tree limbs and leaves. The Silver Fox slowed down and I caught up to him and then heard a third crash from behind. This time we both heard a loud roar from a beast that I didn't want to ever meet. The roar echoed through the air and I did not want to look over my shoulder.

At the bottom of the hill, a small creek stood before us and without stopping we ran forward and I slipped on a rock and my foot fell into the cold water. I paused only a moment to free my foot from some mud and then ran faster, trying to keep up to the Silver Fox. After I crossed the creek, I climbed up the steep bank in front of us and saw two trees fall right on the other side of the creek where we had been.

The Silver Fox stood at the top of the embankment and had his hand out. I took it and he pulled me up the side and I scampered up as quickly as I could. Another roar ripped through from across the creek and we did not stay to see what creature made the noise. I did not wish to look back, but did. I caught a shadowy glimpse of a large foot stomping down on the trees behind me and saw two trees break apart into shreds from the force of the footfall.

"Stop!"

I looked quickly around and stopped but nearly crashed into the Silver Fox. I looked up at what he had found and knew not what to say. Standing in the trail directly in front of us was a small hut that stood on what appeared to be chicken leg stilts. The one leg twitched and went up with the entire hut being balanced on the other chicken leg.

"What is that?"

Another roar, much closer this time, drowned out the Silver Fox's answer. He pulled me forward and said, "Climb up and get inside quickly. Come on!"

I saw a rope ladder on the far end of the platform that held the rope and climbed up. The Silver Fox followed up after me and I saw a trapdoor right above my head. A crash right behind us startled me.

"Push up, go, go, go!" The Silver Fox pushed me up and I found the trapdoor opened easily so I climbed the last few rungs up the rope ladder and then pulled myself into the hut. I leaned down and heard another roar from below and pulled the Silver Fox into the hut with me. Once inside, he slammed the trapdoor shut and bolted it.

He leaned against a wall and then I noticed it for the first time. The hut was much larger on the inside than the out. I sat next to him and breathed deeply, wiping the sweat from my eyes. "What was that thing?"

"I don't really know and don't truly care to know." He handed me a handkerchief to wipe my face and gave a quick laugh.

"What's so funny?"

He pointed around the hut. "Looks like we found Baba Yaga's hut. Now we just have to see if she's in here somewhere."

The room we stood in had three doors in front of us. "Well, I guess we better get started." I handed him his handkerchief back and then stood up. "Any chance that thing can get in here?"

"I don't really know." He stood up as well and stared at the three doors.

"Well, let's not stay here and find out." I walked up to the door on the left and opened it. "You ready?" I held the door open for him and moved off to the side to make room for him. "Let's try men first this time."

He smirked at me and led the way through the doorway.

Chapter 8

Jeremiah helped Veronika up the wooden ladder and stopped underneath the trapdoor ahead of him. The hut stayed still and the enormous chicken legs resembled two solid stalks that had not moved. Charley called up from down below. "Do you want me to come up yet?"

He wore his pack on his back and had strapped down his musket to make it easier for him to climb. Jeremiah hung off the side of the ladder and called down, "Head on up. I'll open the door above me and head in. If it's safe, Veronika will come in next."

"Okay, let me know and I will be ready." He kept his hands on the ladder ready to climb.

Jeremiah glanced down to Veronika and lowered his voice so that only she could hear him. "Any idea on what I'll find when I go inside?"

She shook her head. "I do not know what to expect." She eyed his pistols. "Be ready."

"That I always am." He locked his left hand around a rung on the ladder and then pushed up against the trapdoor above. The hatch opened easily and he pushed up to swing the door all the way back. "Here I go."

He climbed up the remaining few rungs of the ladder and pulled himself up into the hut and detected no change in his location. He simply entered into a room that resembled Mamochka Tatyana's hut but had three doors in different parts of the room. A wood stove on the far corner of the room warmed the area and a table with four chairs took up the remaining portion of the room. Herbs, spices and dried flowers hung in different parts of the room.

Jeremiah peeked his head down through the trapdoor in the floor and said, "Come up inside. You have to see this."

Veronika called down to Charley, who started to climb up the ladder, and then she followed Jeremiah into the hut. When she came fully into the room, she cursed in Russian and went over to the stove and shook her head. "I do not believe it. The room is so similar."

Charley finished pulling himself up into the hut and he took the heavy pack off his shoulder. He whistled and rubbed his eyes. "How is this possible?"

"Maybe the hut can read our minds and picked this room as a common area we all know?" Veronika walked away from the stove and headed over to Jeremiah who stood by one of the doors.

He pointed his finger at notches in the doorframe with numbers next to them. "Are these growth marks?"

Veronika nodded. "Every year Mamochka Tatyana measured me and marked how much I had grown."

"I had never seen these marks when I first met you and Mamochka Tatyana." He leaned against the door in front of him and listened. "Do you think Mamochka Tatyana is Baba Yaga?"

Veronika did not hesitate. "No, she is good and I have been with her for years."

Charley saw some bread and cheese on the table and said, "The food here looks like it was left in a hurry." He walked around the table but did not touch the food.

"I think we need to pick one of the doors and go onward. The sooner we find Baba Yaga the better." Jeremiah moved away from the door he stood in front of and then walked over to the second door and listened. "Charley, can you listen at the last one?"

Charley crossed the room and put his ear to the door. "I hear nothing. What about you?"

"I don't hear anything either." Jeremiah looked down and saw that the door in front of him had no knob. The other two doors looked similar in design.

"In Mamochka Tatyana's hut, there are no doors like this so I don't know where they might lead." She pointed to the far wall. "And there is no exit to the hut. The main door is missing."

Charley had moved over to a shuttered window and asked, "Should I try to look outside and see where we are?"

"Be careful." Jeremiah came over to his friend and prepared to pull him back if something unexpected happened.

Charley tried to open the shutter, but it would not open. He pulled with all his strength but the shutter did not budge. Jeremiah then tried to push and pull the shutter but it did not move for him either.

"I think we are meant to stay inside here." Veronika put her shoulder against the middle door and asked, "Should I try it?"

Jeremiah and Charley came behind her with their hands on their weapons. She took a deep breath and then shoved against the door with all of her strength. The door did not open. Charley added his strength and the door did not open no matter if they pulled, pushed or kicked. It remained locked.

At the door all the way to the left, Jeremiah tried to open it, but it also remained locked. Charley ran over to the third door and looked at them both. "Are you ready?" He waited a few moments and then ran against the door, using his shoulder as a battering ram. The door did not open and Charley cursed. He massaged his hurt shoulder and they all suddenly heard a clicking sound. Veronika reacted first and ran over to the trapdoor in the floor but it had already locked shut. She tried to pull it back open, but it would not budge. She banged her fists against the door in the floor, but it only alleviated some of her frustration. "I do not like this. Someone toys with us."

Jeremiah started to respond and three loud clicks, coming from each of the doors, turned their attention back to the entranceways. Without warning, each door flung open and thousands of gallons of water started pouring into the room. The three streams of water would fill up the room in a matter of minutes. The water knocked Veronika over and she grabbed onto a chair to right herself. Charley tried to walk up to the nearest door to shut it but the force of the water was too strong. Already the water had filled the room to their shins.

The roar of the water streaming in was loud and Jeremiah rushed over to Veronika to help her up. He pulled his pistols out and fired at the trapdoor in the floor, hoping to weaken the magic that held the hatch shut. Putting his pistols away, he stomped down on the hatch, but nothing happened. "I can't open it. Do you see another way out?"

Veronika scanned the room and watched herbs and utensils and other kitchen items float through the water. "I will look around, but I cannot see another exit."

Charley waded over to the center of the room and glanced over at the stove. The water had flooded the stove and steam came out of the top. He scanned the room and then decided to look straight up. There, in the ceiling, he saw the markings of another hatch. "Help me. I think there is an opening in the ceiling."

Jeremiah grabbed a chair and dragged it over to Charley. "I'll steady it. Go ahead."

Charley climbed up on the chair and stretched to touch the ceiling. At his touch, the trapdoor opened upward, but no light came from above. "I can't get a grip."

The water had reached Jeremiah's upper thigh and Veronika's midsection. She waded over to the chair. "I will hold the chair. Help boost Charley up."

Jeremiah put his hands out, locked together, and Charley stepped in. With a grunt, Jeremiah boosted Charley up toward the ceiling and he was able to climb through the hatch there. He disappeared for a few moments and called down. "It looks safe up here. Come on up." He had leaned over and reached for Veronika to pull her up.

The water kept streaming in and Jeremiah glanced over. Somehow the water's speed had increased and now the water flew out like jets into the room. The water pressure was so strong that the force nearly knocked Jeremiah over. He stood firm, helping Veronika up and then seeing her safely up through the trapdoor, he climbed on the chair and reached up. The chair nearly tipped over but Charley grabbed his arms and started pulling him up. Gaining purchase on the side of the trapdoor, Jeremiah pulled himself up halfway through and Charley and Veronika yanked him the rest of the way through. He rested on the ground while Veronika shut the door to the water below. With the trapdoor shut, the roar of the water from down below suddenly stopped.

Charley leaned against the nearest wall to rest. Veronika wrung parts of her clothing out and water dripped all over the floor. "Do you think that Baba Yaga is testing us?"

She glanced around the empty room. Off to her right, she saw an ornate door that appeared to be made of gold. Colored jewels adorned the door with odd symbols carved into the metal.

Jeremiah sat up and tried to catch his breath to talk and then said, "I would think it is her who tests us." He took a few more breaths and then joked, "I'm not overly fond of her welcome."

Charley had pulled his musket off his back and dumped some water out. "I don't expect our guns will be of much use here."

Standing up, Veronika continued to wring out the water from her clothes. "Should we try the door?"

Jeremiah held up his hand to caution her. "Wait a moment." He coughed and then pushed himself up and looked around. "I think this is another test."

He walked around the room and stared up into the corners. Charley followed suit and put his hands on the walls walking the perimeter. "I do not see any sort of secret door."

"Let us look around first before we go rushing to the next door. We might set off another trap or be tested with fire this time." Jeremiah stared up at the ceiling and walked around the room. He stopped and asked, "Where is the light coming from?"

Veronika glanced up and held her arm out. "I can see a faint shadow on the ground so the light appears to be coming from the ceiling."

Charley pulled a coin from a pouch on his belt and tossed it up to the ceiling. Instead of hitting the ceiling and coming back down, the coin passed through and never came back down. "Now that's interesting."

Jeremiah rushed over to Charley and asked, "Do you have another coin?"

Charley gave him one and Jeremiah went over to the far corner of the room. He tossed the coin up, it hit the ceiling, and came back down, landing on the floor. Bending down, Jeremiah picked up the coin and tossed it over to Veronika who stood on the far side of the room. She threw the coin above her head and it bounced back down.

"Looks like I found the spot." Charley tossed a second coin up and it sailed through the ceiling and never came back down.

"What do we think? Door or ceiling?" Jeremiah walked over to the door and tried to read the symbols on it, but could not.

Veronika came to stand beside him. "I think we should go through the ceiling. I do not like all the jewels and the gold."

Charley glanced over at the door and then up at the ceiling. "I say we go up as well."

Jeremiah agreed and came over to Charley. He knelt down and said, "Climb on up on my shoulders."

Veronika helped balance him and Charley did as asked and Jeremiah stood up, grunting at all the weight on him but stayed firm. "Hurry up."

Charley reached up and his hands went through the ceiling. He could feel the ends of another trapdoor. He pulled himself up and then disappeared. Jeremiah and Veronika looked up and waited. Several moments passed and he did not return. Veronika put her hands on her hips and asked, "Do you think he is well?"

Jeremiah did not respond and waited in silence.

A full minute passed and then Charley appeared from the ceiling. His head poked through the hole. "You have to come up and see this." He disappeared for a few moments and then reappeared. "It is truly wonderful."

"What do you see?" Veronika asked.

Charley turned back to look and then said, "It's like a …"

In mid-sentence he was pulled away from the hole in the ceiling and disappeared.

* * *

Phoebe followed Father Karl into the crypt of the church. The room's temperature dropped considerably and Isabelle shivered next to her.

"Where are you bringing us?" Phoebe asked.

Father Karl shut the door behind him and then leaned against the wall. "We will not be heard down here and can speak freely. This room is hidden from the world. For hundreds of years, we warlocks have used magic to protect and sanctify this room to help others."

Isabelle stood apart and hugged herself to keep warm from the cold. "How are you going to help us?" She stayed close to Phoebe.

Father Karl held up his hand to silence her. "I will show you where you need to go. Come." He walked over to a corner of the room and pulled away a tapestry covering the wall. Behind the large rug, a floor to ceiling mirror had been fitted into the wall.

Phoebe rushed over and stood before it. Clouds swirled within the mirror and an eerie light shone out to light the room. Father Karl stood behind Phoebe and put his hands on her shoulders. She glanced up at him and asked, "Can you find my mother and show her to me?"

"Yes, I can." He smiled at her and touched the mirror. The light increased in intensity and the clouds began to swirl.

"How is that possible though? I have tried to find her and it is as though she is no longer there. I can't feel her presence anymore. She is silent to me."

"You search for her, but I search for what she carries in her heart. Watch." Father Karl turned to Isabelle and motioned for her to come closer. "Come closer and do not be afraid. I will help you both."

Isabelle stood beside Phoebe but remained quiet. Phoebe reached out and took her hand. Father Karl leaned forward and spoke in Latin. He talked quickly and with great passion and then touched the mirror again. The clouds within the mirror cleared and a man's face materialized and floated before them. He was speaking but they could not hear his words or see to whom he spoke.

Phoebe leaned forward and touched the mirror. "That's Jeremiah." She watched him turn away from the mirror and then fade away. "Do you know him?"

Father Karl waved his hand over the mirror and Jeremiah faded away and the clouds returned. "I helped raise him when he was a boy. I found much promise in him and then he headed off on his own when he grew older. But he is in my heart and I in his. I look after him and can follow him."

"But where is my mother? Are they together?" Phoebe put both her hands on the mirror and peered in as though she looked through a window.

Father Karl smiled. "The secret is simple. Watch." He waved his hand over the mirror and the clouds cleared a second time and Cinderella appeared. She stood in a room, glancing up at the ceiling. She also talked to someone who could not be seen.

"Mother!" Phoebe put her hand on her Cinderella's face. "How did you do this?"

Father Karl pointed at the mirror. "She holds Jeremiah in her heart. Wherever she is, I can find him in her."

Cinderella turned away from the mirror and walked out of view. Phoebe pulled at Father Karl's arm. "Can you bring her back? I want to see more of her. Please!"

Father Karl waved his hand over the mirror and the vantage point changed and they now saw Cinderella walking toward them. She wore strange clothing that Phoebe had never seen before.

"Can she hear us?" Isabelle watched Cinderella as she walked through a maze of corridors.

"No, she cannot and we cannot send a message to her or receive a message. But I do know where she is."

"Where is she?" Phoebe asked. "Can you help us get to her?"

"Yes, I can, but it will not be easy." Father Karl backed away from the mirror and folded his arms across his chest. "She is on the Otherside."

Phoebe turned away from the mirror. "Where is that?"

Isabelle blessed herself with the sign of the cross. "It is not of this world. A place full of darkness and death."

Father Karl nodded. "And yet there you must go if you wish to find your mother."

"I will go anywhere to find her. I am not afraid." Phoebe faced the mirror again and watched Cinderella stop and stare out at them.

Father Karl looked to Isabelle. "And what of your choice? Will you go with her?"

Isabelle thought for a moment and went next to Phoebe and put her arms around her. "Yes, I will go with her. I will not desert her."

Phoebe hugged her and asked, "When can we go?"

"Now if you would like, but be warned that I do not have the power to send you directly to her. I can send you to another who will help you on your way to the Otherside." Before either of them could say a word, he touched the mirror and the clouds returned. "But the way will be dangerous and filled with trouble."

Isabelle hesitated a moment and then said, "Then send us on our way so we can go."

Phoebe held onto Isabelle's hand. "Yes, send us on our way."

Father Karl concentrated and closed his eyes. "When the mirror opens, you both will need to walk through hand in hand and the journey will be complete. Are you ready?"

They both nodded and Father Karl touched the mirror again. A bright purple light shone from the mirror and both Isabelle and Phoebe covered their eyes with their free hands. They saw clouds take shape within the mirror and prepared to walk through. Father Karl kept his eyes closed and mumbled a few phrases in Latin. The clouds began to swirl and turned pink in color within the mirror. Still Father Karl spoke under his breath and his right hand began to glow like the sun. He opened his eyes and Phoebe caught a glimpse of the power that he carried within. The clouds cleared from the mirror and they saw a man with a big beard. He leaned forward and his nose appeared to almost touch the mirror's face.

And then, from afar, they heard a voice emanate from the mirror. "Who is it that calls me?" The person who spoke had a thick accent that Phoebe could not place.

Isabelle and Phoebe huddled together as the voice boomed like thunder. Phoebe recovered first and asked, "How is it that we hear him?"

Father Karl ignored her question and he answered the man. "It is I, Father Karl, from Dresden. I have found the child you seek. I wish to send her and her companion to you."

The man leaned in closer and his gaze turned toward Phoebe. "Excellent. Bring her closer so I can see her more clearly."

Father Karl did as asked and Phoebe stood directly in front of the mirror but still held onto Isabelle's hand. The older man stared at her and from her vantage point she could see up his nose. He nodded and said, "Your mother will be pleased to know that you are safe."

Phoebe chanced a step forward and asked, "Who are you and how do you know my mother?"

The old man did not smile as he replied but remained distant and cold. "I am Vladislav, counselor to the Tsar of Russia and I have sent your mother off to find Baba Yaga."

"Who is Baba Yaga?" Phoebe turned to ask Father Karl but she saw that Isabelle had covered her mouth with her hand in fear.

"She is a witch who lives in the Russian north and is rumored to steal little children. Her legend is known all throughout Europe." Isabelle came forward and asked, "Why did you send Cinderella off to find Baba Yaga?"

Vladislav shook his head. "It was not my idea, but the Silver Fox's. It appears that he and your Cinderella thought it best."

Phoebe grabbed Isabelle's hand. "The Silver Fox is with my mother? We must go. She told me stories of him and I cannot believe she would trust him. Something must be wrong."

Vladislav nodded. "You are wise to think that. I wondered too if his magic had enchanted her. But it did not. She is desperate and wishes to find you. Come to me and I will help you."

Phoebe saw Father Karl back away from the mirror. "Tell us how to get to you and we will come."

"Simply walk forward and through the mirror."

Phoebe did as instructed and she vanished through the mirror. Before Isabelle could follow, Father Karl snapped his fingers and broke her grasp from Phoebe. She remained before the mirror and Phoebe vanished from sight. "Wait. I have a message for you before you go."

Isabelle turned to Father Karl and waited. She knew what would come.

"The emperor wanted me to warn you. Remember your promise to bring Phoebe to Cinderella and continue to block out her powers. If you are loyal, your family will be fine." Father Karl moved closer. "Do you understand?"

"I do. Tell the emperor that I will do as promised." She turned away from him and looked deep into the mirror's clouds. "May I go now?"

Father Karl put his hand on her shoulder. "Yes, but never forget your promise to the emperor. He will know if you try to betray him and your family will suffer. Do you understand?"

"I do." Isabelle walked onward and vanished through the portal.

When she blinked, Phoebe and Vladislav stood before her. "What took you so long?" Phoebe ran to Isabelle and she saw that they were no longer in the church's crypt but had crossed through to Vladislav.

In the mirror, they saw Father Karl. He waved to them and said, "Be safe on your journey. I wish you both luck." He backed away and clouds filled the mirror on their side. Phoebe waved at him but it was too late for he had already vanished.

Vladislav came to them and said, "Come, you will need to rest. Tomorrow you will meet the Tsar and then continue your journey."

Isabelle and Phoebe followed, tired and unsure of what they had just decided to do.

* * *

I had lost track of how long we had wandered through the corridors of Baba Yaga's hut. Time all seemed to flow together. "Does any of this look familiar?" I glanced down the corridor and then turned back to the Silver Fox.

"It all looks the same to me." He pointed down the hall. "Let's keep going and see what we find."

I led the way and after a few more minutes of us walking through an empty corridor we came to a door. The Silver Fox tried to open it for me, but it was locked. I went to listen at the door and it opened for me without my even trying. "Looks like I have the magic touch."

"Seems so." He pushed the door inward and said, "Ladies first."

"Thanks." I pushed past him and the room was dark as night. But in the far corner, I could hear crying and see a tiny bit of light. The crying sounded familiar so I rushed forward and the light shifted in the room and I realized that I stood in the house I grew up in. The crying came from the bed in the corner of the room and I knew right away where I was. I spun around and tried to find a door to get out. I did not want to stay here. I rushed over to the door and tried to open it but it was now locked.

"Who is there?" I heard the girl's voice from the bed and I froze.

"It's just a friend." Heading over to the bed, I stared into my own face as a child. How young I looked.

"Will you be bringing back my mother?" The girl sat up and her eyes were red from crying.

"No, I cannot do that. She is gone." I sat on the edge of the bed and went to comfort my younger self, but she moved away. I could not see where the Silver Fox had gone, but he appeared to not be in the room.

"She promised me that she would never leave me. She promised. Now my father is gone and she as well. What will happen to me?"

"Your father has been sent for. He will be home soon." He would come back and within the year he would be remarried again and my life as the Cinder girl would begin.

"It's all my fault. I should have let her rest and not tell me another story." She broke out in tears again and covered her face with her hands.

I remembered this day and had tried to block out most of the memories. I did not want to be here. I truly did not. I reached out to hug my younger self, but she turned on me. "Leave me alone. Do not come near me!"

I backed away and saw the change in her face. The hardening had already begun. She turned on me and just screeched at her loudest. I tried to cover my ears, but the sound washed over me along with all the hurt. The girl scratched at her face with her nails and screamed, "I should have saved her. I should have tried. It's my fault!"

"No, it's not. Truly, she had already left you before last night." I blurted the words out and regretted them as soon as they were said.

"What did you say?" The girl stopped crying for a moment and focused on me.

I took a deep breath and faced her. "She had already left you and wasn't truly with you last night. She had crossed over to the faerie world and had been cheating on your father with the Silver Fox. You only thought she truly cared for you. You were not only abandoned by your father, but by your mother as well. She took to the faerie world like a drug. That is the truth."

Her face erupted in anger. "You lie!"

"No, I do not. For a long, long time, you will blame yourself and it will hold you back and that will not help you any. I swear to you that it is the truth. It's the truth that for the longest time you will not want to see and believe." I moved closer to her and put out my hand. "Come, I will help you."

My younger self thought a moment and then took my hand in hers. When we touched, a surge of energy flowed through me and she gasped and then clenched my hand tight. I remembered all the nights I had cried alone and feared that I would become an orphan. I never knew when my father would return, and when he did, he loved me, in his way, but no one had truly helped me.

"Please, do not leave me." My younger self clung to me and I wrapped my arms around her.

"I will never abandon you." I held her close and could feel her breath against me. Her tears fell and she sobbed against my chest.

I detected a presence beside me and remembered the Silver Fox. He stood beside me like a statue. "We must go on."

"We must take her with us. I can't leave her here." I sensed her tensing up against me and holding me tight. She would not let go.

He stood close to me and put out his hand. "We must go. It is time for us to leave. You must trust me on this."

"No, I won't leave her here. I will not abandon her. Don't you see that now I have a chance to fix everything? I can make it all right. I can do this."

"You will come with me. I will not be denied." His voice changed and a dark turn edged into it. "Let her go and move on. It is not wise to dwell on the past."

I held my younger self tight against my chest and turned away from him and held my hand out in defense. And then I saw it, my hand lit up and a joy flowed through my veins. Somehow, some miracle had happened to grant me back my magic. "Leave us now. Before I make you leave." I concentrated and could feel a well of energy building up within me.

The Silver Fox simply smiled. "I do not fear you. You will come with me now!" He reached for my hand and I tried to lash out at him, but he negated my magic. He pulled at me with both arms, trying to separate me from my younger self. She cried and screamed, but the Silver Fox pushed me hard back against the wall and I fell back and clung tightly to the girl I was. She then pulled away from me and turned on the Silver Fox. With a gnashing of her teeth, she raised her hand and unleashed unholy hellfire on him. The blast of energy streamed out of her hands and I could feel her hatred. I raised my own hand to cast my magic at the Silver Fox but nothing happened.

A deep, dark ache filled me and I could call no magic to me. Sensing my need, the child before me turned back around and I noticed something changed in her face. I could not place the difference in her, but she reached out for me and I clasped her hand and pulled her close. When she rested against me, I wrapped my arm around her protectively and raised my hand again at the Silver Fox. My hand lit up with bright white fire and I sent a wave of my magic at him. He crumbled to the ground and his clothes were singed. His arms covered his face and he rolled over and pushed himself up. And there I saw as he had begun to change into the fox deep inside.

He yawned and his mouth seemed to split apart and his features changed, turning into part man, part fox. He rushed forward and grabbed at the girl's hair. She tried to fight him off and I prepared my next spell at him, but he pushed me away and knocked the girl across the room. His strength impressed me.

"Run, now. Please!" His spoke in quick bursts and stood between me and my younger self.

"No, I cannot leave her." I rushed forward and tried to get past him.

He pushed me back against the wall. "Look at her. Truly look at her!"

Another blast of magic hit him full on and I stared hard at the girl. Her face had changed. No longer did she look like me. A sinister grin had broken out across her face and her arms had elongated with her hands ending in long black nails. Her hair color changed before my eyes becoming black and thin wisps. In moments, the girl I thought she was had become something totally different. She looked more creature than human. "Don't abandon me. Please, stay!"

Her voice was a deep screech and no longer sounded like me as a child. I had been fooled. The Silver Fox pulled himself up once again and he backed away and pushed me to the door. "Get out of here."

I raised my hand and willed my magic to return and again nothing happened. Sensing my loss, the child creature came closer and addressed me though the Silver Fox who stood between us. "I can give you back your magic. We can be together forever and then we can go find your daughter. The three of us will be happy forever. Come with me."

Temptation came to me and I ached to feel the flow of magic through my limbs another time. It had felt so good. The Silver Fox turned on the creature and ran at me, pulling me to the door. He raised his hand and spoke a word in a language I did not understand and a glowing wall went up behind us. The creature banged against it but could not get through. I had a moment to think and wanted to stay. I could make everything all right. I could help this poor creature and I would have my magic again and then use it to find Phoebe. Then all would be right. I had all these thoughts rush through me and then the Silver Fox pushed me through the doorway.

I tumbled forward and fell into the corridor and he shut the door behind us. A wave of emotion surged over me and I began to cry. "I wanted to stay. I truly could not find it within me to leave."

He looked at me with pity and I despised him for it. "The seductive pull of some is not easy to ignore."

A look of pain crossed his face and then he clutched at his side and fell over. He let out a harsh animal sound and his features blurred to be more human than fox. A few moments later the pain subsided and he pulled up his shirt and we both stared in disbelief. A large patch of his skin had turned golden.

"Damn." He gingerly touched the spot and then moved his hand away.

"Are you hurt?" I kneeled down next to him and tried to touch his golden skin, but he pulled away.

"No, I'll be fine." He banged his fist against the ground and then looked up to me. "I haven't quite told you the entire truth." He pulled his shirt back down and leaned against the wall.

"What haven't you told me?"

"It's true that that I'm maturing and going through puberty, but that's not all." He glanced away as though to see if the door behind us had truly been locked and said, "I'm also changing into a good faerie."

A smile broke out on my face and I simply helped him up so we could move on.

Chapter 9

Charley crouched over the trapdoor in the ground and shouted, "You have to come up and see this." He turned back around and took a moment to take in the scenery. The trapdoor had opened on a large hill that that looked out over an expansive forest for as far as he could see. Leaves of many shades of green filled his field of vision. The air, warm and humid, hung heavy in the air. Wispy clouds floated over another hill about a mile away. He stuck his head into the trapdoor and called, "It is wonderful!"

He saw Jeremiah down below but could not make out what he said. Veronika stood beside Jeremiah and he said, "It's like …"

From behind he heard movement and turned to see a large cat-like animal running toward him. He fell back away from the trapdoor and reached for a knife he carried on his belt. The large cat sprung at him, its golden fur and dark spots beautiful and yet dangerous to behold. With the knife in his hand, Charley scrambled to his feet and crouched into a defensive position. He had placed his musket on the ground after he had climbed up through the trapdoor and doubted he would have time to grab the weapon, aim and fire.

The large animal took a few steps forward and then let out a roar that rumbled in its chest deep and low. Charley tightened his grip on his knife and he glanced to his left and then to his right. He wondered if he could sprint to the edge of the hill's top and then slide down the bottom. If he fell too fast, he would tumble down the side of the hill and die. If he went too slow, the big cat would pounce on him and he would become its dinner.

"Okay, big guy, it's just you and me." Charley brandished the knife and flashed it at the animal. "I have my girls to get to and I really would like if we just went our separate ways. Neither of us would get hurt and we'd both be happier. What do you think?"

The cat kept its eyes on him and let out another low roar that rumbled in its chest. Charley looked for a sign that it was ready to spring at him and he kept his knife ready.

"This isn't going to end well for me, is it?" Charley stood firm and did not make any sudden moves. He kept eye contact with the big cat and prepared to run. Only a few feet in front of him, another option was to run and try to climb back down. He expected he would be torn in two before he even took one step into the trapdoor.

The cat stopped moving and he expected it to spring at him in any moment. With the knife in his hand, he knew what he would do. He glanced up at the sky and said, "Ginny, if I don't make it out of this, I'm sorry. I truly am."

A loud whistle from behind caught the big cat's attention and Charley's as well. He spun around and saw a woman clad in animal skins. Her hair jet black with red paint over her eyes and on her cheeks. She wore no top but had a long necklace in her hand. She shook it at the cat and it backed away.

"Yaguara!" She pointed at the big cat and walked forward, positioning Charley behind her.

"What did you say?" He kept his knife at the ready and watched to see what the big cat did. For now, the large beast stood its ground.

The woman rattled her necklace of beads again and rushed forward yelling. The cat froze for a moment and then sprinted off down the side of the hill.

Charley took a moment and relaxed a bit. "Thank you."

The woman pointed at the retreating big cat and said, "Abáûera."

"I don't understand you." Charley put his knife away and then put his hands together in supplication. "My name is Charley. What is your name?"

The young woman looked at him with a puzzled expression on her face. She spoke a string of words, quickly and with almost a clicking intonation to some of the words and then waited as if for him to reply.

"I have no idea what you just said." He pointed again to him and said, "Charley." Then he pointed to her and asked, "Name?"

She touched her chest and replied, "Iara."

He smiled and said, "Nice to meet you, Iara. Let me show you to my friends." Charley went over to the trapdoor but it was gone. No trace of it remained. He dropped to his knees and started brushing away dirt, searching for the trapdoor but could not find it. He looked up to Iara and asked, "Where did it go?"

She stared at him and again said a bunch of words that he could not comprehend and then she used her spear and pointed off toward the horizon. Charley ignored her and kept searching in the dirt but she poked him with the spear and pointed at the sky. He glanced up and followed where she pointed.

"Now what?" Off in the distance he saw a large mountain with smoke streaming out of the top.

Iara shook her hands in the air and pointed at the mountain. "BOOM."

"Wonderful. Just what I need—an erupting volcano." As if in response, the ground shook and more smoke poured out of the top sending a huge plume of ash into the air.

* * *

Veronika helped boost Jeremiah up into the ceiling. He reached the top of the trapdoor and found the opening shut. "The opening's closed." He hammered his fist against the stone that had appeared over the opening. "I cannot get it open."

He tried to find a better purchase to hold him up but he could find nothing to support him. He pounded his fist against the rock and it felt smooth and cold. It would not budge.

"I cannot hold you much longer." Veronika's face was red and she strained to hold him with her cupped hands. Arms stretched, she exhaled and took short breaths. "Hurry up."

Jeremiah pounded with his fist against the rock with no result. He pulled himself up as far as he could and used his shoulder to shove up against the rock, but it still did not move. "I will try one more time. Hang on."

He started to push up against the rock and then his world tilted sideways. The room suddenly shifted and he heard Veronika cry out in surprise. Grabbing on to the sides of the trapdoor, he hung on as the room repositioned itself.

Veronika tried to find something to hold on to but the ground, which had now become a side wall, was smooth and she started sliding down. Below her the wall was missing and a bright white light emanated from the open space.

She started to yell in Russian and Jeremiah could not understand her. She continued to slip downward to the opening and the white light and then vanished. Her screams could be heard for a few seconds and then faded away. Jeremiah let go from the trapdoor and slid down after her. He kept his hands at his sides hoping to control his slide, but he quickly slid downward into the awaiting opening. When passing through, he smelled a fragrant rush of plant life and then he started falling. He tried to see down below but could see nothing until it was too late. He splashed down into a warm lake and could now hear a waterfall near him.

He tried to keep his pack on but the force of the impact knocked it off along with his two pistols. For a moment he sank downward into the water. He heard the rumble of the waterfall and opened his eyes and thought he saw Veronika in front of him. Swimming to the top, he broke the water's surface and gasped. The sound of the waterfall drowned out his cry as he sucked in more air. He swam away from the sound and came to rest on a beach next to Veronika. She lay on her back, chest heaving, and took in as much air as she could.

They rested there for several minutes, listening to the pounding waterfall and birds calling to each other. Veronika rolled onto her side and asked, "Are you hurt?"

Jeremiah shook his head and touched his right ankle. "I hit the water hard but I am fine. How about you?" He sat up and looked around. "Can we still be in the hut?"

Veronika felt the gritty sand between her fingers. "I don't know." A call from a bird startled her and she glanced back to the jungle. "I have never seen a place like this."

Jeremiah sat up and felt the warm sun hit his face. "We might be in South America. A long time ago when I was still a boy I worked on a boat and we encountered jungles like this."

"Do you think Charley is here?" Veronika walked over to the edge of the jungle and could hear animals scurrying around. The smell of life surrounded her and the humidity in the air quickly warmed her up.

"I think Baba Yaga plays with us and we are meant to be tested together." He glanced up at the sun. "We should gather some food and water and get some shelter."

The sun had already begun to dry her wet clothes. "Which direction should we go?"

Jeremiah stared out at the water in front of them. "First, let me go get my backpack. I might be able to salvage some of the supplies that I had in there."

"I will scout around this area and see if I can find some fruit to eat." Veronika headed into the jungle and stopped. "Should I be worried about any wild creatures?"

"Watch out for jaguars and big snakes." He headed off into the water.

"You are not joking, are you?" She paused at the edge of the jungle.

"No, I'm not. Don't touch any frogs and watch out for mosquitoes. They carry disease. I've seen the strongest of men die from a simple bite." He headed farther into the water and turned back, "Don't go far. I'll be right back."

She shook her head and hesitated before walking into the jungle. Once she did so, she heard insects buzzing, more birds calling and the lush green life surrounded her. The trees bore no fruit but she walked on a bit and heard some small animals scurrying ahead of her. She kept onward, glancing up from time to time, and stopped at a tree. Far up above her, she saw some green bananas. She glanced around and then heard a shout from back at the lake. The voice did not sound like Jeremiah's.

Running back as quickly as she could, she broke out of the jungle onto the beach and saw a young boy watching Jeremiah swim out of the lake. He wore a purple undergarment and a beige wrap tied around one leg. Two black streaks of paint covered each cheek. When he noticed Veronika, he pointed his stick at her in a defensive position and spoke quickly in a language that she did not understand.

Jeremiah stopped at the edge of the lake and Veronika came next to him. Dropping his pack to the beach, he squatted down and pulled out some rope. "Would you like this?" He offered it to the boy and stayed at his level.

Veronika knelt down on the sand and kept her hands out, pointing to the gift of rope. "Do you think he understands what you are doing?"

The boy ran up to Jeremiah and grabbed the rope, but still held tightly onto his pointy stick. He looked to be no more than six or seven years of age. His skin brown and his hair jet black, but cut short. Looking at the rope, he felt it between his hands and then tied it around his waist like a belt. Then he smiled at his handiwork and his teeth were bright white.

Jeremiah glanced over at Veronika. "Now what?"

"Just stay still and let us see what he does."

The boy adjusted the rope around his waist and then stopped. He sniffed at the air and held his stick at the ready, looking up at the sky. He then ran forward and grabbed Veronika's hand, pulling her toward the jungle. He pointed up and then grabbed her hand again and pulled her toward the jungle. "Should we follow him?"

"Yes, go, just go." Jeremiah ran after them and he heard a loud rumbling sound. The ground shook and he heard an explosive sound from off in the distance. Once inside the jungle, he glanced up through a break in the trees and saw a mountain with huge plumes of smoke streaming out of its top not too far off in the distance.

Veronika pulled him closer to her and stared up. "What is that?"

"It's a volcano." The ground shook again and they held onto the trees and tried to keep steady. The little boy tugged at both of their hands and they followed him deeper into the jungle. When the earthquake stopped, he hid them under the thick leaves of a tree and motioned for them to be still. When they looked up at the sky, they could see the ash plume getting closer.

"What are we going to do?" Veronika asked and stared up at the ominous sky.

"We have to get under some cover soon." Jeremiah looked at the volcano and more ash shot into the sky. "I don't like the looks of that."

"We should pick a direction and get moving. That ash cloud is moving quickly toward us." Veronika allowed the little boy to play with her hair. When Jeremiah did not answer, she asked, "Which way should we go?"

"I don't know. I truly don't." Jeremiah turned away from the volcano and pulled Veronika up off of the ground. "But you're right. We need to get going. Come on."

The little native boy led the way deeper into the jungle and off in the distance the volcano rumbled again as if to let them know that it had not gone to sleep.

* * *

Phoebe and Isabelle followed Vladislav into the throne room. The Tsar stared down at a map on a large rectangular table lost in thought. The sun shone through the large windows and Vladislav stopped in front of the table. The Tsar ignored them and continued looking at the map.

Isabelle curtsied and Phoebe did the same, not knowing what to do. Vladislav moved off to the side and stood tall, staring straight ahead.

"You must be tired from your long journey." His flawless French surprised Phoebe.

"Thank you for your hospitality," Isabelle replied.

Phoebe nodded and kept quiet, unsure of what she should or should not say.

"The more I look at this map, the more I become frustrated and hopeless." Alexander knocked over a wooden horse figurine placed on the western borders of Russia. "My scouts tell me that Napoleon has crossed into Russia with his grand army. I have gathered my troops and am prepared to fight them, but against all my wishes, I've been advised to allow Napoleon in and to draw him farther back. Most of Europe has fallen to Bonaparte and now he comes for me. He once called me brother and friend. But you two care not for these matters." He walked over to Phoebe and asked, "You look much like your mother."

"You've seen her?" Phoebe could not contain her excitement. "Can you take me to her?"

"I know where she has gone, but do not know where she is." He looked down on Phoebe and by her chin tilted her face up to look at her. "She has gone to find Baba Yaga. An old hag of a witch from stories told to me when I was a child."

"Then we will go there as well. I must find my mother." Phoebe did not turn away but stared up at the Tsar. "She needs my help."

"We would be glad to assist you any way we can." Isabelle spoke in a low voice and kept her head down.

"Vladislav, what do you think I should do?"

"Do with what, Your Excellency?" Vladislav asked.

"If you were me, what would you do?" He turned away from Phoebe and pointed at the map. "Hundreds of thousands of French are invading Russia as we speak and I stand here like a fool."

Vladislav remained quiet.

Isabelle chanced a response. "You are only a fool if you play into Napoleon's hands."

"And what would you know about any of this?"

"I am a witch and I see many things." Isabelle lifted her head up. "We can help you."

"Thousands of my people will die and the advice I am given is to allow Napoleon to destroy my towns and allow my people to die. I cannot allow that."

Vladislav came forward and stood over the map. "Your Excellency, drawing him in and meeting him but withdrawing does make sense."

"He believes himself invincible and, if you taunt him, he will come." Isabelle kept her hands folded in front of her and stayed calm. "My sisters and I have watched him a long time. His faith in himself is his weakness. He believes he cannot be beaten."

"No one is invincible. We will all fall one day. Even me." He joined Vladislav at the map and said, "Though I am greatly tempted that I now have what he had held so dear."

"He let us go." Phoebe came forward and looked down at the map, not understanding all the arrows and markings on it. "I think he has given up on me."

"You are a pawn to him in his game. You will help him get to your mother."

"I don't understand."

"You don't understand because you are a child." Alexander turned around and pointed at Isabelle. "But she knows of what I speak."

Isabelle did not say a word.

"Now you two can help me, and in return, I can assist you." Alexander smiled. "Our arrangement will be beneficial to each of us."

"What do you want from us?" Phoebe moved away from the Tsar to be nearer to Isabelle.

"You will stay here as my guests and I will let Napoleon know that I have you both. He will not be pleased to learn that I have Cinderella's daughter."

Phoebe chanced a response, "We cannot stay here."

Isabelle tried to cut Phoebe off and said, "We would be happy to stay here as your guests."

"No, I cannot stay. I have to go find my mother. I don't want to stay here."

Alexander came before Phoebe and looked down at her. "You will do as I command. Do you understand?"

Phoebe crossed her arms and shook her head. "No, I don't wish to stay here. I have to go find my mother. She needs me."

A slight flush of color broke out on Alexander's neck and he bent down to look Phoebe eye to eye. "You will do as I say. There will be no argument on this. It is what I want."

Isabelle rushed to Phoebe's side. "Your Excellency, we will gladly stay here in your palace as guests."

Phoebe pushed Isabelle away. "No, I will not stay."

Alexander's face turned red and he smashed his fist into his palm. "You will do as I say. Nothing can change that. You are not strong enough to resist me."

Vladislav appeared beside Phoebe. "But I am strong enough." Alexander reached out and tried to push Vladislav to the ground, but his hands went through empty air as Vladislav had raised his hands in defense. His right hand glowed white with power and he had put his other arm around Phoebe. "Your Excellency, you do not wish to do this."

"You dare to rise up against me?" Alexander rushed to the table and reached for a ceremonial sword. He pulled the blade from its scabbard and rushed at Vladislav.

Isabelle ran to Phoebe's side and pulled her from Vladislav. She took her to the far corner of the room and they watched as Alexander rushed forward with his sword drawn.

Vladislav stood firm and said, "Lower your sword. The child must be allowed to pass. I have foreseen it."

"I do not care what you have seen or not seen. You will die at my hands for defying me." Alexander rushed forward and threw his full weight into his swing.

Vladislav pointed at Alexander and he dropped to the ground as though he had run full force into a wall. The sword fell from his grasp and slid a few feet away. Alexander did not get up. Vladislav turned around and rushed over to Isabelle and Phoebe. "You must hurry and leave here before he awakes. I will take care of him and you will be safe if you leave now. Come with me."

Isabelle grabbed Phoebe's hand and said, "Thank you for helping us."

"You must go find Baba Yaga. Head north and you will find her. If you hurry, you still have time to find Cinderella." Vladislav hurried out of the room and two guards stood at attention. They appeared to be mesmerized, staring off into space as though they had heard none of the fighting within.

Phoebe glanced back and saw Alexander still passed out on the floor. "Why are you helping us? I don't understand."

Vladislav rushed down the hall headed toward the stables. "Napoleon must be stopped and if you stay with us then you will bring the entire grand army upon us. Alexander does not see that. He is a good man, but often indecisive and a bit excessive with his emotions."

"Won't he be upset and have you imprisoned or killed when he awakes?"

"All will be well. When I am done with him, he will think he simply had a bad dream and he will call me for my aid with the massive headache he will have when he wakes. Do not worry about that. But instead, heed my advice. Head north and look for Baba Yaga. Do not sway your course. Napoleon is coming and he will destroy us all. Your mother or you must bring Baba Yaga back to defeat Napoleon. It is the only way." Vladislav brought them out a back door and walked them over to several horses.

"And if we fail or stray from the path?" Phoebe asked.

"Then you will die." Vladislav pointed at the horses and handed them a bag of coins. "Now go."

Isabelle took the money from him and Phoebe said, "Thank you." They turned from him and ran to the horses. He watched them go and wondered if they would be strong enough to succeed or if they would fail. Many failed and only a few ever survived from his visions. He wondered which they would be. As though in response to his musings, Phoebe turned back and smiled at him and waved.

Chapter 10

Napoleon slouched on his horse and stared down at the battle scene. He had won another victory but each time the costs were dearer for his grand army. He turned away from the smoke and ruins before him and a fresh bit of hope coursed through his body. He clenched his right hand tightly around the reins and took a deep breath.

"Your Excellency, come have some rest." His aid took his horse and led him back to the main encampment.

"Leave me for a moment. I want to continue to look out on our victory."

The aid nodded and then left him and Napoleon pulled himself up and fought against fatigue. They had fought hard today. He turned away from the remains of the battlefield and looked east deeper into Russia. His army would keep advancing until no one stood in resistance.

He turned around and motioned for the aid to help him off his horse. His tent had been erected with haste and he went inside and dismissed everyone around him. He needed quiet. Inside only a cot and a rug thrown on the ground acted as adornment. Crude, but effective.

"Attend me." He raised his right hand and allowed his magic to pour forth. Before him, a portal opened in thin air. "Report and tell me what you have learned."

An image began to take shape in the air around the portal he had opened. A woman's face came in close and then she backed away so that he could see. Isabelle brushed a lock of hair from her forehead and said, "Your Excellency, I obey."

"How is Phoebe and our plan?"

"She is sleeping and in good health. We head north to find Cinderella." She appeared to want to say more but turned away, looking at something behind what Napoleon could see. When she turned back, she lowered her voice. "We will do our best to find her."

Napoleon massaged his aching shoulder and thought for a moment before he replied. "Does she suspect you?" He leaned closer to her floating image before him. "I cannot have you fail this task. All depends on it. Do you understand?"

Isabelle lowered her eyes to the ground. "I will not fail you. You have made it clear that I would never see my family again if I do." She fought back tears and said, "Phoebe does not suspect me. She trusts me without question."

"I am happy that we understand each other so clearly. I would hate to see harm come to your children during a time of war." Before she could respond, Napoleon said, "Then if she trusts you, bring her to Moscow and my army and I will meet you there."

"But Cinderella is up north and we head that way now. It will be difficult to convince her and turn around."

"Be resourceful and convince her otherwise. I've changed my mind and need Phoebe in Moscow." Napoleon sat on his cot and leaned back. "Am I understood?"

"I understand you clearly." Isabelle lowered her head and remained quiet.

Napoleon heard a tap on the tent's door and he closed his fist and broke the connection. The vision of Isabelle before him faded away. "Enter."

"Your Excellency." A messenger rushed into the tent, bowed before him, offering him a letter.

"What is it?" Napoleon focused his attention on the man before him.

"I bring a message from our scouts." He offered the note to the emperor.

"Just read it to me." Napoleon shifted on the cot and tried to find a more comfortable position. "Quickly."

The messenger bowed and then opened the letter. "The enemy retreats and falls inward deeper into Russia. They fall back past Moscow."

"And we will keep driving forward. We will crush Alexander and his people. We will not fail." Napoleon glanced down at the messenger. "Is that all?"

"There is more. Moscow is being evacuated and the Russian army is withdrawing farther eastward."

"Alexander plays games with us. He draws us in, closer and closer. Will he destroy all of Moscow too? We will not stop. We French will dine in Moscow in a week. Would you enjoy that?"

The messenger nodded but remained silent.

"Go now. I have work to do." Napoleon dismissed the messenger. Once he left the tent, Napoleon leaned heavily on his side to relieve the pain in his back. "But first, even I need rest."

* * *

The giant plum of smoke slowly headed their way. Charley took Iara's lead and started to climb down the hill. He slid partway, and grabbed onto some bushes but kept his footing all the way down. Once under the cover of the trees, he turned toward the approaching cloud of ash and could hear another eruption inside the volcano that shot more ash into the sky. From off in the distance, a loud explosion echoed through the area and the birds in the trees around them flew off in fear.

"What the hell was that?" Charley searched for a place to hide, but did not know where to go.

"Boom." Iara made a motion with her hand and then pretended to drop something from the sky and enacted an explosion with her hands.

Charley could hear another set of explosions going off inside the volcano and saw bits of lava spraying out of the top. "We need to hide. What is the best way to go?" He saw trees all around him and knew he wouldn't head toward the volcano, but where else to go he did not know.

Iara pointed off to the left and said something in a quick burst of words and then ran off at a fast pace. Charley did not hesitate and followed her through the jungle. From behind them, another explosion could be heard, but this one was much closer. After a few seconds of silence, Charley thought he heard a musket being fired and then another explosion. His ears began ringing but he did not stop to turn back. Iara ran onward, weaving through the jungle, leading him in a westerly direction. They saw a few monkeys headed their way and many birds that flew away from the madness behind them.

"Where are we going?" Charley called after Iara but either she did not hear him or did not know how to respond.

Charley jumped over brush, vines and passed through large ferns, scratching his arms and hands desperately trying to keep up with Iara. She kept running at her fastest and weaved through the jungle heading westward.

Without warning, she stopped and Charley skidded to a halt behind her. "Did you lose your way?"

She turned on him and raised her hand, silencing him. She closed her eyes and closed her left hand into a fist and it began to glow in an eerie blue light. Iara mumbled under her breath and Charley watched in awe. From behind, another loud explosion rocked the ground not too far off.

"I think we better get moving. Standing here isn't a really good idea. We need to find cover or we won't make it."

Iara ignored him and he went to grab her hand but she pulled away. She opened her eyes and pointed back the way they had come.

"What? You want us to go back there? We can't do that." Charley reached for her arm to pull her in the direction they had been running but she avoided his grasp.

She smashed the end of her spear into the ground and rattled off a string of words that he did not understand and then pointed the spear toward the direction of the explosions.

"I understand. But we need to get to …"

Iara ignored him and ran back the way they had come. For a moment, Charley stood still watching her recede into the forest and then said, "Ginny, forgive me."

He ran after her and braced himself as the next explosion went off far off to the north. He heard a whistling sound in the air and then a crash and another explosion went off again far away. The volcano rained down fire on them. When his hearing cleared, he again thought he heard returning musket shots.

Iara still ran forward and came to a small stream. She slid down the bank and splashed on through the water without stopping. Once on the other side, she waved Charley onward and then pulled herself up the bank using some vines. Charley followed and when he caught up to her she had stopped, hiding herself behind a tree.

She pointed ahead and Charley looked in the direction and could see movement. He saw two men ahead in dark blue uniforms. One of them stopped and aimed his musket into the bushes ahead and fired.

A second soldier rushed over to him and yelled, "Cease fire. They're too far away. You'll not hit them and just waste ammunition. Now come on."

Both men slung their muskets onto their backs and jogged away. Moments later a loud whistling broke the temporary calm and from behind them Charley could hear the impact of the fiery piece of lava as it crashed into the forest floor. The impact exploded near them and sent a shockwave through the area. The ringing in his ears took some time to subside and Iara pointed at the men and inched forward.

He nodded and followed after her, remaining as quiet as he could be. The two soldiers had taken cover behind two trees, covering their ears and faces from the explosion. Iara rushed forward and raised her left hand. It glowed a brilliant blue. The one soldier reached for his musket, but before he could unsling his weapon from his shoulder, Iara pointed at the sky.

"DANGER. FOLLOW ME. SAFETY." Charley heard her words in his head. She had not said a syllable.

"It's that witch woman the captain was talking about." The closest solider shouted too loudly to his friend. "She's helped us before. Let's go!"

Charley came out of hiding and waved to the soldiers. "I'm lost too, but she's helped me so far."

Iara put her finger to her lips and pointed in a direction away from the volcano. "GO. NOW. NO TIME."

She lowered her hand and then took off at a fast pace. Charley and the soldiers ran after her and from behind them they could see the approaching ash cloud headed their way. After a few minutes of hard running, the thick humid air hung heavy around them. Charley stopped to take a break and wiped sweat that dripped off his forehead and into the corner of his right eye. From behind, the volcano rattled the ground again and another large plume of smoke shot up into the sky. Charley glanced up at the upward grade in front of him and shook his head. "Ginny, I could use a bit of help here."

He bent over and took a deep breath and felt an arm on his shoulder. He turned to the right and Iara's look of concern conveyed the words she did not speak. "Yes, yes, I know. I need to hurry up. But I'm tired and haven't slept in a long time."

Iara stopped and turned her head upward to look back at the volcano. Gray and menacing, the first wave of ash would hit them soon. And then they all saw it. Dozens of small bits of lava flew through the air out of the volcano and were headed toward them. The ejecta hit the ground and the following explosions rocked the surrounding area. Charley covered his ears and covered his face in the confusion and chaos. Before another set of ejecta could hit the ground, Iara pulled him away and in his head he heard her voice. "GO."

The two soldiers had stopped to watch as well, but followed Iara's lead. The noise from a second wave of explosions deafened them and they ran up the dirt hill. Charley stayed close to the rest of the group and pushed hard to make it to the top. Once there, he glanced back behind them and saw the cloud plum had nearly reached them. Ahead, he saw the two soldiers had begun the run down the hill. He followed Iara's lead and as in slow motion saw one of the soldiers trip and fall forward, flailing his arms. He hit the ground hard and slid several feet before coming to a stop. His companion had not seen him trip and kept running at full speed, but Iara and Charley stopped to help him.

Charley helped him up and could see a cut on his cheek. "Are you okay?"

"Yeah, I just tripped. Stupid of me." He stood up and shook his right leg. "I'm a bit shaken up but I'll be fine."

A gunshot from down the bottom of the hill caused the three of them to turn. The other soldier fell to the ground clutching his chest. Five men in white, blue and red uniforms rushed out of the trees below aiming their muskets at them. Their leader shouted in French and although Charley did not understand a word, he understood enough. He started to raise his hands in surrender when the ground around him moved and suddenly six men who had been hiding in the jungle around them fired at the French soldiers below. Charley threw himself to the ground and Iara took his lead. One of the dark blue uniformed soldiers motioned for them to crawl with him into the woods. They followed his lead and came to a hole in the ground.

In a thick English accent, he yelled, "Climb down. Now!"

Iara went first and Charley came right behind her just as the ash cloud hit them. The hot ash flew past them, blocking out the daylight and any visibility they had had. The English soldier climbed down into the ground with them and pulled close the trapdoor above them. From down below, Charley could see torchlight. "Where are we?"

At the bottom of the wooden ladder, the soldier closed another trapdoor above them and pointed down the corridor ahead. "Welcome to the English base."

Charley coughed into his hand to clear the ash from his throat and wiped his eyes as well. He looked on ahead and tried to whistle but it came out as a cough. "You built all this? I'm impressed."

Iara kept her hands at the ready and pointed ahead. The solider nodded. "Well, it's mostly natural caves but we made the best of it that we could." He coughed into his sleeve to clear his mouth of ash and said, "Let's get moving."

He led the way and Charley let Iara go before him. He turned around and could still hear the sound of gunfire from up above. "Will they be okay up there?"

"I hope so, because if not we'll be in a world of trouble if the French come down here after us." The soldier trotted off at a brisk run and Iara followed.

Charley looked up and said, "Ginny, when I get back I'm never going on a trip again. I swear."

He took off after Iara and hoped he wouldn't hear any noise behind him.

* * *

Jeremiah stood before me and I could see the look of fear on his face. Up in the sky, he saw a huge plume of ash erupting from the volcano that took up much of the open view above the tree canopy. He turned away from me and said something that I could not hear. He needed help and fast. I reached out to him and my hand passed through his. I was not there.

I awoke from my dream, took a few moments to erase the nightmare from my mind, and saw the Silver Fox stretched out near me. He still slept and snored softly. More spots of golden skin had covered his arms and neck. Even his signature white frock of hair had started to turn golden in color. I sat up and tried to clear the dream I had had from my mind. Both Phoebe and Jeremiah had been in my dreams of late. If I did not dream of the one, I dreamed of the other. The only way I knew to help either of them was to keep going forward. The corridor ahead ended in a door and I suspected that we would have another adventure today. How many weeks we had been wandering around in the hut I did not know.

The Silver Fox heard me stirring and woke. "Bon matin." He rubbed his eyes and then scratched a golden spot on the side of his neck.

"Morning." I stood up and glanced around.

He turned away and said, "I'll go wait for you by the door."

Some days we were lucky to find a bathroom in the hut, but today was not one of those days. I walked a little away down the corridor and then squatted down to release my water. I didn't have much time alone, but in the few moments I did have to myself I thought of Phoebe and of Jeremiah and hoped they were well. After finishing, I walked back up to the door and said, "Do you think we should go in here today?"

I touched the large wooden door. It had been painted white and still smelled of fresh paint.

"What I think isn't relevant. What do you think we should do?" The Silver Fox crossed his arms and waited for me to reply.

"I think we should go forward. I'm tired of wandering around in circles. I want to face this Baba Yaga and convince her to help us defeat Napoleon."

"You think it'll be that easy?"

"I don't know, but I have to try. We've been in here long enough and our supplies are getting low." I put both of my hands on the door and asked, "Is she far away?"

"She's behind this door. I thought a good night of sleep would help you before we faced her." He stood behind me and waited. "Go ahead and open the door."

"Why didn't you tell me she would be right here?" I failed to hide my frustration with him.

"Because you would have wanted to press on and I already told you that I thought you needed sleep more." He scratched a golden spot on his hand. "You have to trust me."

"Let's just get this over with." I turned away from him and pushed against the door and it opened easily. The door creaked on its hinges and a bright light shone from inside. I could only see an empty room. Turning back to the Silver Fox, he nodded and I walked inside. He followed right behind me and I saw a large stone chair in the corner of the room. A slight figure sat in the throne hidden in shadow. The rest of the room was empty and a mysterious, yet constant light shone through the back walls. The light lit up the room but most of the throne fell in shadow.

"There's no turning back now," the Silver Fox whispered and then continued to follow me.

On the throne, the figure appeared to be an old woman of slight build with white hair that fell past her waist. Head bowed forward and hands on the arms of the throne, I could not tell if she heard us or if she even lived.

"Is she awake?" I hesitated and stood in front of the throne.

At my words, she opened up her eyes and hissed at me. Her eyes burned like white orbs and her white hair came alive, like Medusa, swirling all around her. The door shut behind us with a bang and I raised my arm in defense.

"Who disturbs me?" Her voice, old and barely recognizable, echoed throughout the room.

"My name is Cinderella and this is the Silver Fox. We have come to ask you for help."

She hissed again and leaned forward in her throne. "I help no one. I am Baba Yaga. The witch, the old crone, the one alone. Leave me be."

I glanced over to the Silver Fox and he took the lead. "Your Malevolent One, we have travelled far to beg a boon of you."

She flicked her hand in the air and the Silver Fox flew against the wall, pinned there against his will. He struggled to free himself but could not.

"I do not wish to be disturbed." She turned to me. "Leave me."

Fear coursed through me, but I took a step forward. "I cannot leave without your help. You are my only chance to find my daughter. There is no turning back for me. I have to stay."

I expected to be flung against the nearest wall, but she only laughed. "You are young and unwise, but have courage. I often do not see courage. Tell me more."

"There is a great warlock emperor in the world who calls himself Napoleon. He has kidnapped my daughter and taken over most of Europe and marches through mother Russia as we speak. I need your help to defeat him." I finished my well-prepared speech and added, "Please."

"You are a fool to fight in the wars of men. Let the men fight, kill themselves and then the women will rule and peace will settle across the land. I have no desire to help in the pettiness of men." She focused on the Silver Fox and he struggled to talk but could not free himself. "My patience is waning and I ask you again to leave. The next time I will not ask."

The door behind me opened. I did not know what to do, but I knew that I could not fail. I had to find a way to convince her. "No, I cannot leave."

She raised her other hand, but I pressed on, "You are alone, separate from this world and I expect by choice. I do not know what hurt you so that you holed yourself up in this hut away from the eyes of the world, but the people need you. I need you."

"Do you think you can play with me so? Do you want to know why I came here and hear about the nightmare that I have lived through? Do you truly?"

"You cannot be all evil. I don't believe anyone is that. I will hear your story if you are willing to tell it." What a fool I was.

Baba Yaga motioned me forward with her finger and I resisted her. A look of surprise crossed her face. She tried again and I do not know what she expected to happen but I stayed on my feet unharmed.

"Tell me your story. I will listen."

She looked at me askance as if to see through me and waved her hand at me. I took several tentative steps forward and she hissed at me. "Come closer."

I did as she asked and I could see the blue veins underneath her wrinkled skin. Her white hair flowed all around her and I tried to ignore the stink emanating from her.

"Closer!" She reached for my face and I allowed her to touch me.

When her hand made contact with my face, her smooth hand felt warm to the touch. I had thought it would be cold. Baba Yaga closed her eyes and concentrated and I kept my eyes open. Her mouth moved and I heard her mumble some unintelligible words under her breath. Yet I stayed firm and did not shy away. She opened her eyes and let go of my face. "My magic does not harm you. How is that?"

"I do not know."

From behind me, I heard the Silver Fox squeak, trying to talk, but Baba Yaga flicked her hand again at him and the force of her magic increased, knocking him unconscious against the wall.

"No one has ever faced me as you do."

"I need your help. Without it, I cannot find my daughter or rid the world of Napoleon and bring winter down upon his army to destroy him."

She squinted at me and then scratched a wart on her neck. "But there is something more that you are not sharing with me. What is it? Who else do you fight for?"

I remained quiet and glanced away.

"You fight for love." She grinned a toothless smile at me and laughed. "Tell me, who do you love?"

I needed her help and without it I would fail. Looking back at her, I stared into her face and said, "Jeremiah."

"The witch hunter?" She responded right away and reached for my arm. "He is the one you love?"

"Do you know him?"

She cackled and the long hideous laugh turned into a cough. "So much time has passed that I had forgotten. I remember now. I remember."

"What?"

She yanked at my arm and squeezed it tight. "He chose you. He chose you over me!"

* * *

Veronika tried to mimic what the little boy said, "Ra-ja."

He shook his head and pointed at himself. "Raga." He said it again and the name flowed off his tongue.

"Raga." She spoke faster and put the syllables together.

The little native boy smiled and nodded.

"Your name is Raga." She offered him her hand and he backed away.

Jeremiah climbed down a tree and sat down on a rock. "The volcano is far away but the cloud of ash is blowing to the north. Still, we should leave this area in case the next cloud comes our way if the wind changes."

Raga pointed at the sky with his stick and made a rumbling sound. He shook his head and then pointed in the opposite direction.

"I'm with you. I think we should go the other way as well. I don't know how violent the volcanic eruption will be, but we better stay away from it." He stood up and then stretched. "Raga, lead the way."

Raga grabbed Veronika's hand and pulled her deeper into the jungle.

She followed him and Jeremiah did as well. "Where do you think he's taking us?"

Jeremiah kept a close watch but could see no one else around them. "I do not know. I'm hoping to his people and that they are friendly."

The sun beat down on them and the jungle kept in the heat with its oppressive humidity. Veronika walked right behind Raga.

Several hours passed and Raga brought them to a small village. He ran ahead to a man dressed in a dark blue uniform. Speaking quickly, he pulled at the man's leg and pointed back at them.

Jeremiah stayed back in the jungle. "Well, I wasn't expecting that."

Veronika hung close to Jeremiah and pointed at the five tents set up ahead of them. In front of the largest tent, a wagon with large wheels rolled to a stop and another man climbed out. Raga convinced the closest soldier to turn around and he pointed right at them both.

"Looks like it's too late now. We might as well come out and smile." Jeremiah led the way and Veronika kept close by him.

The soldier reached for his musket and pointed it at Jeremiah. "Stop or I will shoot!" His thick English accent caught Jeremiah off guard.

"We mean you no harm." Jeremiah froze and then put up his hands. Veronika did the same.

The solider whistled and waved over to two of his fellow soldiers who were unloading the wagon. They put down the boxes they carried and ran right over. And from behind one of the tents, another solider, a bit older than the others, rushed over and asked, "Who are you two and how did you get here?"

"Hello." Jeremiah waved but kept his hands in the air.

Raga spoke quickly and then pointed deep into the jungle.

"What did he say?" the older soldier asked.

The youngest soldier kept his musket trained on Jeremiah and said, "Raga says they fell out of the sky and saw the volcano erupting and they have not caused him any harm."

The older solider rubbed his brow and asked, "How did you fall from the sky?" He did not wait for them to answer and added, "Tell me the truth. I need to know."

Jeremiah glanced over at Veronika and then back at the older man. "We were in Russia and then fell through some sort of hole and landed in a lake."

The old man thought for a moment and then said, "My name is Benjamin and that's Taylor over there." He pulled out a pipe from his shirt pocket and stuck it in his mouth. "Do you smoke? You are going to need it."

Benjamin bit down on the pipe and offered another that he had in his pocket to Jeremiah, but he shook his head and refused.

Benjamin shrugged and put the second pipe away. "Now if I could only find a light." He waved over to one of the soldiers who brought him a burning stick from the natives' fire. Benjamin took his time lighting his pipe and then inhaled and blew the smoke out in small circles. "You and your friend here have landed in South America."

"What are you doing here so far from home?"

"Those bloody French." He scratched the back of his neck and then said, "You can put your hands down now."

"What is going on here?" Veronika had lowered her hands and Jeremiah had followed her lead.

"We are in the middle of a war against the French. Napoleon sent his troops here to take over the land." He pointed all around him. "This area is rich with minerals and Bonaparte needs resources to keep his wars going. We are here to stop the French." He smiled and opened his arms up to them in welcome. "You are safe with us."

"You don't seem to be too surprised to see us," Jeremiah said.

"That is because you are not the first people to bloody drop out of the sky." Benjamin pointed over to Raga. "We saw it with our own eyes. He just appeared out of the sky and fell straight down into the trees. We even found a jaguar that way too. Scared Taylor here right out of the privies."

Taylor had put his musket away and pointed off the way Jeremiah and Veronika had come. "Sir, I think we should head on out. The volcano might erupt again soon."

Veronika wiped the sweat from her head. "Can we have some water before we go?"

Benjamin pulled a wineskin from his pack and tossed it over to her. "Of course, here you go, miss."

"Do you think you can help us get back to Russia?" Jeremiah looked up at the sky and thought he heard a rumbling sound from the volcano.

Benjamin ignored his question. "Taylor, go tell the rest of the troops that we need to pack up and move onward. The bloody volcano is erupting again."

Raga ran over to Veronika and grabbed her hand. He clung to her leg and would not let go. Jeremiah scooped Raga into his arms and asked, "Should we head back into the jungle? Is that the safest place?"

"Nah, come with me." Behind them, three soldiers had already broken down the tents and ran into the jungle. The wagon was pulled off and soon gone from sight. Benjamin led the way and opened a trapdoor in the ground. "Come on, get on down in there. It will be a tight fight for all of us, but we will be fine."

Jeremiah could feel the ground shaking from the erupting volcano and could hear the eruption off in the distance, but couldn't see it. Veronika led the way, climbing down the wooden ladder and then Raga followed. Taking one last look behind him, Jeremiah heard another large eruption, but all signs of the makeshift village had disappeared. He climbed down the ladder and Benjamin followed behind him and locked the door. They could still hear the volcano erupting overhead.

"Keep heading straight down." Ben yelled down. "Wait for us once you get to the bottom."

Veronika climbed down as quickly as she could. She lost count of how many rungs they had climbed, but eventually she made it to the bottom. She held Raga in her arms and could not see much but knew that she stood in an open area. She could not feel the walls and saw only torchlight up ahead.

Jeremiah reached the bottom and finally Benjamin, who walked over to the wall and grabbed a torch from a holder. The flickering light lit their surrounding area but still they could not see much in the dimness.

Veronika kept Raga close and asked, "Where are we?"

Benjamin led the way and said to Veronika, "We're in a natural cave system that connects all through this area. We'll be safe down here. There are some people I wish you to meet."

"Who?" Jeremiah followed along and ran his hands against the walls.

"We're almost there." Benjamin led the way and they passed a room that several men worked at, staring at a map laid out across a large table. He ushered them along quickly before they could ask any questions.

At the end of the long corridor, Veronika stopped at a large wooden door that blocked her way. She turned around and asked, "Should I go inside?"

Benjamin walked to the front and grabbed hold of the door's handle and pulled. Slowly the door opened. Raga clung to Veronika's leg and refused to move forward.

Holding back, Jeremiah stood behind Benjamin and blocked Veronika's path. He held his arm out protectively and asked, "What is inside there?"

"Come on, you will be fine. There's no one to harm you." Benjamin lit another torch with his own and the room lit up in full light.

Hunched over a book, a woman had covered the sides of her face with her hand, deep in thought. She had a blanket pulled over her and appeared oblivious to her surroundings. In the far corner of the room, a man and a woman sat at a table talking in low voices. On seeing the additional light in the room, the woman with the book pulled herself up straight in the large stone chair that she sat and asked, "What's going on? Who turned on the light?"

At the table in the back of the cave, Charley turned away from Iara and waved to Jeremiah and Veronika, smiling. "I never thought I would see you again." He rushed over and hugged them.

Jeremiah ruffled Charley's hair and then a look of surprise came over him. "Mab, is that you?"

Dressed in the same uniform as Benjamin and the other soldiers, Queen Mab simply smiled. "Jeremiah." She put down her book and said his name and nothing more for a few moments. Not standing up, she reached out toward him and asked, "Is it really you?"

Jeremiah did not take her offered hand and continued to stare at her. Down to the tiny mole on the right side of her throat, it still amazed him that Mab appeared identical to Cinderella.

She let her arm fall back onto her lap. "Yes, it is."

Charley interrupted the awkward moment. "It's a long story, but Iara here saved my life and then we met up with these British soldiers. They brought me down here and showed me to Mab."

Jeremiah did not know what to say. But Mab ignored Jeremiah for the moment and addressed Veronika. "You've come to rescue me. Thank you!" Veronika looked on confused. Mab reached out and took Veronika's hand and pulled her close.

Veronika turned toward Jeremiah and asked, "How am I supposed to rescue her? I don't understand."

Hearing her question, Mab patted her hand and said, "Well, aren't you here to take my place on this stone throne?" She squeezed Veronika's hand and smiled.

Chapter 11

Phoebe glanced down at her meager meal and sighed. Their supplies had run low. The stale bread that she tried to eat did not satisfy her appetite.

"Where can we get more food?" Phoebe held her growling stomach.

"My hunting skills are not as sharp as I would like." Isabelle ate the last of her bread. "The good news is that we will be at Moscow soon and we can resupply there."

"We have been walking for weeks. How soon until we get there?" Phoebe stood up and looked ahead down the trail. "I often wished I could fly like some witches. We would have been there by now."

"I do not know. I'm not quite certain how we'll find Baba Yaga, but we will know when we get there."

From behind a hill, the sound of cannon fire silenced them. Isabelle jumped up and started scanning the way ahead, but she could not see anything. When the cannons stopped firing, Phoebe asked, "What do you think that is?"

Before Isabelle could answer, they heard a horn in the distance and then the cry of thousands of men as they charged into battle. Musket shots soon followed and additional cannon fire. Phoebe joined Isabelle but she could not see anything ahead either. Isabelle put her arm around Phoebe and pulled her close. "It might be Napoleon and his grand army fighting the Russians."

They listened to the battle for a few more minutes and then began to clear up the remains of their meal. "Should we go see the battle and watch from afar? I've never seen one before."

"You should not be so cavalier with what you ask. Battles are bloody messes for both sides. There are no victors." Isabelle finished packing and slung her pack on her back. "Come on, let's go."

Phoebe hesitated and stared off at the hill. "But what if that's the place we need to be?"

"I am not taking a child to a battlefield. It wouldn't be safe for either of us." Without turning back, Isabelle kept walking along the path.

Phoebe crossed her arms and replied, "I'm not a child. I'm thirteen now and I think we should go see if we can help."

"Help with what? Do you know what we would come across if we went there? Do you?" Isabelle rushed up at Phoebe and pointed at the hill. "Men would be lying all along the valley. Some will have lost limbs from the cannon fire and their blood will have soaked the fields. A battlefield is a hell that I would not wish on anyone, not even my enemy."

"But we could help save some lives." Phoebe did not back down.

"You know not what you ask. We have no supplies and if we could help save some soldiers, which side do we help? And how would you fend off the survivors? Some of them will want to rape you. What you ask is foolhardy and we're not going there."

Phoebe put her head down. "I just wanted to help."

"And I thought the same once and saw my husband torn to shreds from a cannonball. Nothing I did could save him." Isabelle turned away and tried to hide her tears. "You are too young to see such things." She turned around and rested her hand on Phoebe's cheek. "You are the future and have such opportunity and I don't want to see you hurt. Do you understand?"

"I do. I am just tired of wandering and not getting anywhere. I want to meet this Baba Yaga so she can help us find my mother and we all go home."

Isabelle handed Phoebe her pack. "Come on, let's go and we will keep heading toward Moscow. I don't think we're too far away." She sniffed the air and pointed the way.

"How are you so sure?" Phoebe followed along and tried to ignore the return of cannon fire behind them.

"I may not be able to fly but I have other witch powers and knowing my way around is one of them." She set a steady pace and did not look back. "If we keep walking, we will reach Moscow before nightfall."

The rest of the day went without incident and at times Isabelle would look back behind them expecting to see Napoleon's army rushing forward on their horses, but that did not happen. Instead they settled into a steady pace and remained quiet much of the day. At sunset, they reached the city and saw many people packing and leaving.

"The news must have reached here that Napoleon is approaching." Isabelle led them through the chaos of families packing their belongs into wagons and fathers carrying children on their shoulders. The exodus had begun.

"Where are we going to go?" Phoebe moved out of the road so that an old man could pass her. He wore a heavy pack on his back and nearly knocked her down trying to get past.

Isabelle came to help her and said, "We have to get off these roads." She looked around at the buildings around her. "We will head to the nearest convent. In time of need, the nuns should be able to help us." Isabelle took Phoebe's hand and led the way through the busy street.

After several blocks of negotiating through the bustle of people, Isabelle came to an old church and pointed to the sign. "We will be safe here. Come."

Phoebe followed Isabelle up the steps and turned back, watching the people go past. She heard Isabelle knock, but did not turn around. She leaned against the railing and held her stomach. She did not remember her last good meal.

The door opened and a tiny woman answered speaking Russian. Isabelle spoke in English and then in French but Phoebe lost interest. The immensity of it all overwhelmed her. A brush of hot wind caught her hair and she closed her eyes to protect herself from the grit and dirt that blew at her. When she opened her eyes, she saw yellow spots floating before her and the next moment she saw the world turn sideways. The sounds of horses and people bustling past the church slowed down and she crumbled to the ground.

She heard voices and saw people reaching out to her, but could not answer. To rest would do her good, so she closed her eyes and gave in. Gentle arms picked her up and she heard frantic calls to her, but she did not answer. It would do no good. She could not respond even if she wanted.

* * *

Late in the day, Phoebe awoke in a small room lit by several candles. Isabelle sat at the foot of the bed watching her. "Are you feeling better?"

The smell of stew perked her up. "I am so hungry. Can I have something to eat?"

Isabelle brought the bowl of stew over to her and helped feed her a few spoons of broth. The warm liquid coursed through her body and she smiled. "This is good." She took a break for a moment and put her hand on her hip. "My side hurts from all the walking we have done. Please tell me that I can rest here for the night. I'm so tired."

Isabelle offered more stew to Phoebe and she accepted. "Yes, we are safe. The nuns have taken us in. We can rest here tonight. And that is what you need to do, just eat and rest."

Phoebe ate a bit more stew and smiled. "I can do that."

"I was worried about you." Isabelle pushed back Phoebe's hair. "It has been hard on the road and I am sorry."

"It wasn't your fault. You got us here and we're safe now."

Isabelle shook her head. "Napoleon will be at the city's gates tomorrow. Then his men will be all through the city." Isabelle stopped and squeezed her hand. "You remind me a bit of my oldest daughter. She also doesn't complain and would be willing to go through much. I think you would like her."

Phoebe stopped to eat and said, "Maybe one day I could meet her and we could be friends."

"I would like that and I think she would too." Isabelle turned away to hide her tears. "Maybe one day that could happen."

Phoebe ate more of her stew and watched Isabelle. "Once we find my mother, we can then be together and all will be well."

Isabelle wiped her nose and took a deep breath. "You are right. Once we find your mother, then everything will be right like in a fairy tale."

She smiled and took hold of Phoebe's hand. Phoebe put down the stew and pulled Isabelle close. "We are all that we have right now. But we'll be fine. I just know it."

Isabelle shook her head and turned away, hiding her tears as best she could. "You are right. All will be fine."

* * *

I had traveled too far to give up now. The old woman on the stone throne watched me intently when I did not respond. She taunted me again. "You know that, don't you? He chose you over me."

"What are you talking about?"

"Your precious Jeremiah. The witch hunter. We were searching for you and I fell in love with him but when I told him that he chose you."

"None of this makes sense. When did this all happen?" I came closer to her and tried to read her expression to see if she were lying to me.

"It all happened a long, long time ago and it doesn't matter now. All that matters is where I am." She raised her arms and pointed to all around her. "I am here and all is lost. I paid the price for love just as you shall."

I could hear the Silver Fox mumbling in his unconscious state behind me. Baba Yaga had allowed him to fall to the ground. I turned away from her and went to his side. His eyes flittered open for a moment and after a few moments he recognized me. "She's tougher than I expected, isn't she?"

"Come with me." I helped him up and brought him before the stone throne. He sat propped up against the wall and did not speak. He simply watched us.

"Now that you have found me, am I all that you expected?" Baba Yaga leaned forward on her throne and waited for my reply.

"I need you to come with me. We must defeat Napoleon." I stood within arm's reach of her. "Please, if you have any compassion left, help me."

"I have no compassion. There is nothing left in me but hate and regret. All the rest has burned away over the years. All of it." She held up her arm that was all skin and bones. "Look at what is left of me. And I chose this to help him. I thought he would come back for me and that my sacrifice would make him love me more. And, if not, then it would absolve me from all my crimes. But it did none of that, none of it. All that happened is that I rotted away here for year after year."

I looked down on her with pity. "But I don't understand. Who did you sacrifice yourself for?"

Baba Yaga shook her head in disgust. "For your damned Jeremiah. Are you not listening to me?" She pounded the arm of the stone throne. "He and his friend needed to get back here to find you and I went along. Now it's been more years than I can remember and all is lost. All of it. My youth has been squandered and I've turned into a witch that little children fear. At night my spirit leaves the Otherside and I haunt the dreams of others." She coughed into her hand and then spat on the floor. "Can't you see that I'm stuck here on this stone throne? And you talk of me leaving here. I can't do it. I've tried for many, many years." She strained to pull herself up but the throne stuck to her.

"You have to come with me. Together, we can defeat Napoleon!" I stood before her and she simply laughed back at me.

"You and your fox came too late. I am finished and can go nowhere." She hung her head down and began to sob. "Finished I am. I lost it all. I am nothing."

I turned away and rushed over to the Silver Fox. More of his skin had turned golden in color and his hair had started to change to a shade of bronze. I propped him up against the wall and he opened his eyes. "Are you doing as badly as I think?"

Baba Yaga still sobbed on the stone throne and I turned back to him. "Yes, you could say that. Are you hurt?"

"I have felt better." He cringed and scratched at a large patch of gold on his throat. "If you help me up, I can try and convince her that all is not lost."

"Do you really think that's going to help?" I squatted down and put his arm over my shoulders and lifted him up.

"No, I don't, but would you rather I just sat here and pretended to be half-dead?" He grinned at me and took a few steps forward. "Come on, walk me over to her. I'm not done yet."

I took a few steps and he did not fall so we headed over to stand before the throne. The Silver Fox raised his hand in greeting to Baba Yaga. "I think we might have gotten off on the wrong foot when we first met. Good day." He pretended to tip a hat and bowed slightly. I steadied him so he did not fall. Always the showman, the Silver Fox did not appear to have grabbed her attention. He shuffled forward and asked, "Are you okay?"

Baba Yaga glanced down at him and stopped sobbing. She asked, "We are all trapped here on the Otherside. No, I am not all right."

The Silver Fox glanced back at me and then turned to Baba Yaga. "I've been trapped before. All of us have, but we cannot give up hope. I have magic that can help." He lit his hand up with a blue fire. "Please, let us help."

I came closer and took her hand in mine. "What do you have to lose? To sit here and wait for no one to come, or to get up with us and help us defeat Napoleon. Together we can do it. We three can change the world. Please, it's not too late. It's never too late. We can make a difference. We just need to try."

I tugged lightly on her arm and she turned to me and I saw into her face. The wrinkles, the regret and pain. Her face softened a bit for me and she turned her lips upward into an awkward toothless smile. "I will try to leave this stone throne for you. But you must take my place while I'm gone."

The Silver Fox shook his head. "No, all of us are leaving together."

Baba Yaga turned on him. "That is not how it works. The stone throne needs to be sat on and it must be her."

"I don't understand. We will help you up and then we can leave together. Forget about the throne. Just come with us." I pulled again at her arm and tried to get her to move, but she refused.

"You both know so little. The throne is what holds the worlds together. The Otherside and the Earth are joined in this one spot. When the seat is occupied then the worlds can intersect and magic, faeries and light can be in the world." She turned away from us and stared up at a point beyond what we could see. "Even now I feel her still there on the other throne waiting for me to make my choice. It all makes so much sense now that I think about it. But I was too young to understand."

The Silver Fox covered his mouth with his hand and whispered to me. "Do you have any idea what she's talking about?"

I nudged him to be quiet. "I need to find my daughter and in order to do that Napoleon must be defeated. He has her and I will do anything to stop him."

Baba Yaga squeezed my hand. "Anything?"

"Yes, I would do anything for her." I stood tall and thought about my Phoebe. I owed her much for not being there for her in her time of need.

"Then sit on this throne and I will go with your fox to destroy Napoleon. I would be absolved of all my past wrongdoings and I can move on in peace." She held my hand tight. "Will you do that?"

The Silver Fox tried to intercede but I pushed him away and said, "Yes, I will. I'll sit in your damn throne if it will help save my daughter."

"And your precious Jeremiah." Baba Yaga completed my unspoken thought for me. "Then I am ready to go."

"Good." I kept her eyes locked on mine and pulled.

The Silver Fox said something that I did not quite hear but with a gentle pull Baba Yaga stood up and I saw the tendrils of the stone throne be pulled out of her. The stone throne seethed for a moment and the living tendrils flowed back into the stone. She stumbled forward into the Silver Fox's arms and before he could stop me I took Baba Yaga's place.

A shock of cold went up my spine but I felt no different after that. I placed my hands on the throne's arms and more coldness seeped into me. I chanced to try and get up and, to my surprise, I could. I settled into the throne and saw Baba Yaga bent and broken in the Silver Fox's arms. And then a tickle went up my legs, back and shoulders. A thrust of power coursed through me and I opened my eyes as if for the first time. The world spoke to me and I could hear the magic and pulsing of time as it swirled around this point. A power rushed through me and I could see across space and time. A glimpse of Jeremiah swirled by and I saw him searching for me with Charley. Men and horses with smoke and fire hung all around Napoleon and his grand army. And not too far away, my dear Phoebe. I saw her face. She had grown so much in the time we had been apart. Too much time had passed. I knew what I had to do.

"Are you ready?" I clenched the sides of the stone throne, looking at Baba Yaga.

The Silver Fox looked doubtful. "Ready for what?"

"I'm taking her on a little journey."

Baba Yaga stood up straight and life appeared to have returned to her. "I am ready as well." She stood on her own and years of time looked to have fallen from her. Still old and willowy, she no longer appeared to be on death's door.

I smiled and with the ease of a child laughing, I opened the dreamline and took us through. We would not be lost and trapped in this place. I could see her now. My Phoebe waited for me and needed my help. Napoleon was all so near and I could save her and millions in the process. It all had to do with me again and my choices. I opened the floodgate within me and the stone throne gave me its power and the world went black as we fell through time and space.

* * *

Phoebe opened her eyes and for a moment she was unfamiliar with her surroundings. The early morning sun shone through the window and its warmth raised her spirits. The chill in the air could not be easily erased, but she played along imagining that she was back in America. All she needed to do was to stand up and open the door and she would see the fields of grass stretching far off toward the horizon. In such an expanse, she could truly be free. But then she took a deep breath, stretching, and the illusion faded away. She could smell the burning embers in the air. Each day the fires came closer and closer.

Isabelle opened the bedroom door. "Bon matin!"

"Good morning to you as well." Phoebe sat up and rubbed her eyes.

"Would you like some breakfast?" Isabelle started to put away clean clothes and sheets into the small closet in the room.

"Yes, I would." Phoebe dressed quickly and asked, "How long have you been up?"

"I couldn't sleep." She looked away.

"Did the fires keep you awake?"

"The sisters told me that Count Rostopchin has ordered the entire city burned." Isabelle stopped putting the clothes away and sat down on the spare cot in the room. "We will need to leave soon."

Phoebe stared out the window and not too far off she could see columns of smoke. "We are trapped here. I want so desperately to go home. To see my mother again and for this war to end."

"Come have some breakfast and we will start our day off right." Isabelle shut the closet door and headed to the kitchen.

"You are right." Phoebe followed her and they went through the hallway to the kitchen and she saw no one. "Is today another feast day? Is that why no one is around?"

Isabelle ignored her. "Would you like some bread and cheese for breakfast or something a bit warmer?" She turned into the kitchen.

Phoebe followed and entered to see Napoleon sitting at the large table. He smiled at her. Isabelle walked to his side and she thought to flee but from behind she saw several of his men appear with their weapons drawn. "How?"

"How is not important, but what you can do for me is." He straightened his hat that he had placed on the table. "I still search for your mother and thought you would have found her by now, but I was wrong."

Phoebe ignored him and turned on Isabelle. "It was you. It has always been you all along. You brought him to me."

Isabelle came forward. "I had no choice. My children. He said he would …"

"Enough." Napoleon banged the table with his fist. "We are not here to discuss that now. I want two things from you and I will make them simple for you. I want you to hand over your power to me and I want your mother."

Phoebe shook her head. "I have nothing to give to you. You lied to me and said you would set me free. All of it was untrue."

"Welcome to the ways of the world." Napoleon took his riding gloves off and placed them on the table next to his hat. "My grand army has travelled through Europe and Russia to get here and still I search and search. I am tired of searching. I am going to count to three and when I hit three you will give me what I want or you will die."

Isabelle turned back to face him. "That is not what you promised." Two soldiers entered the kitchen and grabbed Isabelle and held her back. "You told me that you would not harm her."

"I promise many things. And I once did have patience, but these damn Russians are burning their own cities down rather than to surrender to me. Today I will have what I want. One …"

Isabelle struggled but with her arms held tight she could not move. "You promised that she would not be harmed. Please!"

Phoebe saw movement behind her and a man with a scar on his forehead advanced on her. "What do you want me to do? I don't truly know."

"Give me your power. Relinquish it to me and I will spare your life. It is simple." He tapped his fingers on the table. "Two …"

"But how do I do that? I don't know how. Please, I just want to find my mother and go home. I've never done anything to you. Please." Phoebe backed away from him and bumped into the soldier behind her.

"I am tired of waiting. I have waited enough. This is your last chance. Turn your powers over to me now or you will die."

Phoebe clenched her fist and tried to spin up her power and readied for what would come next, but Isabelle burst free from the two soldiers with power and speed unlike anything Phoebe had ever seen before. Her arms shone like the sun and she rushed forward with her hands all afire with witchcraft. Napoleon glanced up at her and raised his right hand. "Three …"

A dark wave of sound emanated from him and all the light in the room vanished. A forceful wave of dark energy knocked Phoebe back against the nearest wall. And she saw what happened, Isabelle ran straight into his attack and it ripped through her, tearing through her body and continued on through the entire room. The floor shook as did the walls. Plates, silverware and glasses flew off the shelves and Phoebe held her breath until the wave of energy passed through them all and she heard only ringing in her ears. Isabelle's fire went out. She collapsed before the table and she clutched at her chest. The three soldiers in the room crumbled as well and blood seeped from their eye sockets, nose and ears. They made no sound as they died. Their deaths were swift and brutal.

Phoebe covered her ears and watched Isabelle continue to crawl toward Napoleon. He glanced down at her and moved his boot away from her hand. "You will be able to see your mother and children soon I should think."

Isabelle tilted her head up at him and blood coursed down her nose. She fixated on him with a look of hatred. "I will kill you."

"No, I think not. Your mother is dead as are your children and in a few moments you will be gone as well." He peered down at her like she were an insect. "But I wanted you to know all this before you died. Do you understand? I wanted you to know."

Isabelle turned from him and caught Phoebe's attention. "Forgive me." She faced Napoleon one last time and said, "You'll never have her power. I've protected her from you. There is nothing you can do to take her magic from her. Nothing." She croaked and her voice sounded burned and broken.

Phoebe watched her take her last breath and then Isabelle's head hit the floor.

A look of annoyance crossed Napoleon's face and then he glanced away from Isabelle's corpse with disgust and turned on Phoebe. She pushed herself back against the wall and all the fight within left her. He crossed the room with great speed in a few strides and pointed at her. "Do not make me count to three again. Do you understand? Now give me what I want."

Phoebe nodded and prayed. She prayed for her mother to come rescue her or the strength to smite him down. She took a deep breath and then exhaled and neither happened.

Chapter 12

Jeremiah eyed Mab with suspicion and asked, "What are you doing here?"

Mab banged the stone chair on which she sat with the palm of her hand. "It's a long story, but I'm not going anywhere. I need to be exactly where I am and I need her help."

Charley came over to Jeremiah and asked, "Did you ever find Cinderella in that hut?"

"No, we didn't. Not too long after we were separated, Veronika and I fell through a portal and landed here." He pointed over to Raga who cuddled up against Iara. "He helped us escape from the erupting volcano."

Benjamin crossed his arms over his chest and asked, "You all know each other?"

Mab snapped her fingers and Benjamin tossed her his skin of water and she took a quick drink and then wiped her mouth on the sleeve of her uniform. "Jeremiah and I go way back. We've been great friends through thick and thin. Charley I just met but he seems like a nice enough guy. But Veronika, now she's special."

Jeremiah shifted uncomfortably on leg to leg. "I still do not understand what you are doing here and why are you sitting on that stone throne?"

Veronika had backed away and stood near Raga and Iara. She eyed Mab warily and kept quiet.

Mab looked down at the stone throne. "After I dragged Napoleon away when we last saw each other, I tried to trap him in the future. I held him for a bit but his power was too strong and he escaped. But I had another ace in my pocket. I don't like to lose. I had brought us to the stone throne." She pounded her hand on the arm of the throne. "As long as I sit on this throne, I can cast my magic out and block Napoleon from using the dreamline. I have him trapped in the present. He can't use his magic to travel great distances any longer."

Veronika edged forward a bit and said, "But Napoleon has still won all of Europe and he's marching on Russia. He's been unstoppable."

Mab rolled her eyes. "I'm stopping him as best I can, but I need help and allies. The Silver Fox has helped me one last time." She turned to Charley and said, "I always knew he would come in handy one day and come through for me."

Jeremiah came closer and asked, "What has he done to help you?"

Mab folded her arms across her chest. "Why do you ask?"

"You know why."

"You wonder if Cinderella still lives and if she's found him." Mab leaned forward in the stone throne. "Am I right?"

"Yes, you are. I worry about her. Charley and I have been trying to find her for months and I wish to make certain that she is safe."

"That she's safe?" Mab started to say something to him, but she stopped and then turned to Benjamin. "Is it safe from those crazy French lurking about up there or is the volcano ready to blow us all to hell?"

Ben tried hard to hide his smirking. "We're fine. I have placed guards all along the way and we would have been notified if there were any danger. Those nasty French haven't discovered us."

Mab turned back to face Jeremiah. "She is well, but she will need your help. The good news is that she's found Baba Yaga's hut and the other stone chair. The bad news is that she's decided to sit down and learned that if she gets up that she'll lose all her power and never have a chance to save her daughter." Mab closed her eyes. "I can sense her sitting on the other throne and together we're using magic to keep Napoleon locked in place. Now we just need to drive the little bugger into the cold and then Mother Nature will rip him to shreds. We've almost won."

Veronika kept her arms around herself and asked, "But aren't we in Baba Yaga's hut as well?"

"Well, yes and no. You went inside the hut, but then you went through a gateway and traveled through to the Otherside. On your timeline, we're technically decades in your past." When Mab saw everyone looking more confused, she shrugged and said, "Trust me, it's a bit complicated."

Charley started to ask a question, but the ground began to shake and they heard a loud crashing sound from far above. Benjamin steadied himself against the nearest wall and said, "The volcano is erupting again. I will go check with my scouts."

Mab watched him run out of the room and she gripped the sides of the throne, holding on.

Jeremiah moved out of Benjamin's way and asked, "Do you need my help?

Benjamin shook his head. "Stay here and I will be back soon."

"Hang on to something." Mab gripped the throne harder and then the first pieces of ejecta landed above them. They were still far off, but the room shook and the torches flickered as the door opened and Benjamin left. The successive shockwaves from the earthquake continued to rock the room. Dust and bits of rocks fell on them all from the ceiling above.

Veronika held onto Jeremiah's arm but stood near Iara and Raga. He had started to cry out in his native language and Iara tried her best to comfort him as best she could in the far corner of the room, waiting for the earthquake to stop.

Jeremiah braced himself against the closest wall and watched the torches flicker. After a few minutes, the shaking lessened and the sound of falling rocks and mud from above faded to a low rumble. Mab brushed some dust off of her uniform. "The volcano is unstable and it'll erupt again soon, but we should be safe here for a while." She motioned to Jeremiah and waved him over.

He came over to her and accepted her hand. "What is it that you want?"

"First, let me tell you about your precious Cinderella." Mab patted his hand and then stopped joking. "I'm sorry. I shouldn't jest with you. I should be happy for the two of you. I really should." Mab kissed his hand and then let him go. "I missed you and had always hoped we could be together again, but I have seen you with her and know that your heart is with her. It's just hard for me. Can you understand that?"

"Yes, I do." Jeremiah kept quiet and thought it best to say no more.

Making a deep sigh, Mab turned away from him and addressed Veronika, "I hope you haven't a thing for him. He'll only break your heart."

Veronika blushed and also remained quiet.

Mab put out her left hand and it began to glow white and pure. "While we're waiting for Benjamin to come back, let me show you how she's doing."

On the wall to the left, an area began to glow and spread out, spiderlike, until the entire area lit up like the light from the moon. Mab leaned forward and orchestrated the glow on the wall until it focused into a clear picture. Cinderella sat on a stone throne. She stooped forward and had dark circles under her eyes. What she stared at they could not tell.

Mab kept the image clear for a few moments and then dropped her hand in fatigue. "Going so far into the future is challenging. But she is well." She snapped her fingers and the torches came back on and lit the room with their flickering light.

"How do we get back to her?" Jeremiah glanced over at the wall. "Could you send us to her?"

Mab shook her head. "Me, no, I don't have that kind of power, but she could." She pointed at Veronika.

Veronika shook her head. "I cannot do that. I have no magic powers."

"And you are a liar." Mab pointed at her accusingly. "I know who you truly are and can see through your illusion. I'm not as gullible as the others."

Veronika backed away. "I do not know what you mean." She glanced over to Jeremiah. "She is frightening me. Truly, I do not know what she speaks about."

Mab paused and held her gaze for a moment and then said, "Tell me about your mother and father."

"They were killed when I was small and I was raised by my Mamochka Tatyana." She looked to Jeremiah. "Tell her to stop."

Charley stood by Veronika to protect her and she hid behind him.

Jeremiah turned away from Veronika and stood in front of Mab. "Stop this. You are frightening her. We have traveled far together and need no more riddles. Stop playing games with us and tell us what you know."

"Is this how you treat me after all I have done for you?" Mab shook her head.

"Mab, please, we need your help. Tell us what you know." He lowered his voice and spoke from the heart.

"You have never needed or wanted my help before, but you are right. I have been lonely here and being stuck to this chair has not made me any better. I want so much to get up and to leave here. I want to be free again. I'm tired of being the one who is left and abandoned. Can you understand that?"

Jeremiah took her hand in his and kissed it. "Then get up and walk away."

"It's not that easy. I can't just do that."

"Stop allowing yourself to be held back. Get up, cast off your chains and start again. You are a strong woman. You can do it." He let her hand go and stepped back. "Just get up."

Mab smiled and she gripped the sides of the throne and looked poised to stand. "I so much want to do that. I want to just stand up and leave here. I could walk right through that wall, rip open the dreamline and head to any place within my imagination." She closed her eyes and then took a deep breath. "But I can't do that. I just can't. I need to stay here for a little while longer."

"Do not complain to me then about being abandoned and trapped. If you want to get up, then do so. Or if you choose not to leave here, then help us. Help us get back to Cinderella so that we can help her."

"Everything is always so simple with you. If I were to get up and leave, then Napoleon would be able to travel through the dreamline again. I block him. This chair acts as a barrier for him. He's walled from the dreamline and he cannot come here. He wants to visit here so that he can bring back gold and resources that would help him crush the rest of his enemies in his own time. But I stop him and have to remain here to keep him from coming to this time. I wish I could leave, but I have to stay. Someone has to stop him and for right now that person is me."

"Why are you sacrificing yourself then? What do you really do this for?" Veronika hung by the door and she kept Raga close.

Mab faced Veronika and said, "Because of love. I loved Jeremiah and treated him badly. Now I want him to have a chance to be happy. And if that's with Cinderella, then so be it."

"Then help us get back and we can end all of this." Jeremiah kneeled beside the throne. "If you do truly love me, then help me …"

A pained look crossed her face. "Please, do not say anymore. If I could help you now, I would. It is not within my power to do so. I use all of my strength to stay here and power the throne. Look behind you. She is the one who can help you."

Veronika pulled farther away and stood behind Charley. "I do not know what she means. I have no such power."

"Tell him what your real name is."

"My real name is Veronika."

Mab shook her head and wagged her finger at her. "No, it's not. Your real name is Baba Yaga. Tell him that."

Veronika froze at the sound of the name. "No, that's not possible."

"But it is and you have created all of this. The hut, the tests you've put them through, everything. Only you can get him back to where he belongs."

Veronika ran over to Jeremiah. "She lies. I do not understand what she means."

"Do not understand or pretending not to understand?" Mab asked.

Veronika turned to Jeremiah. "I swear. I do not know what she is talking about. Mamochka Tatyana raised me after my mother and father died and I have been on my own since then."

Jeremiah looked to Veronika and then to Mab. In the corner, he saw Iara clutching Raga close to her, protecting him.

"I can feel the flow of magic within you, but you hold it back for some reason. It is blocked within you. Why is that?"

"I cannot use magic anymore. I have sworn not to do so ever again." Veronika crossed her arms and stared down at the ground.

Charley chanced a question. "Is it true that you have magic?"

"Yes, it is, but please do not ask me to use my powers. I swore that I would never again." She backed away from them and looked small.

"Unless you choose differently, we will all be stuck in the past and the volcano will bury us within these tombs. I cannot send you back. And the only way we can stop the emperor is for you to go back and reclaim your throne. You must return to the stone throne and sit on it. You must reclaim it and face your fate." Mab paused for a moment and said, "It is the only way."

"No, I will not go back." She glanced up at Jeremiah. "I cannot use magic again. I swore that I never would again."

"But why?" Jeremiah edged closer to her with his hand out. "Help me understand."

"Because I killed my parents with my magic." She crumbled to the floor and covered her face with her hands and started crying. "It was all my fault."

Jeremiah went over to Veronika and knelt down to her. "All will be well."

"No, it will not. She has to use her magic and we do not have much time." Mab leaned forward and stretched out her hands toward the ceiling, concentrating. "The volcano is going to erupt again soon. You have to leave or you'll be trapped here."

Benjamin came running into the room with a gun in his hand. "The bloody French troops are in the jungles not too far from us. We're shutting all the entrances and exits down to hide. And you are right, the volcano is starting to rumble again. It's going to be a rough night." Benjamin helped Iara and Raga out of the room. "I'm going to try and get them to safety, but whatever you're going to do on that throne, you better do it quick."

Mab nodded and raised her left hand that began to glow with magic. "I will do my best to hide our position. Tell your men to get underground now."

Benjamin ran out of the room and they could hear him barking orders to soldiers out in the rest of the caverns.

Charley came by the stone throne and stood near Mab taking his cue to give Jeremiah some room.

Jeremiah sat next to Veronika on the floor but did not reach out to her. "Is there any way I can help?"

She sniffled and shook her head at him.

"Please, we need your help. At least talk to me."

Mab scoffed. "She's just pretending. Don't pay her too much attention. Like it or not she'll show her true colors and come around. Girls like her always do."

"No!" Veronika stood up and faced Mab. "I will not use my magic again. I swore it off and no one can make me use it if I don't want."

"Then we'll all die here. But I can see right through you." Mab ran her hand through her long hair. "How did you kill them? Lose your temper?"

"Stop it!" Veronika clenched her fists at her side and then she started to say something in Russian.

"Cursing at me isn't going to frighten me. Listen, stop playing this game and use your magic."

Veronika turned away and then the ground shook violently. The earthquake was much stronger this time and the ground rattled horizontally. Charley stumbled forward but caught himself on the nearest wall and Jeremiah held Veronika close, protecting her. A loud explosion that sounded to be nearly on top of them caused dirt from the ceiling to fall on them. From outside their room, they could hear Raga cry out from another cave and men running to safety. The torches flickered as dirt fell on them. Mab stood firm and her left hand cast an eerie glow on everyone.

She closed her eyes and focused her power. A white light shone around her and when she opened her eyes she frightened even Jeremiah. Her eyes glowed with white magic and she spoke in a language that they did not understand. Her power pulsed out of her like a shell that grew over them, covering everyone in the room and beyond. The wall of light passed through them and Jeremiah shivered as it passed him.

"I will protect you all but I do not know how long I can hold this shield." Mab kept her eyes closed and concentrated. Her hands were out as though she kept two walls at bay from crushing her. "Veronika, come to me."

Another large explosion went off above them but too far away to do any real damage. Veronika turned back to listen to the fading rumble from falling ejecta and then ran forward to stand before Mab.

She kept her eyes closed. "I would not ask you to use magic to harm anyone, but you were given a power to help people. What you choose to do then is up to you." She strained and pushed her hands out. "I am going to need your strength. If you don't help me, we might not survive the next blast. Do you think your parents would want that? For you to die by being buried alive?"

"But I can't." Her voice was small.

"Just give me your hand. I will coax the magic out of you. Hurry, we don't have much time."

Veronika hesitated and then quickly reached out and grabbed Mab's hand. She closed her eyes and Mab opened hers and they were normal. "Hold on. The next bomb has dropped. It's right above …"

A pulse of light flew out of Veronika into Mab and then out across the room. Directly overhead they heard a loud explosion and then parts of the cave's ceiling caved in. Rocks fell onto the far corner of the room and Jeremiah moved away to the opposite side covering his head with his hands. Charley fell to the floor and covered himself as well. The room rocked uncontrollably. Mab grunted with the effort but forced her shield out around them and up above. For a few moments, the explosions continued and then suddenly stopped.

The torches flickered again and this time Veronika eased up and she gave more freely of her magic. A blue light surrounded her and surged into Mab. Together the two of them took a deep breath and then their magic shot out of them like a large bubble that quickly grew and flew out past them and was absorbed into the floor and ceiling, covering the rest of the underground caverns.

Jeremiah listened and the next explosion went off far away from them. Mab kept focusing her magic, but she opened her eyes and Veronika opened hers as well. "See, I told you it wouldn't be that hard to do."

Veronika smiled but she withdrew her hand from Mab and slunk back to the far corner of the room with her shoulders slumped. "You were right. I did kill my parents. I lost my temper and lashed out at them when I was little and they were no more. It was all my fault."

Mab took pity on her. "It will be okay. I can help you—if you trust me."

Veronika nodded her head and sat on the floor and began to cry.

* * *

The Silver Fox scratched the back of his neck and then pulled up his shirt sleeve and stared at his arm. His skin tone had changed entirely to a soft golden hue. "No, no, no. This can't be happening. I don't want it to be happening. Stop!"

On the floor in front of him, Baba Yaga moaned but she did not respond to him. Her eyes fluttered and she remained unconscious. He ran back to the stone throne and watched Cinderella. Eyes closed, she breathed steadily and faced the wall. Images flickered past faster than he could see. From time to time, he could see a flash of insight into where she travelled but the image lasted only for a second or two and then the images would increase in speed again and become blurry.

"Come back to me."

Cinderella ignored him.

"Fox." Baba Yaga croaked his name.

He ran back to her and skidded across the floor to pick her up in his arms.

"Are you waking? Can you hear me?"

Baba Yaga opened her eyes. "It is almost complete."

"What? What is almost complete?" He shook her as she started to fade off again. "Tell me."

She grabbed his arm and squeezed. "I will not be here soon. All will be changed. But you must promise me something. I do not have much time."

"What is it that you want from me?" He waited for her to speak but she turned away from him and smiled. He saw that he was losing her. "Speak to me! What is it that you want me to promise you?"

She turned back to him and became fully awake. "Take care of Cinderella. Watch over her. Mab has given me another chance. I am free …"

"Mab? Did you say Mab?" He pulled her close. "Please, don't go. Tell me more."

Baba Yaga closed her eyes and she vanished from the room. The Silver Fox held empty air. "Wait! Please, don't go!" He jumped up and looked around the room. No trace of Baba Yaga remained.

He covered his face with his hands and breathed. He was alone now. No one would help him and Cinderella sat on the stone throne still.

"Cousin."

The Silver Fox turned toward Cinderella and watched her lips move.

"Cousin, come here."

Wary, he walked to the stone throne. "Who are you?"

Cinderella opened her eyes and he could see she was not herself. "It is Mab." She held his gaze and put out a hand to him. "I have only a short time. Listen to me. The timeline has changed. Baba Yaga is gone. I am from the past holding Napoleon at bay. Help Cinderella here. She can defeat him. Do not desert her. Do you hear me?"

"I do. But what about …"

"I see you have changed and I am happy for you. I will see you soon. Do not fail Cinderella. Help her. Please. Please, help her." Cinderella closed her eyes.

"Wait, where did Baba Yaga go? I don't understand." The Silver Fox reached for her hand but she blinked and was gone. Cinderella turned back toward the wall with her eyes closed. She fixated on a spot that he could not see. Images of the Russian countryside flashed across the wall. He could see French and Russia soldiers engaging in battles that lasted only for a few seconds. The scenes would change and then he could see the carnage. Thousands of men cut down, the wounded reaching out for aid, but the images would move onward. Always onward and onward as though she searched for someone.

"You will find him. And I will be here for you. I will not leave you." He glanced down at his hands. Both had turned golden in color. He then ran his hand through his hair and could feel the difference in texture. Auburn now in color, he expected his transformation was now complete. Across the room, he saw a mirror and walked toward it. He stared at his changed form. His hair color had changed entirely. None of his silver hair remained. His face had changed too, becoming fuller with a light scruff of a beard. Pulling himself up to his full height, he looked at his reflection and said, "When I was a child, I spoke like a child, I thought like a child, I reasoned like a child. But when I became a man, I gave up my childish ways."

Cinderella called out behind him and she struggled on the stone throne. He turned away from the mirror and ran back to her. "I am here. All will be well." He glanced up at the rapid fire of images flashing across the wall. "I hope."

* * *

I would have him now. On his knees and he would crawl, begging for forgiveness but I would only laugh at him. And then I would hear his pleas for mercy and would ignore them. I would open my heart and let all the cold, fear and hatred escape and would wrap him up in a dark embrace and bring him down to hell.

"Cinderella, wake up." The Silver Fox nudged me and then took a step back.

I jolted awake and for a moment I had forgotten my surroundings. I still sat in the stone throne, but I had slumped to the one side and apparently fallen asleep. "What happened to your hair?"

"I've changed." He answered matter-of-factly and then walked up to the far wall and stared out at a scene projected there.

"Are you comfortable with that?" I yawned and stretched my arms up high, relishing the movement. My legs still were asleep.

He turned back to me. "It's time that I grew up. I have a lot to make up for what I did in my youth."

"How long have I been away?"

"About a month."

I tried to stand up but had no strength in my legs to do so. "But I thought I had only been gone for a few minutes." I glanced around searching. "Where is Baba Yaga?"

"It's a long story, but she's gone. We're on our own now. But tell me, what happened to you?" The Silver Fox gave me a cup of water and I accepted.

"I opened the dreamline and went through. I concentrated on Napoleon and went toward him but he resisted me. I can't describe it. It was as though I blocked him as he kept trying to get away. The faster he ran, the harder I had to chase after him and hold him in front of me. I could never reach him, but he could not get away." I drank some water and rubbed my temple. I had a headache and felt groggy.

"I heard from Queen Mab while you were gone. She told me that she's holding Napoleon at bay, keeping him here. You only need to go back and find him so that you can face him. That is the only way."

I massaged my temple with my hand and rested for a few minutes. I then gathered myself and focused my strength and said, "Yes, you are right. I just need a moment to think on how best to capture him."

I ran my hand through my hair and heard a voice. It was him again. Napoleon. He tried to run from me, but could not. I raised my hand and the wall focused on what I could see into view. He rode his horse, heading back to Paris. His horse trotted off the scene and my attention focused on his immense army that marched away from a city.

"I still cannot find Phoebe, but he is leaving Moscow. It is done."

"Are you certain that he has her?" The Silver Fox watched the scene play out on the wall.

"I can sense her, but she is being hidden from me and her magic is muffled. I need to go back and try again. I will need to chase after him with ice and snow and freeze his army into submission."

I turned away from the Silver Fox and lost interest in him. He was a distraction for me. Now that I had such power, I would use it and I could clear my mind of anything not worth my time. I took a deep breath and drew in the power from the stone throne. The coldness in it flooded into me and I took it all within my heart and it gave me such a rush. I remembered my mother and I saw her leave me each night to be with the Silver Fox. Abandoned, I remembered playing with my toys all alone. My father out on his boat, sailing the world making deals with other merchants to sell silks and spices and all sorts of great and wonderful things, but none of the gifts he brought me could give me what I needed.

Then after my mother died, I truly was alone. My stepmother and stepsisters tortured me and later I looked to the prince but he could not save me. My poor Henri who was my biggest mistake came into view and I laughed at him. I would leave him now. I would leave them all and anyone who did not stand by me would be against me. I lashed out and blue light streamed from my hands into the wall and I fed it strong with my icy hatred. I would find Phoebe and I would bring her back to me and right all the wrongs and then I would give this all up and go back to being a simple mother who looked after her daughter. I would fade from history and no one would ever know that it was me who defeated Napoleon and saved the world. I would do this to save Phoebe and give her the chance I never had.

The wall changed and I saw Napoleon again on his horse. I sent my hatred and cold at him and smiled. No more being nice and waiting for people to treat me kindly and with compassion. Now that I had the power of the stone throne, I would use it and then give it up and move on. I could beat all of this and I would be forever strong.

Napoleon bent his head down against the snow and I sent a strong wind against him. I drew on the stone throne's power and sent all of it at him. All of it. His horse turned away for a moment, but he resisted me. And still, I could not find Phoebe. I searched high and low and I sent out my tendrils of ice that sought her, but I could not find her.

"Phoebe!" I shouted out to the gray sky and I stood on the cold battlefield. The Russians had been defeated yet again, but their numbers grew each day. Now with Napoleon on the run, I could freeze him and the spirits of pestilence and insanity would feed off of his grand army and I would watch and smile. Now justice would be mine. No longer would I be ignored. I could control my own destiny and I had had enough of the little man playing general.

An advisor of Napoleon's came up to him and said something to him and I could not make out the words, but Napoleon kicked the sides of his steed and headed off. Maybe he finally realized his predicament. I released more cold at him and I would let it freeze and I would be so happy in the cold. Enough of being nice and of smiling and doing what was right. I had had enough. And I would win where others failed, without ever having to send another to do my bidding. Napoleon would fall and though I might lose my own soul in the process, the world would be a better place. If only I could find Phoebe.

"Phoebe!" I called her again and I could hear my voice echo in the small room with the stone throne, but I did not want to go back there yet. Not yet.

Instead I searched far and wide, hoping to find her but I could only see the snow and the grand army, or what remained of it, heading back to Paris. I still had not the understanding of how to use my newfound powers and the doubt that crept within me, I buried it deep. Now would not be a time to think of what was right or wrong. There was only one right. I needed to find my daughter. I had waited more than two years and could not wait much longer.

"Cinderella."

I heard my name being called from far away and I realized that someone had been calling for me for some time. I simply had not heard the voice.

"Come back to me." The Silver Fox appeared before me and the room materialized around him. I brushed imaginary snow from my shoulders and saw his look of concern. "Can you hear me?"

"Yes, I can." I tore myself away from the wall but kept the cold building up within me.

"I'm starting to lose you." He held up his finger. "Focus here."

I turned away from him and prepared myself to go back out on the battlefield. I would continue to chase after Napoleon and face him. He would not be able to defeat me and I would win. For all time, I would be victorious and for once I would have succeeded where others had failed.

"Look here now!" The Silver Fox lit his hand with magic and raised it at me. His spell whipped my head around and I saw him rush me.

"Do not interfere." I willed him to kneel, but he resisted.

"Cinderella, listen to me." He still moved toward me and I could not force him down. "You must resist or I will pull you off the throne."

"No, you will not take this from me. No one will." I clung tightly to the arms of the throne and felt the rough stone and the coldness there. "I will find her."

"Who are you looking for?"

"My daughter. I search for her."

He came closer and was only inches from me. "And what is her name?"

"She's my daughter. Her name is …" I could not remember. I turned away from him and focused on the wall.

He grabbed my chin and righted my face and asked again, "What is her name?"

"Whose name?" I could see his lips moving but I could hear voices now from behind me. They whispered to me and I could not make out their words yet, but I knew that the secrets they held would give me great power.

"Your daughter's name. The reason why you came here. The purpose for your sitting on the stone throne. What is her name?"

I closed my eyes and listened to the whispers and lost my focus.

A sting on my cheek snapped me back to the room. He had slapped me.

"I am the Silver Fox and I command you to hear me." His voice boomed throughout the room but it made no difference to me. He raised his hand to slap me again and I could see a look on his face. A look of concern. I glanced down at my own body, seeing how tired and weak I was from the stone throne. I looked for her. For my daughter and her name, the name that meant so much to me had faded. I turned my head to the left and thought of something else and then turned to the right and I searched for her name. I remembered what she looked like but could not place her name. Her name. Her blond hair and her smile and the times we laughed. The name came to me then.

"Phoebe." I smiled and focused on the Silver Fox. "My daughter's name is Phoebe."

"Good. That is very good." The Silver Fox took my hand and he flowed some of his warmth into me. "I almost lost you to the stone throne. Do you hear me now? Are you with me?"

"Yes, yes, I am here." I shook the cold from me and concentrated on the warmth in his hand. "It is so hard. The power is too great and I want to lose myself in it."

"I think you should get up now. I don't know if I will be able to bring you back if you start to fade away again."

I nodded to him and tried to get up but could not. "I can't get up."

He frowned and tried to pull me but could not. A panic rushed through me. "I think I'm stuck."

The Silver Fox pulled at me one last time and I did not budge. It was as though I was one with the stone throne. He took a step back and put his hand on his chin. "You're stuck. This is much worse than I had ever thought."

My heart beat fast and I tried to get up again, but could not. "What are we going to do?"

He shook his head and remained quiet for a moment and then said, "I don't know. I truly don't."

Chapter 13

Charley walked past the cot in which Iara slept with Raga cuddled next to her and he smiled. "They could not get out of the caves before the eruption but they weren't injured."

Jeremiah led Charley out of the small room and weaved his way through the fallen debris in the caverns. Dim torchlights flickered, casting an eerie glow throughout the underground tunnels. "Let's head back to Mab and she if she's finished talking with Veronika."

Charley yawned and covered his mouth with his hand. "I could use some sleep myself. It's been a long day."

"I agree." Jeremiah stopped and turned to his friend. "I want you to know how much I appreciate all your help in finding Cinderella. You've been away from Ginny and your children and now you're stuck here with me far from home."

"There is no point being upset about it. That will not get me home faster to them. Best thing I can do now is stay positive and find a way to get back to them." He patted Jeremiah on the back. "Come on, let's go see what Mab is up to."

"Wait a moment." Jeremiah blocked Charley's path. "I've known Mab for a long time. If she tries to deceive us, do all you can to get back home. Will you promise me that?"

Charley kept silent for a moment then said, "I can't promise that. I understand what you say but I would do what I can to help you and then we'd get home together."

Jeremiah shook his head. "But if you can't save me, go home to Ginny and your children. Do not worry about me. Mab might not try to trick us, but I wouldn't be surprised either."

Charley nodded and said, "Or, she might have changed. It's possible."

Jeremiah agreed. "You might be right. Maybe the lack of sleep is just causing me to be paranoid."

They continued down through the corridor and only a few soldiers were still awake and on duty. When they entered the cave with the stone throne, Veronika sat slumped against the far fall resting. She raised her head at their entering. "You're back." She stood up and pulled Jeremiah back out into the corridor. Charley left them alone and sat on the floor far away from Mab who appeared to be sleeping.

Veronika struggled to speak and in her thick Russian accent asked, "May I speak with you?"

"Of course." Jeremiah followed her into the next cave and together they sat down on the cold floor.

Veronika crossed her legs and folded her hands in her lap. "I have spoken with Mab and I wanted to apologize for how I acted earlier. I do not like to talk about my past and Mab frightens me a bit."

"She has a tendency to do that. She often gets right at the core of a thing and then digs at it, knowing she'll get a reaction. Right or wrong, it's her way."

"Do you think she will be able to help me?" Veronika pulled back her hair from her face.

"She will, though there are always unforeseen circumstances that come up in working with Mab. I doubt she's told us everything and what we don't know is what I fear." He pointed down the end of the hall. "Though she probably is using her magic to spy on us right now."

"In the morning, we will need to leave her and find a way back through the dreamline. She told me that she can help me but that I will need to make a choice."

Jeremiah shook his head. "I don't know if I would trust everything she told you." He kept his gaze on her and she turned away from him. "What is the choice that Mab says you have to make?"

Veronika put her face in her hands and sighed. "I will have to use my magic again. And the last time I did that, I lost control and my parents suffered. I still see their faces in my nightmares. They call me to stop hurting them with my magic and I cannot do so." She moved her hands away from her face and showed Jeremiah her tears. "She says that I am Baba Yaga and that it is my destiny to sit on the stone throne and that I can help you all get back home."

Jeremiah moved closer to her and took her hands in his. "To help us get home, can you tell me what happened with your parents?"

Veronika turned away and could not look Jeremiah in the eye and said, "When I was thirteen, my mother and I argued about my not being able to go to learn about my powers. Both my parents forced me not to use magic or acknowledge it. I would be punished if I used any of my powers. One day when my mother caught me using my powers in my room, she struck me. I will never forget that moment. She slapped me across my face and yelled at me to never do that again. I had simply been levitating a toy top that I had, making it spin around the room. No one saw it but me, but my mother did not want me to do even that.

"When she went to slap me the second time, I unleashed my magic on her and threw her across the room. My father came in and tried to stop me, but I threw him back as well. I lost control and my magic kept them at bay for too long. They could not breathe as I held them against the wall of our home. I just screamed and outside it had started to rain and the thunder started, blocking out their screams as they died. I killed them. It was my fault."

Jeremiah patted her hands lightly and said, "There is nothing you can do to bring them back. You will need to learn to forgive yourself and move on."

"I do not know if I could ever do that. I am broken inside and I cannot see how I could ever become whole again." She took a chance to look at him and reached out to him. "Hold me, please."

She fell into his arms and Jeremiah held her but at a distance. She snuggled her body against him and stayed close to him. He looked up at the ceiling and patted her back gently. "It will be okay over time."

Tears began to fall down her cheek and her voiced cracked. "It has been six years and still I carry this cross with me. I feel no more healed than after the first day. Mamochka Tatyana says that I need to use my magic and to learn how to control it. But instead, I just refuse to use it at all. I have caused too much damage already."

"Mamochka Tatyana is wise. Trying to bury who you are will not save you."

She hugged him close and stared up into his eyes. She watched him for a moment and moved to kiss him.

Jeremiah pulled away and held her at arm's length. "I cannot."

"I am sorry. I should not have done that." She pulled back from him and already her walls began to go back up.

"I am in love with Cinderella." He released her from the hug and smiled. "You are young yet. It has taken me many years to find love and now nothing will stop me from finding Cinderella again. I will find her and help her. It is what I need to do. Do you understand?"

Veronika brushed some stray hairs from her cheek. "She is a lucky woman to have found you. Most men would not be as honorable as you are." She moved away from him and then stopped. "I wish that you both find each other again and are happy together. You deserve that."

"Then help me. Tell me if there are any memories you have of being Baba Yaga."

"How can I be Baba Yaga? I am nineteen years old and only have the memories of my childhood. None of this makes sense to me."

Jeremiah shrugged and pointed around the room. "We were in Baba Yaga's hut and now are in the past. I know no more of any of this but we have to find a doorway to get back home. I have to find the stone throne there and help Cinderella."

"But how do we do that?"

"There is a way. There is always a way." A ghost of Mab stood in the doorway before them and they both looked up in surprise.

"How are you off the stone throne? Did you not tell us that you could not leave it? I don't understand." Jeremiah pulled himself up and went over to her.

"I still sit there and only a shadow of me is here." She spun around and they could see the torchlight shining through the apparition." She turned back on them and said, "I knew that she would not be able to resist your charms. Not many women can." She walked into the room and the man's uniform she wore did not fit her well. "And you found out more of what I needed to know."

Veronika stood up and backed away from the doorway. "What do you want from me? I have told you all that I know."

"I want you to go back and to sit on that stone throne. I will remain here and I will continue to man the throne in this time. That is the deal I will make with you. Together we will trap Napoleon and we will freeze his grand army to nothingness. He will be defeated and head back to Paris in shame. Then the armies of Europe will advance on him and tear France to pieces. He will be cast down and sanity will return to the world. Do you agree?"

Veronika shook her head. "I am a simple country girl who is a witch. I am not Baba Yaga."

"Exactly. But in my timeline, you become Baba Yaga. You are the witch and choose to sit on the stone throne. Your spirit travels all around becoming a nightmare for little children. All of this is what you are destined to become. I will send you back to where you belong. But you must promise to do your part. Do you understand?"

Veronika turned to Jeremiah. "But I don't want to go back and become an old witch. I want to be me."

Jeremiah started to say something, but Mab interrupted him. "It is your destiny and the more you fight it, the more it will come to be. You have to go and take the throne from Cinderella. If you don't take back your rightful spot, then history will be changed and others will suffer."

Veronika shook her head. "Maybe that's a good thing. Can you send me back to when I killed my parents with my magic and I can change that? I know so much more now. If you could help me do that, then I could stop all of this from happening. I would be fixed and then none of this would have to have happened. It would all go away."

Mab shook her head. "Trust me, I've tried to change my own timeline many times and it never works out right." She looked to Jeremiah for help. "Tell her."

Veronika looked to him and he saw the hope on her face, but knew his words would bring no solace to her. "It is true. Mab and I have a complicated history and what she says makes sense. I cannot tell you what to do. You must do that for yourself."

"Accept responsibility for your actions and go back to help another. It might break the chain of destruction that you are in and can set your path straight." Mab came over to her and squatted down in front of her and went to touch her arm but the vision of her passed right through Veronika.

"But I don't want to grow up to become an old hag that everyone hates. It's not fair. I want to be different. I want to be me." Her thick accent became worse as she stammered out the last few words.

"But in the future, you have tricked Cinderella and she is now on the stone throne where you used to sit. You have traveled away, trying to escape and are now here with us. But you don't belong here. You've tricked yourself into forgetting who you are so that you can start again and give yourself another chance. If you help us, you will also be helping yourself." Mab turned around and pointed toward the next cave and the stone throne. "Go back and this will all be fixed."

"And I will become an old hag that people fear." Veronika wrapped her arms around herself. "It does not seem fair."

"Life is not fair. But you have to go back or many will die."

Veronika kept silent for a long time and Jeremiah sat still and said nothing. Mab kept quiet as well and finally Veronika said, "I cannot do it. I do not want to go back."

"But you've made Cinderella take your place on the stone throne decades in the future from now. It's not fair to her." Mab stood up and put her hands on her hips. "I need her to defeat Napoleon. You must go. We need your help."

"I have not done anything. I lost my parents and now I simply want a chance to live and be happy." Veronika turned to Jeremiah. "I cannot go back. It is not what I want to do. Can you understand?"

Mab shook her head. "You will be making someone else suffer and the war that Napoleon will continue will kill hundreds of thousands of people."

"But I have no memories of what you accuse me of. I don't remember coming back into the past and changing my life. I just remember what happened to my parents and I want to learn how to move on from that."

"Then accept your fate and go back." Mab crossed her arms. "Do it or you will have lost your soul."

Veronika pulled herself up and said, "I will not go back. I do not wish to go!"

Mab lowered her head and pulled herself within. She did not lash out, but simply asked Jeremiah, "What will you do?"

Jeremiah had stood as well and he put his hand out to Veronika and asked, "Why don't you sleep on it tonight and decide in the morning?"

Veronika shook her head. "No, I have decided. I am not going back. She cannot make me go back!"

Jeremiah rushed forward and grabbed both of Veronika's arms. "She may not be able to force you back, but I can." He slipped behind her and locked his arms around her tight. Before she could respond, he lifted her off her feet and dragged her out of the cave.

Mab said not a word, but a smile broke out on her face. She floated out of the room, twirling her finger and followed Jeremiah into the next room.

Veronika had begun to scream but Jeremiah pulled her into the next cave. Charley woke up with a start and jumped up.

Mab came awake on the stone throne and motioned with her hand. At her wave, the door to the cave closed shut and locked.

"What's going on?" Charley asked.

"Help me get her onto the throne!" Jeremiah struggled and pulled Veronika up off her feet. She struggled and screamed.

Charley ran over to Jeremiah and grabbed his arm. "Jeremiah, stop. Please."

He pulled away from Charley and dragged Veronika to the stone throne. Veronika tried to escape but he had her arms locked down tight.

Charley put himself before the stone throne and Mab raised her arm and flicked him away. Hit by an invisible force, Charley fell to the side into the cave's wall.

"No!" Veronika screamed as loud as she could and she kicked her legs and pulled straight down, trying to fall out of Jeremiah's grasp, but could not.

"Throw her onto the stone throne and I will take care of the rest!" Mab opened her arms waiting for Veronika.

Charley picked himself up off the ground and ran at his full strength and then threw himself at Jeremiah's legs. Unable to withstand the lunge, Jeremiah fell hard onto the ground and Veronika fell free as his hands unlocked from the grip he had on her. She scrambled away from the stone throne and raised both of her hands before her. They both lit with a brilliant blue glow.

Jeremiah sat up but Charley had him in a headlock. "Jeremiah, think what you are doing. Would Cinderella want you to get back this way?"

"This is the only way back. She has to sit on the throne." Jeremiah did not struggle but watched Veronika.

Mab turned to Charley and said, "The only way you'll ever see your wife and children again is to have Veronika sit on the throne. Do you want to be stuck here until you die, knowing that you could have gone home?"

Charley tightened his hold on Jeremiah. "What if I sit on the throne and the rest of you get to go back? There must be another way."

Mab shook her head. "It must be Veronika. She has the power to open the dreamline. You and Jeremiah do not."

Veronika's chest heaved up and down. "All of you leave me alone. I want to get out of here."

"And where would you go? The French will find us here soon enough. We can only hide here for so long. Or the volcano will blow its top entirely and we'll be buried down here for eternity. Come sit on this throne and open the gateway. Let me lead them back to Cinderella and fix the mistake you have made in the future."

"But I do not understand. How could I have tricked Cinderella and come back here?" Veronika heard banging on the door behind her. She expected that Benjamin and his comrades would burst through the door soon enough.

"There is nowhere for you to go. Come sit on the throne."

"Don't do it! There must be another way." Charley held Jeremiah back as he struggled to get up off the floor.

Jeremiah reached out to her with his one free arm. "Please, Veronika, we have to get back. There are too many lives at stake. Napoleon must be defeated."

Veronika turned to him. "Do you love Cinderella so much that you would risk all for her?"

"It is not that I would risk all for her, but I love her. I want to help her."

"Even if it means destroying my life?" Veronika pointed at him and the light around her hands changed in color to a brilliant fiery orange.

"No, you are right. I am desperate and a fool. I am tired and want to go home and find her. If my sitting on the throne would open the dreamline, I would do it, but I have no power like you. My powers of hunting are different than yours and Mab's. We need your help and the only way I know to get home is for you to sit on the stone throne."

Veronika addressed Mab. "How do I know that what you say will even work? All of this might simply be a trick to get you out of your trap. Maybe Napoleon put you there because you deserve to be there and it's your prison."

Mab nodded. "Yes, I could be trying to trick you. All of that could be true, but I tell you that it is not." The soldiers continued to pound on the wooden door. Sooner or later they would break through. "You do not have much time. What do you want to do?"

Veronika walked up to Jeremiah and lowered her hands. He did not struggle and Charley let him stand. She reached out and grabbed his hand in hers. "I will sit on the throne for you because I see the love that you have for Cinderella."

She turned to face Mab. "I choose this for what I did to my parents. It will be my penance."

Charley pushed past Jeremiah. "Veronika, please, if you do not want to do this we can find another way."

The pounding on the door became louder as they heard the soldiers smashing the butts of their musket rifles against the door.

"And where would I go? In a prison cell or, worse, in a lab where these soldiers would try to harness my magic? There is no other choice. Let me do this and it will be done. I am tired of all this." She hugged Charley quickly. "Thank you but I have made up mind."

Jeremiah remained quiet and Charley took a step away. Mab reached out her hand to Veronika and said, "Take my hand and you will release me. I will come off the stone throne and you will take my place. Are you ready?"

Veronika nodded and took a step forward. She looked back at Charley and Jeremiah and said, "Remember me." She turned away from them and then grasped Mab's hand in hers. Mab pulled Veronika forward and in a blink of an eye they switched places. Mab stood before the stone throne holding Veronika's hand while she sat in the stone throne.

For a brief moment, a look of panic crossed Veronika's face. She pulled her hand away from Mab and put both her hands on the throne's arms. She stopped moving and then turned her head away to listen and said, "I hear her. She is calling for help."

Jeremiah moved over to Mab and asked, "Is this supposed to be happening?"

Mab pushed him away. "Just stay back."

Veronika raised her hands and both ignited in fire. "I see the doorway to her. I see it. It is all so wonderful."

Mab pushed Jeremiah and Charley forward. "Go with her. Go back to your time and bring her with you. I will stay here and keep anyone else from using the stone throne. Do you understand?"

Veronika concentrated and a gateway opened in the wall to their right. She appeared to be dazed and lost in concentration. They could almost see through to the other side. Mab ran forward and pulled Veronika off the throne and took her place.

"Mab, what are you doing?" Jeremiah lifted Veronika off the ground and held her in his arms.

"I wanted to see what she would sacrifice for you and now I know. And I needed to know how far you would go to save Cinderella." Jeremiah went to argue but she held up her hand and shook her head. "Be quiet and just do what I say. Go find the woman you love and get out of here. I'm starting to get cranky and might change my mind."

Jeremiah gave her a quick hug. "Thank you." He ran over to the far wall and Mab raised her hand and the swirling light grew larger on the wall. In moments, a portal appeared showing another time and place. She pointed and said, "Go!"

Charley did not need any further urging. He helped Jeremiah with Veronika but she woke and stood on her own. She took a few steps toward the stone throne and looked to say something but Mab held up her finger. "Go help him and know this: Each of us deserves a second chance. What you decide to do with that is up to you. Do you understand?"

"Do you mean that I can change my fate?" Veronika's face lit up.

"Go back and make wise decisions and you'll see." Mab turned away and heard the stone throne groan and Veronika vanished. The soldiers broke through the door into the cave but they were too late. She settled herself into the stone throne and sat up straight. She had one last job to do and then she would be finished with all of this and she could not wait for that to happen.

* * *

I opened my eyes and saw the Silver Fox standing over me. He frowned and asked, "Can you hear me?"

When I did not answer, he shook me hard, but I had already begun to fade again. The world pulled me down and I stared out at the wall next to me and I hung on no matter how tired I had become.

"Cinderella." A sharp sting woke me and I came back to him. The Silver Fox's face hung right in front of me. His full frock of auburn hair with no trace left of white. A second slap across my face brought me back. "Stay with me."

"What do you want?" I begrudgingly turned away from the wall and let my thoughts wander back to the Silver Fox. The winter cold I had sent at Napoleon and his grand army would not dissipate in the few minutes I spared talking to the fox.

"You must eat and drink. Here." He handed me a cup of water and I took a sip. The water went down smoothly and I took another sip. He then offered me a bowl of mushed fruit. I took a few bites and swallowed and then rested my head back against the stone throne.

"Thank you." I glanced down at myself and I tried to move my legs but could not. "How long has it been?"

The Silver Fox began to wipe down my arm with a rag that was warm and wet. "It has been several weeks." He washed my other arm and then rinsed the rag in a bowl of water. "How do you feel?"

"Tired, extremely tired." I met his eyes and smiled. "Thank you for taking care of me. I expect that I haven't been easy to care for."

The Silver Fox came closer and asked, "Would you be willing to try and move?"

I raised my arms over my head and then tried to pry my leg off the stone throne. I could still wiggle my toes but my leg stayed glued. "Yes, but I can't seem to move from here."

"Let's try all the same." The Silver Fox grabbed my left leg and tried to lift it. "Can you use the throne's magic to help me?"

I concentrated and willed my leg to move. It did slightly and the Silver Fox reached down and grabbed a bucket of water with his other arm. Before I could react, he pour the water underneath me. The warmth from the water surprised me and I called out. When I looked down, I could see my filth being washed away. The smell reached my nose and I nearly retched. The Silver Fox dropped the bucket and went for another and dosed my legs and lower area with another full bucket of water. The warmth spread through me and this time I was more prepared.

"You can put your left leg down now." He then pulled up my right and it came off the throne but only long enough for him to pour over another bucket of water. When the Silver Fox had finished cleaning me, he put down my leg and towel dried me.

Tears came to my eyes. "I'm sorry." A lump caught in my throat and I lowered my head and cried.

The Silver Fox kept drying me and began to hum a song. The music rose up and its melody washed over me. He finished drying me and then began to massage my legs. I could feel the blood flowing back into them and life returning to me.

I wiped the tears from my eyes and gathered myself. "Thank you." I knew not what else to say.

The Silver Fox kissed the back of my hand in a fatherly way. "I will not give up on you so you must keep fighting. You have almost won. Don't give up."

"I won't." I wiggled my toes and leaned forward as far as I could. "I do not know what to do. How am I going to get out of here?"

The Silver Fox raised his hand and it lit with his magic. "I will continue looking for a way to get you off this throne. I've tried breaking it, smashing it, pulling you off and last week you had agreed that I try to cut you out, but nothing has worked." He touched my legs with his magic and warmth flooded through my limbs. "I will not give up on you though. I owe it to your mother. I'll keep trying."

"I'm so tired though." I rested my weary head back on the stone throne. The warmth in my legs from the Silver Fox's magic spread through the rest of my body and the sensation tingled through my tired limbs.

"Take things one moment at a time." The Silver Fox grabbed my hand. "I believe in you." He pointed at his changed skin color and messed with his frock of auburn hair. "Anyone can change if they want to bad enough. If we work for it, we can do anything. Do you understand?" He squeezed my hand and then caught my eye. "I am here for you."

"Thank you. I feel so helpless." I turned back to the wall and said, "I need to go back now. I must continue to fight. I can see him. He still does not know that it's me who sends the winter's cold at him."

The Silver Fox closed his eyes and poured his strength into me. "Go defeat him. Take my magic and vanquish him. Eradicate him and his army from the field and then you will find Phoebe. Once Napoleon is defeated, you'll both be free. Go!"

I nodded and turned my head full toward the wall. Its white surface shifted in an instant and I could see Napoleon on his horse, in the cold, and those around him had begun to fall into the pure white snow. I willed myself to go and I did, leaving my body behind. I passed through the wall and out into the battlefield and could smell the desperation of the men. They were too far from home and the cold would freeze them and sickness would do the rest.

I cast my hope out like a net and searched for Phoebe but could not find her. Instead I focused on Napoleon and tried to find him so that I could confront him one last time. I had not much strength left and the world seemed so distant and cold. I walked through the field in front of me like in a fog, not seeing the people around me. I was a spirit and the men near me trudged on, unable to see me. The snow blew in the air and I saw men pulling their coats up tighter around their faces, desperately trying to block the wind and the cold from their faces and hands. But I dug deep into my hatred and I tapped into it and channeled all my despair into the cold. The cold flowed through me and I, like a ghost, walked on. I would find him again and he would tell me where Phoebe was or he would die. It would be that simple.

Chapter 14

Napoleon turned back and watched the long line of his troops behind him. He dismounted from his horse and handed the reins to the nearest person. Pushing past his advisors, he stormed into his tent and still the cold did not leave him. In the corner, Phoebe stood with her hands tied behind her back against a pole. A dirty rag tied around her mouth inhibited her from talking. She stared at him with hatred. He could see her scrutinize him as he walked into the tent.

Tired, he shrugged the snow off his coat and threw his hat down on a cot in the corner. "I am emperor of all of Europe and this is what it has come to. I have a hovel in the middle of a frozen wasteland as your mother's spirit chases me back home." He clapped his hands together to shake the remainder of the snow from his gloves and then threw them down on the cot as well. "I have no patience left. I have been patient with you for a long time and still you resist me. But now I have come to give you your final choice. I have only one question for you and only one."

Napoleon pulled a knife from his belt and held it before him. He walked over to Phoebe and pulled down her gag. "Are you ready?"

Phoebe's eyes were red from crying and she said, "I will not help you."

"It is not a matter of your help." He held the knife up to her cheek and placed the blade there. "Will you give me your powers?"

"My mother will come for you and she will destroy you and all that you have stood for. I do not fear you any longer." Phoebe held his gaze. "I already told you that I will not help you."

Napoleon took the blade from her face and shook his head. "It must kill her to know that she will never find you. I have hidden you from sight and there is no way she can find a trace of you in the world. She will think you dead."

"She will come for you and rescue me. I know it. But you have a choice, you can let me go and she might spare you. I can convince her of that." Phoebe leaned forward but the thick wooden pole behind her did not move.

"I do tire of all this war. And winter has come early, but I will need to return home and build a bigger army and then return to crush all of Russia. I might have lost this part of the war, but I will return and be stronger."

Phoebe closed her eyes and reached out her senses. "Your magic is being dampened as mine. I can sense it. You fear my mother and some power holds you back." She tried to tug free from the pole and wiggle her hands from the tied rope that held her, but she could not. "Please, we can stop all of this. We can all be happy."

Napoleon laughed. "The only happiness I crave right now is a warm fire and to be back home."

"But you cannot do that. Your magic is weak and you have to travel on horseback all the way back to Paris with my mother at your heels." Phoebe turned away and stared at the wall of the tent that faced east. "I can sense her looking for me. She is out there always. And she will find me."

Napoleon rushed her and held the knife again at her throat. "Not if you're dead. I will ask you one last time and then I will wash my hands of you. Will you give me your powers?"

He appeared crazed and Phoebe recoiled from him. She had pushed him too far and there would be no going back. She had stalled as long as she could but there was only one last trick she could try. It might give her some time. Any amount of time would be better than none. Putting her head down, she started to cry. "I do not know how."

Her tears came in full force and the sobs wracked her body. The cold bit at her and she fell forward crying still, but the ropes held her up. She would not see her mother again and their times together would be no more. Her mother would not see her grow and marry and have children of her own. The full force of her fate washed over her like a wave and she could not sustain it and cried.

Napoleon put the blade away and lifted her face up with his hand. "Let your guard down and I will do the rest. Do you agree?"

Phoebe cast a last glance to the east and sent a silent prayer out to her mother. It was the best she could do. "Yes, I do. Make it quick."

A small smile broke out on Napoleon's face and he could not contain his happiness. "Good, you finally see reason." He held his right hand in front of him and it began to glow in a pulsing red light that seemed to match the beating of his heart. He held his hand before her and then closed his eyes. And then, without another thought, he placed his hand on her forehead and he sensed no resistance in her. How many times he had tried this he could not remember. But now, at the end, she had succumbed to him. He could sense her untapped power and he went toward it and gathered it all up. His smile did not fade and with renewed strength he began his task. Her magic would be his and nothing of her would remain. He had won.

* * *

Jeremiah blinked and realized that he had reappeared. The journey back was completed. He still held Veronika by the hand and had pulled her close to him. Charley stood by his side rubbing his eyes. The walls around them were white and it appeared that they had returned to Baba Yaga's hut.

He let go of Veronika's hand and faced her. "I want to apologize for trying to force you onto the throne. It was not right of me. I am ashamed that I acted that way."

She massaged her wrists where he had held her and replied, "You scared me back there. I didn't know that you had such anger in you."

He did not turn away from her and said, "There is much darkness in me that you do not know of. I have done things in my life that I regret."

She stayed silent for a few moments and chose her words with care. "Then that means both of us have done things we have regretted. It will take me some time to fully forgive you, but for now let's work together to find Cinderella and help Charley go home. Agreed?"

"Agreed. That seems fair." Jeremiah nodded and then turned away from her.

Charley went forward to check the nearest door and found it unlocked. "We are back, aren't we?"

Veronika said, "It sure seems that way. The corridors and the doors look very much like the inside of Baba Yaga's hut."

Charley opened the door and peeked behind it. The way looked safe enough. "I guess we should get going and go onward. But before we do, what's our plan?"

Jeremiah looked behind them and saw a dead end. "I think we go onward, find Cinderella and help her defeat Napoleon and get you home. Sounds easy enough, right?"

Veronika came over to him and asked, "But how exactly do you plan to do all that?"

"I'll let you know once I figure it out." He smiled at her and began walking down the corridor.

"I commend you for your bravery, but as for your plan, I think it needs some work." She followed after him and then stopped to listen. Veronika turned around and asked, "Did you hear that?"

Charley nodded. "Yes, someone's whistling. Come on."

They ran down the opposite end of the corridor that opened into a large room. In the center, they found a large stone well and Jeremiah saw a tall, thin man with auburn hair and fancy clothing pulling a bucket of water up from the bottom.

"Hello, can you help us?"

The Silver Fox glanced up and a big smile beamed on his face and he tied the well rope down and ran over to Jeremiah and hugged him. "You made it!" Upon seeing Charley, he hugged him as well. "Cinderella is off chasing after Napoleon's army and she could use the help." Veronika came forward and he stopped. "You look familiar. Who are you?"

Jeremiah put himself before Veronika. "And who are you?"

"I'm the Silver Fox, of course." He offered to shake his hand.

Jeremiah and Charley both put their fists up in a defensive posture. Jeremiah pointed at the Silver Fox and asked, "What have you done to Cinderella this time?"

The Silver Fox took a step back and put up his hands. "I haven't done anything to her. I am helping her."

Jeremiah inched forward wary. "She told me all that you had done to her. How did you escape your prison?"

"Does it matter? All that matters is that I'm here with Cinderella and am helping her. I can bring you to her." He kept his hands up and remained still.

Charley leaned over to Jeremiah and said, "I do not trust him either."

Veronika pushed forward past Jeremiah and Charley. "Let us hear what he has to say. Maybe he has changed."

"I doubt that." Jeremiah hung back and lowered his fists. "Why should we trust you?"

Charley kept his fists raised and stood close to Veronika to protect her.

"I am a faerie and see why you would not trust me. I admit that I have done horrible things to Cinderella, but I served my time and have changed." He pointed to the end of the corridor. "I can take you to her and, if it will make you feel more secure, I will go as your prisoner. We do not have much time and standing around arguing all day won't help any of us."

Jeremiah pulled some rope from his backpack and the Silver Fox offered him his hands. With much skill, Jeremiah tied the Silver Fox's wrists together.

While Jeremiah bound the Silver Fox's hands, Veronika pointed over to a pile of food piled in an alcove. "Where did you get all that?"

"I found out which doors opened into different places so that I could gather some supplies. We have been here a long time." He stared at her, looking her up and down. "But you do look familiar. There's something important about you. I just can't place it."

"And what about you? You seem changed. Cinderella always described you by your long white hair." Charley pointed at his hair and skin. "What has happened to you?"

"I've grown up. It's a faerie thing." He shrugged. "But we should go and get back to Cinderella. She is in a bad way. I must be honest with you." The Silver Fox led the way down the corridor and said, "She is on this stone throne and I cannot get her off."

"Bring me to her." Jeremiah kept calm but forceful.

"Of course." The Silver Fox led them to the end of the corridor to another door. "Are you ready?"

"Just bring us to her." Jeremiah kept at the ready for any sign of trickery.

The Silver Fox motioned to the door's handle and said, "I could use a little help." He held up his tied up hands and then smiled.

Charley opened the door and inside the room they saw a long rope hanging from far up in the ceiling. Where the rope ended, they could not see as the ceiling stretched beyond their reach but only in a small section of the room. The Silver Fox glanced up through the large hole in the ceiling and said to Veronika, "Gently tug the rope three times."

She looked to Jeremiah to whether she should listen and he nodded. When she grabbed the rope, she gently tugged three times. A bell at the top rang and they heard a roaring sound as though a fire had been ignited. And then from above, they could see a wicker basket, large enough to fit a half dozen people begin to descend. Above the basket they saw a large red balloon. When the basket touched the ground, the Silver Fox motioned toward the balloon and said, "After you."

Jeremiah, Charley and Veronika climbed inside and then helped the Silver Fox in. Jeremiah looked up but could not see around the balloon and then asked, "Is it far?"

"It's not too far. The throne room is just at the top and off to the side. This place is full of some wondrous things. You should see the fish pond. It is simply amazing." The Silver Fox pointed to Charley and asked, "Can you tug the rope again?"

Charley did as asked and they heard a fire roar again and could see a flame above them in the balloon. The fire warmed the air in the balloon and slowly they began to rise. In moments, they were high off the ground.

Veronika held on tight to the basket's railing and glanced down. "This is fun." She watched as the ground below faded away.

The Silver Fox glanced up at the red balloon and then leaned closer to Jeremiah so that he could whisper to him. "Prepare yourself. She truly is not in a good way."

Jeremiah nodded and folded his arms across his chest, but did not say a word. A few minutes later the balloon stopped when they reached the top. Charley climbed out first and then helped each of them out of the basket. The Silver Fox kept silent and led the way. At the end of another corridor, they walked into the large throne room and the nearest wall was lit up with images of battle and destruction. They entered the room and the lighting increased. In the center of the room, facing them, they could see the stone throne and the shell of a woman who sat on it. Jeremiah took a few hesitant steps forward and then ran full out to the throne.

He stopped when he reached her and fell down on his knees. Her long blond hair had gone thin and her body appeared wasted away. She was a slight of a thing now consisting of only flesh and bone in such meager portions that Jeremiah feared she would waste away before him. He looked at her eyes but she stared off trying to locate something he could not see. Her eyes are what appeared most alive, the irises frantically moving from left to right. She breathed ever so slightly and Jeremiah could see the bones beneath her sallow-colored skin.

He reached out and touched her knee but she did not respond. Her skin felt cold to the touch. Jeremiah spun around and confronted the Silver Fox. "How could you have let her get like this?"

"Me, you're blaming me?" The Silver Fox bristled and then shook his head. "I tried everything to get her up off of that damned throne. And I can't do it. She won't budge."

"But you let her sit down on it. You knew what would happen to her. You knew!" Jeremiah's anger rose up and he made no attempt to contain it. He rushed toward the Silver Fox. "She's only a pawn for you. It's always been like that, hasn't it?"

The Silver Fox said nothing and his face remained neutral.

"Tell me! You planned this all, haven't you?"

"There is nothing that I can say to convince you that I did not plan this." The Silver Fox pointed at the scenes playing out on the far wall. "But someone needs to stop this war and she's doing that." The winter snow blowing across the field that Cinderella stared out at showed the destruction that had been caused. "And it's working. Just a little bit longer and Bonaparte will be defeated."

"And what will happen with what's left of Cinderella? She'll be a husk with nothing left inside."

The Silver Fox shook his head. "She wants to find her daughter and have her magic back so this is the choice she's made. It's not my fault she's unable to let it go."

"Not your fault?" Jeremiah turned from the Silver Fox and asked Charley, "What do you think of this?"

Charley looked sheepish but found enough of his voice to say, "I don't think he forced her to be on the throne. It's up to us to find a way to convince her to get off it." He caught Veronika's eyes. "With Mab having changed the past, Veronika didn't become Baba Yaga so she was never on this stone throne. That's changed everything."

The Silver Fox came over to Veronika and stared at her. "You saw Mab and she's helped you? I can see the resemblance in the old woman you will become. History has been changed." He walked over to a spot on the floor and looked down. "Now you've never sat on the throne and the timeline has been rewritten. Everything has changed and I don't know how that helps or hurts Cinderella."

Veronika did not look away from the Silver Fox and said, "Mab sacrificed herself for me to give me another chance. I didn't sit on the throne long enough to become Baba Yaga. Maybe I can help Cinderella off this throne by taking her place. I'm willing to try."

The Silver Fox shook his head. "It doesn't work that way. The person on the throne has to want to get off and Cinderella won't want to do that until she finds her daughter. But there might be another way."

Jeremiah asked, "And what would that be? Probably something convenient to help you, isn't it?"

The Silver Fox ignored his taunt. "The stone throne needs blood. I can see that it's taking it from Cinderella as I've watched her all this time. Faerie legend has it that only the blood from a person who loves the one trapped on it will work. That might free Cinderella."

Charley shook his head in doubt. "How do we know he's telling the truth? Maybe he just wants to trick us into doing this."

Jeremiah ignored Charley and asked, "Well, how much blood does it want? A few drops?"

The Silver Fox shook his head and laughed, "Of course not. It would want all of the person's blood. All of it."

Veronika crossed her arms deep in thought. Jeremiah turned to her and asked, "What do you think? Is he telling the truth? Is that the only way I can free her?"

"I do not know. My timeline has changed and I do not have any of the throne's secrets."

Charley interrupted and asked, "But did the stone throne communicate anything to you when you were on it before Mab pulled you off?"

"Let me think." Veronika closed her eyes and placed her mind back to when she had sat down on the throne.

Jeremiah watched her and stayed wary of the Silver Fox. "Anything that you could remember might be of help. Please."

Veronika kept quiet a few more moments and then said, "I remember the cold shock going up my back when I sat down. The throne felt comfortable and then the backs of my legs and any part of me that touched the throne felt these tiny pinpricks as though needles had bored into me." She opened her eyes and faced Jeremiah. "I think it did drink of my blood in tiny amounts."

The Silver Fox went over to Jeremiah and said, "It does not matter what you think of me and of my motives. I tell you true that I want to see her survive. I have made many mistakes in my past but I am changed. I want to see Cinderella defeat Napoleon, but more than that I want to see her survive and be reunited with her daughter. But I tell the truth. The stone throne needs your blood."

Jeremiah faced Cinderella and said, "Then it shall have it. All of me." He held her gaze and then walked toward the stone throne, ignoring the pleas from Charley and Veronika.

Chapter 15

I had cast myself off into the deep coldness, searching for the emperor or for Phoebe, but I could not find either. I sat still in the cold stone throne and had lost track that I still had my body. My heart and will searched for a way to bring Phoebe back and the power that I had through the stone throne made me strong, but I knew that I could not last much longer. My body had become too frail, wasted and tired, but still I searched on.

    I glanced down below and like a bird my spirit flew, unseen, over the men. Tens of thousands of them marched through the snow and I pulled the cold from the north and it listened to me. I used the cold like a weapon. It bit deep into men and I saw wounds fester with gangrene. I no longer needed Baba Yaga for I had become her. My cold would chase them back to France and they would never return to Russia. I lost track of days and the hours, hearing the Silver Fox calling me to return for food and rest. But I needed to press on for I did not know if I could return and then come back again. I needed to find Phoebe. I stood on a hill, like a ghost, staring down at the remains of Napoleon's army. I remained motionless and allowed the snow to swirl through me and I felt nothing but the emptiness. I closed my eyes and listened.

    For a moment, all I could hear was the snarling wind and then a brief gasp caught my attention. Phoebe. I heard her in pain. To the north, I could sense her. I willed my spirit forward and I flew over the broken bodies of many men, moving without a sound and invisible to those around me. Time passed and I found a tent far off in the distance. Larger and more elaborate than any of the others, I knew that I had finally found Napoleon and Phoebe was with him. She was in danger and I sensed her fear. Gathering my strength, I ignored the pleas for me to return and rushed forward over the sleeping men, carrying with me only my coldness and hatred. The snow began to fall harder, but still no one could see me as I was a ghost.

    The tent's walls could not stop me and I rushed through and saw Phoebe tied to a wooden pillar. Napoleon stood in front of her with his right hand glowing red tightly around her neck. He had his eyes closed and Phoebe tried to free herself, but could not.

At my arrival, she opened her eyes and stared right at me. "Mother!"

Her scream broke Napoleon's concentration and he turned to look behind him and saw my ghost of a form. "You have finally come. Now I can have both mother and daughter. Perhaps this is a good day."

I raised my left hand and willed magic to shoot forth and burn him from the earth, but nothing happened. I stood there powerless. My magic had fled me forever and now I had different magic from the throne of stone.

Napoleon squeezed tighter and began to choke Phoebe, but still he kept his eye on me. "Have you come to watch her die or will you surrender?" His hand glowed hot and Phoebe screamed in pain.

Not knowing what else to do, I rushed forward and tried to grab his arm but I could not make contact with him. I was a ghost and could not touch him. He grinned at me, like the devil he was, and pulled more of Phoebe's magic from her. She tried to pull her hands up to grab him or push him away but she remained bound to the wooden pole. "Help me, Mother. Please get him off of me." She choked the words out and could say no more.

"Let her go." I raised my arms and pulled toward me and the air stirred. The light and air answered being sucked into my awaiting hands and Napoleon was pulled from Phoebe. She gasped for air and I could see her left hand lighting up with her magic. I needed to give her more time.

"Tonight it will all be over. I will rid myself of you and have your daughter's magic." He rushed me with his drawn sword but his attacked passed through me.

"If you leave now, I will let you live. But if you stay, I will haunt you for the rest of my days. You will not win, you will not thrive, you will not rest without me whispering into your ear."

I do not know if it were my voice or how I looked, but he paused and did consider my offer. Phoebe saw him hesitate and she burned away the ropes around her and she ran toward Napoleon with her left hand lit with magic. She screamed at him with all her hatred and fierceness and he turned on her and attacked her with his sword.

"No!" I pulled at the air again and the room shifted and went dark. All light and air came to me and I left only the void. He would not win. He would not harm my daughter. I would sacrifice everything for her. The world darkened and I opened my eyes.

Jeremiah held my hand. His face looked white and I saw blood running down his arm, down mine and into the stone throne. "You have come back."

"I must go back. I must. He is about to kill her. Please, let go of me." I tried to pull away but my body was too weak.

The Silver Fox came beside me and put his hand on Jeremiah. "Let her go back. She can finish this and all will be over. He is almost defeated."

I saw that Charley and a young woman stood near the throne and I begged them, "Please, let me go back."

Jeremiah turned toward the young woman. "Veronika, please don't help her. This is the only way."

Veronika and Charley went to Jeremiah and Charley was the first to put his hand on his friend's shoulder. "Let her go. Let her go save her daughter." Veronika hung back unsure of who to help.

"But she will die." Jeremiah clung tighter to my hand and he turned away, looking for an ally but could find none.

"I will help you." The Silver Fox pushed Jeremiah away from me and took his place.

Jeremiah fell off to the side and grabbed at his wounded hand. "You would do that for us?"

The Silver Fox rolled up his sleeve and then took Jeremiah's knife and cut his arm. The blood flowed freely from the wound onto the stone throne. "Yes. She can take my strength and my body and I will leave this plane forevermore and be trapped in the Otherside. For all the harm I have caused Cinderella and her mother, I choose to help you both. I have always loved Cinderella as my own daughter and this is what I can do to aid her."

I tried to push the Silver Fox away but I could not do so. "No, please, just let me go. I don't want anyone's help. I must do this on my own." I tried to pull back from him but my back simply rested against the hard stone back of the throne.

"You will take my strength and I will fade from here forever. Just remember me and call me by my new name. I'm the Golden Fox now. The Silver Fox is no more." I could see that he had already made up his mind. He smiled at me and said, "Good-bye."

The Golden Fox closed his eyes and I felt a surge of energy come into me. I watched and his blood coursed from his body onto me and the stone throne. A brilliant light shone forth from his open wound and I could see him fading away fast. I took a deep breath and then his body vanished within me. I reached out to Jeremiah, but the room changed and the last image I saw was of him rushing to my side.

When the dreamline opened, the light came into being and I saw Napoleon standing before Phoebe. He still had his hand around her neck and she gasped for breath.

"Let her go!" I rushed forward, but I had my body with me now. The Golden Fox's magic had cast me through the dreamline. I pulled him away from Phoebe. Her pale face scared me. She did not look well.

He turned on me and unleashed his hatred. He had great power to defeat Mab and me, but I had a secret now. He could not win against me and the Golden Fox's power. Together, as one, I blocked his attack using the magic of the stone throne and then lit my hand with pure white magic. It had been so long since I had last done that. Real magic and not the sick source from the stone throne. This was magic of the heart and of my spirit and of the Golden Fox's. Entwined together, I rushed at him and my magic burned through his spell of hatred. The red sphere of light that he attacked me with emanated from his right hand, but I put my hand on his chest and yelled, "No! I cast you back. I send you away from here to go back from whence you came. Defeated and never to return again. You will never step back in this land. You will never win as my magic will act as a barrier to protect these people. You are cast off and have lost. Go!"

Napoleon struggled to fight me but he fell to his knees and my spell seared through his and the red light that had streamed from his hand evaporated away like dew on flowers in the heart of a summer morning. His power dried up and I pushed harder and could feel the Golden Fox within me. His magic nourished me and gave me hope.

Napoleon raised his hands over his head to try and defend himself, but could not block my spell. "I will never surrender. I will never lose. I am undefeatable." He pushed himself up to his feet and I expected him to rush me but he turned and pulled a knife from his belt and lunged at Phoebe. And time stopped, or so I hoped. I saw him rushing forward and I expended every last ounce of energy from my body, both mine and the Golden Fox's, toward Napoleon and around Phoebe. I saw her cry out and I could feel the stone throne, pulling me back again. I fought hard and focused and let go of all that I was to win this moment and to be there for my daughter.

Napoleon fell back from Phoebe and I saw her head fall back and she closed her eyes. I sent my last bit of energy at her but it was too late. A shock passed through me and I opened my eyes and again Jeremiah held my hand. The Golden Fox had collapsed at my feet.

"No, no, no. I have to go back. I must go back." I could barely lift my arm and tried to say more but I could not erase Phoebe from my head.

The Golden Fox reached up at me and said in a weak voice, "It is done." He lowered his head and turned away. Jeremiah and Charley moved to help him but it was already too late. Veronika looked on as the Golden Fox fell to the cold floor.

Before anyone could reach his side, a blinding light materialized beside the Golden Fox and took shape. A tall man appeared holding a cat in his arms.

"Tristan?" Charley asked in surprise.

"Yes, it is I." He held his cat Misty in his one arm and bent down to touch the Golden Fox's forehead. A yellow light surrounded the Golden Fox and his eyes fluttered.

Jeremiah stood by me on the stone throne and asked, "What are you doing here?" By instinct, he reached for his pistols on his back, but they had long been lost.

Tristan waved at Veronika and she backed away in fear. "I am here for my cousin the fox. None of you have need to fear me."

I gathered my strength and asked, "What are you going to do with him? He saved my life."

The Golden Fox stirred but still remained unconscious. Tristan snapped his fingers and the Golden Fox vanished from the room. "He will be with me now on the Otherside. That is where all the faeries have gone to. We have moved on from this world onto the next." Seeing that I had started to ask a question, he shook his head. "No, there will be no questions. Trust in that he will be safe and he will be on holiday. For how long, I cannot say, but he will need time to heal and then we shall see."

"See what?" Charley asked.

"I believe it is impossible for you to resist asking questions." Tristan shook his head. "Fare thee all well." He started to snap his finger but stopped and said, "No one has ever escaped from the Otherside. You all are the first. I'm impressed." He tipped an imaginary hat at us and then snapped his fingers and vanished from the room.

Charley came forward and Veronika stared at me with such great fear that I knew that I must be near death myself. But none of it mattered. "Where is Phoebe?"

Jeremiah said, "I do not know." He took both my hands in his and I saw him wince as the cut on his palm was tender still though it had stopped bleeding. "Stand up and let us go."

I began to cry. I pulled my hands from his and covered my face and kept crying. "Just leave me here. It is all done. Napoleon will head back to Paris, the Russians will chase him back there and men will overcome the once great Napoleon. I can see that now. I can see it all. But here I must stay."

"No, I want you to come with me." Jeremiah grabbed my hands again in his. "We will live. Do not say such things. Come with me."

"I can't. Phoebe is gone. I am lost and am too tired. Just leave me be."

Jeremiah squeezed my hands tight. "Please, do not give up. You were once a princess and a witch of great strength. You are a Chronicler. And you are the woman I love. Please, come with me."

I admired him for his strength. I always would. "I can't accept your help. I don't need to be rescued. I just need some time by myself and I will be fine."

"Cinderella, I will say this once and I will only say it once." He pulled away from me and let go of my hands. He stood before the throne and put his right hand out to me. "Please, accept my help. Let go of your pride and take my hand. I am not here to save you. I am here to help you. There's a difference."

I looked around and saw that Charley and Veronika had left the room. I did not know where they had gone, but it was only Jeremiah who remained. I looked at him and saw greatness there. He had a subtle and hard greatness that would be good for me. I had to decide as I always had whether to be saved or to save myself. But this time was different. This time I realized that the choice I made would set me on a path for the rest of my life.

Jeremiah stood there with his hand out to me and I thought about what I would do. Now that Phoebe was lost to me, Napoleon on his downward spiral toward defeat, what would I do? More importantly, who was I but a defeated and tired woman who had wasted so much time, chasing after fairy tales. I did not need Jeremiah to live. I did not need to be rescued, but what would my life be like to have a partner who would support me, listen to me and for me to do the same for him? I had always chased after love, being more in love with love itself. I got wrapped up in the moment, in the person, in the emotion and that delusional feeling of being so much more than who I currently was, but that never lasted or could be sustained. And I crashed to the ground and became broken and alone.

I had seconds left and Jeremiah would lower his arm and turn away forever. I could feel the stone throne under me, around me and that it had become a part of me. I did not know how I would ever leave this room. The doorway looked so far away. But it would be the first step to raise my arm and reach for him. I did so and held his gaze and he smiled at me. He came forward and grabbed my hand and squeezed tightly.

He looked down at me. "I believe in you. Now get up."

Doubt swirled around my head. I dug deep and realized that my magic had truly vanished. I had nothing left but the magic within the throne and that would only keep me a prisoner and I would waste away here until the end of my days. A thought came to me unbidden. I wanted to see the sun with my own eyes and stand on my own two feet. I wanted to walk around in the daylight and learn to enjoy life. An ache came to me and I knew that I had to get up. I wanted to hold Phoebe's body close to mine, to kiss her one last time and then let her go. I had tried so hard to find her and, after all this time, I had, but it had been too late. The whole journey seemed pointless in the end and there was no grand victory. Everything had just petered out and life had gone on.

I leaned forward and my back peeled away from the throne. It was hard but I pushed myself up with my one arm and Jeremiah simply held my hand. He didn't pull at me. He only helped to balance me. I cried out loudly and stood up and fell forward and Jeremiah stopped me from falling and then backed away, but still held my hand. A smile grew on his face. "You did it. I knew you could. Come with me now. Someone has waited a long time to see you."

"How?" I asked, but he did not answer and only smiled. I then saw that Charley had been waving and jumping up and down in joy at the entrance to the throne room.

My heart beat fast. I stumbled forward and never looked back. I think the throne crumbled away. Honestly, I didn't remember or care. I walked to the doorway and Jeremiah stood beside me and I gained more strength after each step. I felt weak and all my muscles ached, but hope kept me going. Hope sustained me. I stepped through the doorway and I was outside the hut. I stood on a platform and beneath me I could see the enormous chicken legs that protruded under the hut. I heard singing and music being played and Jeremiah went first down the stairs. I followed him and I saw at the bottom Charley and Veronika and between them stood Phoebe. Her long blond hair was tattered with dirt and grime and she had blood on her clothes, but she stood of her own accord.

I found it funny how I became so strong after seeing her. I pushed past Jeremiah and nearly fell down the remaining stairs. Phoebe ran to me, and I to her, and I wrapped my arms around her tight. I could smell her and feel her tears running down her cheek onto mine.

"Phoebe!" I called her name and it was one of joy and of such longing fulfilled. At long last, we had found each other again. I held my daughter in my arms and could not stop crying and my tears turned to ones of joy as I held her close. I lost track of how long we stayed that way.

Phoebe kept her arms around me and said, "Thank you for coming for me. I have missed you so!"

I kissed her on the forehead and Jeremiah came up to us and led us to a tent. I could see the remains of Napoleon's grand army all around us. Someone told me later that he had fled in the night and rumor was that he had deserted his army and gone back to Paris in his carriage with his guard. His army had begun to crumble and they had moved onward, without him. That day we ate, drank and played music until the sun went down. I kept Phoebe close to me and that night I slept with her in my arms.

When I woke the next morning, I saw Jeremiah on the floor bundled in some clothes. Charley and Veronika had made breakfast for us and we ate watching the sun rise. I saw the rising sun and the light shone on Phoebe's blond hair and it lit us all up with beauty and hope. I fell back asleep and relaxed for the first time in almost two years. When I awoke, we were no longer in Europe.

"Where are we?" I did not recognize the house that I was in.

Phoebe sat in a chair next to my bed and said, "We are all back in America. I opened the dreamline and brought us to Charley's house. Ginny will want to come up to see you. She has been worried about you." She looked older and wiser now that I had time to really watch her, but still had an air of innocence about her.

"Where did you learn to use the dreamline?" I could feel no magic in my veins and for once that did not bother me. I had more than magic now.

"I had watched you when we were last together. It's a long story, but a witch named Isabelle had kept me from using my full powers so that we couldn't find each other. Now that she and Napoleon are both gone, my full powers are starting to return."

"I am happy for you." I sat up in bed and gave her a big hug.

"Mom, maybe one day you'll regain your magic. Do not give up hope." She returned the hug. "I'm going downstairs to say good-bye to Veronika. She's headed out, going into town, staying with one of Charley's cousins."

I glanced around and saw another bed by me and could tell that someone had slept in it. "Is Jeremiah here as well?"

"He's downstairs. He never left your side while you rested." Phoebe waved at me and bounded out of the room still like a child. "I'll see you later."

I wrapped a blanket around me and had a few minutes to look out the window to see the light snow that covered the ground. But soon I heard someone coming up the steps and Ginny entered the room. She sat at the end of the bed and smiled. "It is so good to see you doing better. When you first arrived, you looked pale and exhausted." She adjusted the blankets on me and asked, "Are you hungry?"

"Yes, I am." I searched around for some clothes and Ginny brought some over to me. She helped dress me and held my hair back as I washed up. I still was weak and it would take some time for me to heal and to regain my strength.

"Thank you for taking care of me."

"I have not done much. It was Jeremiah who took care of you the last three days." She made the bed I had slept in and saw my surprised look. "You didn't know that?"

"I don't remember anything after waking up in the battlefield after we defeated Napoleon. Everything after that is blank." I shivered and wrapped a sweater around me for warmth.

"Let's get you by the fire and I will prepare some breakfast for you."

I agreed and together we came down the stairs and she led me to the kitchen. There I saw the rest of the Radley clan running about, helping to cook and setting the table. Charley saw me first and gave out a happy cry. He had a several month old baby in his arms. He hugged me gently as to not harm the baby and said, "I'm happy to see you doing better."

"Thank you." I allowed myself to be led along into a dining room.

The rest of the children then all came over to me. Ruth, their littlest girl, wrapped herself around my left leg and then tugged at my blouse.

"Did you meet my baby sister yet?" Ruth let go of me long enough to pull her father over. "Her name is Ella. I picked the name after you."

"I am so honored. Thank you all for everything." I could feel tears overwhelming me, but the door opened then and Jeremiah came in from the cold carrying an armful of wood. He went over to the stove and piled the wood next to it.

Ginny leaned over to me and whispered. "It is true that he never left your side while you slept. He's a good man."

"I know." I squeezed her hands. "I'm so thankful for all that you have done for Phoebe and me."

"I'm just glad that Charley came home safe. Raising the girls on my own would not have been easy." She reflected a moment and then added, "And I would have missed him after a while." Her joke caught me off guard and I laughed.

Charley handed the baby to Ginny and then went to give Jeremiah a mug of hot cider and we all sat down to a wonderful breakfast. Jeremiah sat next to me on my left and Phoebe on my right. Charles, Ginny and their children filled out the table. It was a tight fit but we ate, joked and after we cleaned up, the children went outside to play. Ginny took Ella down for a nap and at last Jeremiah and I sat alone by the fire. I could not remember the last time I had a chance to relax and just enjoy the moment. I thought no words would be spoken and we would simply enjoy our time together, but a thought came to my mind and I needed to speak.

"Thank you for coming after me. I shouldn't have left on my own. But I saw a chance and needed to try and find Phoebe." I paused for a moment and then added. "Without your help, I don't think I would have been able to survive. Thank you."

"Next time, I would appreciate your listening to me. We make a good team." He crossed his leg over his other, leaned back in his chair and took a sip of warm cider.

I could smell the cloves and the nutmeg from it and lifted my own mug to my lips. "We do make a good team." I turned away from the fire and risked it all. "Will you marry me?"

I didn't know if he would mind my saying the words, but so much had happened between us over the last two years and I did not wish to risk a chance to be happy. I had wasted too much of my life already.

"Yes, but ..." He stopped talking, paused a few moments and then said, "I have one condition."

"What is it?" I couldn't tell if he were joking or serious.

"You must know that I love you for who you are and not what you used to do. I don't care if you have magic or don't or any of that. I need to know if you're comfortable with that as well. I want us to be happy and to build a life together and not chase after the past. Do you agree?"

I sighed and leaned over to him and punched him in the arm. "You scared me. I didn't know what you were going to ask."

He laughed and put down his mug. "Come here, please."

I did so and sat on his lap and we kissed. I could hear a piece of wood crackling in the fire and his lips tasted like cider. He wrapped his arms around me and then held my face in his hands. "You frightened me. I didn't think I would ever see you again. I thought I had lost you forever and that you had truly gone over the edge and chosen to be lost, but I was wrong."

"I have a long way to go in setting things right, but I know what I want now. I'm tired of chasing after rainbows and of faeries and magic and adventure. I want to build a family with you and Phoebe. I want to build a home. But what about you? You're a witch hunter."

He smiled and tapped me lightly on the forehead. "I found my witch. She's already got my heart. I want to build a home with you and raise Phoebe and to be near the Radleys. Let's buy some land near them and we can raise our children together."

"Yes, let's do that. Together." I leaned into him and kissed him and before I could disengage myself from him, Phoebe came running into the room.

"Mom, can I go hiking with the others and ..." She stopped dead still when she saw us kissing.

I stood up and felt a bit embarrassed and asked, "Phoebe, I know that we have not been together a long time and I will wait if you would like, but Jeremiah and I have decided to marry."

Phoebe smiled and rushed forward and hugged us both. "Can we live near here and have friends to play with and can I go to a real school?"

Jeremiah ruffled her hair. "We were just talking about that. Looks like we all want the same thing."

Phoebe kissed me on the cheek and squeezed us tight and then rushed outside. I could hear her screaming at the top of her lungs, "My mom is getting married. Come here everyone! Come here! And we're going to live right near here!"

I could hear the screams from the other girls and knew that we only had a few moments left before the chaos from outside tumbled back into the house. Soon we would be surrounded again and there would be many questions and hugs and kisses and I welcomed it all. But first, I wanted to kiss Jeremiah again. I kissed him on the lips and I took his hands in mine and said, "Thank you for not giving up on me. I know that I have stumbled along the road and that I have not made things easy for you, but I have found my way. I had to do it on my own. I know that might not make sense, but I can be a prideful person."

"You, have lots of pride? Never!" He laughed and I put my hand on his lips to silence him.

"And you're never prideful?" He tried to take my hand off his mouth to respond but I did not move my hand. I shook my head and then said, "For a long time, I did not think myself good enough to be loved and I kept choosing the wrong person. And then it came to me that I had to love myself first. It's such a funny thing, but then I nearly lost everything again. I needed to find Phoebe and to be there for her. I needed to do that. Can you understand?"

He moved my hand from his mouth. "Yes, I can. We will not always see things the same, but for now, let's enjoy the moment. Let's allow ourselves to be happy."

"Yes, let's."

We kissed again and this time the children all came in. Ginny came into the room as did Charley and we shared with them all the good news. I had found Phoebe, such great friends and I had also found myself. I had always wanted a happily ever after, but there are no such things. There are times of great joy and of sadness and hurt. Life is like that. I realize that now. I realize that I am blessed and loved beyond compare and it started with myself. I needed to make a simple decision to love myself. I know it sounds trite and strange, but to love myself is a lesson that took me a long, long time to learn. I hope you do not take as long to learn the lesson. Know it well. For there will be dark days along with the bright and it will be between the two that you most will live and that is where it matters most.

The End of Book 3

Want to find out what happens to Cinderella's daughter Phoebe?

Read the first chapter of Ron Vitale's *Faith: The Jovian Gate Chronicles* (book 1):

Chapter 1

Jacob glanced down at his left foot and cursed. He peeled away the wrap and exposed his bruised ankle. Blood had pooled in the soft, fleshy part by his heel. A red line in his skin marked the spot where the temporary semi-cast bit into his skin. Slightly swollen, his foot looked like a piece of overcooked ham. He touched his foot and could still feel it, which he thought a good sign, and then wiggled his toes.

He heard movement behind him and placed his hand on his gun.

"Here's that bucket of ice water that you wanted." An old man dropped the container next to Jacob and some water splashed out. "I've got some kits here that would heal your foot up *tout suite*."

"No thanks." Jacob lifted his foot with care and then slowly lowered it into the container. The shock from the icy water shot up his leg, but felt good on his swollen foot. "I appreciate your offer, but I don't believe in any of those kits."

"Are you one of those neo-Luddites or whatever they're calling themselves these days?"

"Maurice, how long have you known me?"

"Long enough to know that you still don't get my jokes or know when I'm kidding around." Maurice scratched his butt and then sat on a chair next to Jacob. "But I got to ask you something."

Jacob stared down at the ice in the container and concentrated on ignoring the cold. "Ask away."

"I've helped you in a pinch many times over the years, but this is the first time that you've asked me for a Faraday room. Dropping out of contact for a bit and not being able to be tracked probably means you're in some serious shit. I can get you connected with people who can help you disappear." Maurice waited for Jacob to respond and then said, "I'm worried about you."

Jacob took his foot out of the icy water and said, "I might take you up on that one day soon, but not now. I'm a little banged up, but

I'll be okay. I just need to check out for a bit."

"I'll keep the offer open for whenever you need it. You helped me when I first came off ship, and I'll never forget that. You're from good people, and that means something to me." Maurice patted Jacob on the back. "You need anything else before I head out for the night?"

"Yes, I do." Jacob reached inside his weathered coat and pulled a piece of paper out and handed it to his friend.

Maurice took it in awe. "Where the hell did you get this low tech?" He stared at the picture of young woman. Furtive glance, shoulder-length brown mousy hair with a pretty face. "Last time I saw something like this was in a museum."

"I need you to look for her through your connections. Off the grid. I don't want to be tracked back."

"I'll use my back channels to start looking for her and keep it offline. What did she do?" He handed the photo back.

Jacob put his foot back into the icy water and shivered. "Nothing that I'm aware of, but she's attracted some powerful friends, and I need to find her."

"She get mixed up in the wrong crowd and now her parents want her back?"

"Something like that. It's a bit complicated."

"Complication avoidance is my specialty. Anything I need to be aware of before I start asking around?"

"She was last seen with some Lan'khamire." He turned to Maurice to watch his reaction.

"Jacob, that's some serious shit she's involved in. No one messes with the Kindred."

"I know. That's why I said it's a bit complicated."

"And you're out here, using decades old technology, hiding away in this Faraday room with me. Now it's all coming together. If the Lan'khamire tracked you back here, we'll both be dead by morning. You understand that, right?"

"I do. I wouldn't have come back here unless I had nowhere else to go." Jacob winced and then glanced down to reposition his foot in the water.

"Here, let me see that." Maurice knelt in front of the container, and with care, lifted Jacob's foot out of the water. Swollen and discolored, Maurice probed at different parts of the foot with his thumbs. Touching the sides of the foot, he massaged it and asked, "Does any of that hurt?"

"Nah. It's the back of the ankle." Jacob bent over and measured the spot that hurt with his thumb and index finger. "It hurts here."

Maurice shook his head and grunted. "Let me see." He glided his thumbs down the back of Jacob's left leg from the calf muscle and worked his way down to the heel.

Jacob flinched. "There. Yep, hurts right there. You think it's my Achilles?"

"I don't know, but we're going to find out." Maurice placed Jacob's foot back down on the ground with care.

"I told you that I don't want any help."

Maurice pulled himself up to his full height. In his prime, he was an attractive man, but now with his hair long and white, and his thin and scraggly look, he was a shell of the man he once was. "You're stubborner than a Zebrule! Get up now. I told you that I would help you, and I'm not gonna use any tech on you. I might be old, but I'm not deaf, and I still know a thing or two. Come on."

He lifted Jacob out of the chair and led him into the next room. Careful not to put his injured leg on the ground, Jacob hopped and leaned on Maurice. The lights flickered on, and Maurice led Jacob toward an examination table. The equipment appeared old, but in good condition. Plastic shelves were filled with boxes of medical supplies. "Welcome to my urgent care facility." He helped Jacob onto the table and dangled his feet off the edge. "Get on your belly. I'm going to check to see if you ruptured your Achilles."

Jacob obeyed and shimmied to the center of the narrow table and turned himself onto his stomach. He tried not to rip the paper cloth covering, but failed. "I never knew that you had a full-service facility."

"What, you think that I have a Faraday room just for politicians to fall off the map for a few hours so they can have their side trysts? I've a full medical facility here and can perform most surgeries both on and offline." He rolled up Jacob's left pant leg and then did the same with the right. "You're not the first person who has needed help and wanted to hide away for a bit. It's actually a lucrative side business for me. Keeps me off the streets at nights and weekends."

"You're crazy, you know that?" Jacob smiled and folded his arms in front of him and rested his head there. He looked around the room and saw posters of the human muscular system with separate charts for the foot, knee, and chest.

"Okay, I'm going to test your good leg first." He massaged and pushed together the top calf muscle and watched Jacob's right foot move slightly. "Good, good." Maurice moved to the left leg and positioned his fingers above Jacob's calf. "Does that hurt?"

"Nope."

He moved his hands down farther and squeezed the muscle together as he did for the right leg and saw no movement in Jacob's left foot. "Anything hurt when I do that?"

"Feels tender, but it doesn't hurt," Jacob replied.

"Well, I have good news and bad news. Which do you want first?" Maurice placed Jacob's leg back on the table and his swollen foot hung off the table like a piece of discolored meat.

"Give me the bad news first."

"I can't be for sure, but I think you've torn your Achilles. If you let me do some tests, I can know for sure." Maurice saw that Jacob wanted to speak, but he continued. "With two kits, I can have this fixed up for you fast, and you'll be walking again in about a week."

Jacob interrupted and said, "Can't do kits or tech. Neither are an option."

"You understand that I want to help you, right? I'm not here to hurt you. Do you not trust me?" Maurice sat down on a stool and wheeled closer to his friend.

"It's not that." Jacob reached over with his arm and squeezed Maurice's hand. "I have to do this clean and clear. I can't chance being tracked. Too much is at stake."

Maurice kept quiet for a moment. "You're in deeper than I thought. You're not worried about anyone here in Tycho city, are you?"

Jacob kept silent and shook his head.

"I understand." Maurice ran his hands through his long white hair. "Okay, I got an idea. You're not going to like it, but it's the best that I'll be able to do for you without using kits." He sprang up off the stool and went over to the shelves and rummaged through several of the containers. "Here we go. I haven't used this in a few years, but it'll do the job nicely. Old school and no tech, just like you want."

"What is it?" Jacob pulled himself up off the medical table and swung his legs over the side to sit up. The throbbing in his left ankle bothered him, but he took a breath to focus and allowed the pain to wash through him.

"It's plaster. I'm going to set you up in a nice cast. You'll need to wear it for six to eight weeks and need extensive rehabilitation once you try to walk back down on Earthside, but it'll get you where you need to be. I'll put you in the cast and then give you a medical boot to stabilize it. That's the best I can do."

Jacob turned his foot over and lifted it up to deal with the pain. "Do it. I need to be out of here soon in case they come after me. I don't want you mixed up in any of this."

"It's too late for that, Jacob. Way too late for that." A deep voice, almost monstrous-like, spoke from the doorway.

Jacob reached for his gun and turned around to see who spoke. Over seven feet tall, gaunt, and dressed all in white, the Lan'khamire's face had a tan complexion with skin stretched taut, resembling a desiccated mummy. He had long limbs, and his fingers, longer than a human's, were curled around a pulse weapon. He aimed as Jacob dove off the medical table and fired. A screaming-hot white bolt sizzled through the air and missed but exploded into the shelves on the far side of the room. Jacob fired back, but his two shots went wide into the wall.

Maurice dove down and reached for a control stick in his pocket. He pressed the red button on the stick and the red emergency lights went on and the alarm sounded. The loud noise and flashing light distracted the Lan'khamire for a moment. Long enough for Jacob to take cover behind the medical table and take aim. He fired a shot off, but was too late. The Lan'khamire rushed forward with a burst of speed and threw over the table.

"Come here, now." The Lan'khamire's voice echoed loud in the room, and his commanding voice froze Jacob. "Lower your weapon and attend me."

Jacob's mind resisted, but his body complied. He dropped his gun and knelt on the ground, turning his neck to the Lan'khamire. The alien's emaciated face was almost too perfect with high cheekbones yet hid a mouth filled with rows of sharp pointy teeth. Jacob knew what would come next, but still he could not resist.

The Lan'khamire smirked and then bared its teeth and bent down to embrace Jacob. He would feed on him, but not too much. Oblivious to Maurice, he rolled back his eyes and prepared to feast.

Maurice grabbed a glass jar filled with liquid, unscrewed the top and then rushed up to the Lan'khamire. "Hey, buddy, I got something for you."

The Lan'khamire turned, and on contact, the liquid burned into his skin. Grabbing at his face, the Lan'khamire turned away and lost his concentration. Jacob regained control of his body, and Maurice helped him stumble out of the medical facility. He locked the door behind him and pulled his control stick out of his pocket. "Trish, authorization one, one, two, c, four. Eject medical facility now."

The computer's voice asked, "Can you confirm your command?"

"Dammit, just eject the room now!" Maurice shouted into the control stick and backed away from the door when he heard the Lan'khamire pounding against it.

Jacob grabbed at his leg and saw the door buckling under the force of the Lan'khamire's punches. He searched around for a weapon but could not find one. Jacob pushed back against the wall and waited in fear.

The room's lights went off and the alarms stopped. Maurice heard Jacob's and his breathing and nothing else. The pounding had stopped.

"Medical facility ejected," Trish said without emotion.

The room's normal lights flickered back on and Jacob slumped back against the wall, exhaling slowly.

Maurice pulled himself to his feet and checked on Jacob. "Now let's get that leg of yours fixed."

"What about the Lan'khamire?" Jacob asked.

"He's stuck in the medical facility room somewhere on the surface of the moon. Once his friends find him, they'll come after us." Maurice spoke again into the control stick. "Trish, move the ship now. Random pattern with a twist of Beethoven thrown in."

"Moving rooms now," Trish responded and sounded bored.

"We'll have a little bit of time now, but we have to get out of here fast."

"That's fine with me. I already know where I'm headed after this." Jacob accepted Maurice's help and together they limped down the hallway.

***

Jacob touched the cast that went up to just below his kneecap on his left leg and grimaced. "I'm still in pain."

"Do you want the good news or the bad news?" Maurice washed his hands in a sink and then dried them on a towel.

"Isn't everything bad news today?" Jacob stretched his leg out and tried to get accustomed to the heavier weight.

"You can't bear any weight on your leg for at least six weeks." Maurice held up his hands when he saw Jacob start to protest. "Wait, there's more. I can't guarantee that the cast is going to fix your rupture, and like I said earlier, you're going to need extensive rehabilitation whenever you need to get back down to Earth, but I expect you're not headed that way, are you?"

"What's the good news?" Jacob's scowl hung heavy on his face.

"Well, you're not dead. You're lame as a duck, and if you go full zero G you'll have to deal with all sorts of swelling and pain, but outside of that you'll be good. I think." Maurice gently patted Jacob's cast. "Now tell me what your plan is since you nearly got me killed."

Jacob tried to get up, but Maurice held him down. Jacob acquiesced and leaned back against the wall. "I need to get off the moon and head to Mars. That should get the Lan'khamire off my trail for a bit. There's not too many of them there. And it'll give me a chance to regroup and figure out my next steps."

"So, basically, you don't have a plan, do you?" Maurice shook his head and laughed. "If you have the Lan'khamire after you, going to Mars isn't going to stop them from coming. If he could, I bet our friend back in the medical facility would be walking across the moon's surface now to come after us. You're just lucky he didn't get a taste of your blood. He'd then track you to your grave."

"I know." Jacob glanced down at his leg. "But I need to get out of here. The less you know, the better it'll be for you. Trust me."

"I know you're trying to protect me, but you're not going to get far if you don't make some connections and get some help. You'll wind up drained and left for dead on the surface. It happens enough, and the officials turn a blind eye. Please, let me help you." Maurice went to say more but was interrupted by the computer.

"Destination complete. Navigation reset values randomized and prepared for next departure. Do you wish for me to head to our next scheduled pickup?" Trish asked.

"No, cancel all requests. In ten minutes, take us to the South Pole–Aitken basin." Maurice glanced back at Jacob. "We'll get you off this rock, but I think you'll need a slow ship to Mars. That'll give you more time to heal."

"Thank you." Jacob put his hands around the cast. "Do you have crutches so that I can get around?"

"Once you're in zero G, you'll be fine, but you'll need to take these each day." Maurice handed him a bottle of pills.

"What is it?" Jacob frowned and held them skeptically in his hand.

"It's a blood thinner. With your leg all messed up and being in zero G, you'll need it." Maurice handed him a second bottle of pills. "And take these, too. They're pain killers. Nothing in these will put a nano in your blood. You won't be able to be tracked by either of these. Just take the blood thinner every day and the pain blocker as needed."

"I don't know what to say." Jacob reached out and shook Maurice's hand.

"Don't worry about it. It's the least I can do for all you've done for me over the years." Maurice let go of Jacob's hand and smiled. "I just hope that girl you're chasing after is worth it."

"Trust me, she is." Jacob took out the photo he had and stared at it.

"Well, that's good. Let me go get you a knee crutch so that you can at least hobble around. I know I got one lying around somewhere. Trish, can you locate a knee crutch for me?"

The computer was silent for a few seconds. "Storage room B. I'll have one of the mech droids bring it to you."

Jacob shook his head. "No bots. I don't want them to see me."

Maurice nodded. "Trish, no need to do that. I'll go pick it up as it's only around the corner from here." He turned to Jacob. "You do know that Trish is recording everything we've seen and done, right?"

"But I also know that you regularly wipe her memory and expect you'll do the same as soon as you get me out of here. You'll not want that run in with the Lan'khamire to be saved anywhere."

"You know me well." Maurice smiled. "I planned on ditching the entire ship and starting fresh. Can't be too careful with something like this."

"That's what I thought. And I'd do the same thing if I were you. Trust me, you want no records left. None." Jacob balanced on one foot and hopped over to the nearest counter and practiced moving.

"I foresee an unfortunate accident that takes place with this ship. That's what you get when you use old equipment. It can fail at any time." Maurice walked out of the room and turned back. "I'm just getting you your knee crutch. I'll be right back."

"Doesn't look like I'm going anywhere anytime soon." Jacob balanced on his good leg and put his hands up in the air.

"Why don't you get some rest in the meantime? Put your leg up and look out a port window. It's going to take some time to dock and for me to get refueled."

Jacob glanced at the door and shook his head. "I keep thinking the Lan'khamire's going to burst through any minute and come kill us."

Maurice opened the door and stared down the hallway and saw no one. "That's your adrenaline speaking. It keeps you on edge and alive. If you try to stay that way all the time, you'll burn yourself out and crash hard. Trust me, get some rest. I'll let you know if there are any issues that come up." Maurice headed out of the room into the corridor and stopped to turn around with a smile on his face. "Plus, you'd only be holding me up with that leg of yours."

"Funny." Jacob hopped over to the bed and climbed onto it with care. He pushed the instrument panel and the bottom of the bed elevated. Within a few seconds, he could feel a decrease in swelling in his foot as fluids flowed back out up through his leg. The lighter gravity made life a bit easier for him with his injury, but he expected that if he did have to travel back to Earth that the transition to full gravity would be difficult.

Jacob leaned back in bed and said, "Trish, can you make the port window translucent?"

"Certainly." Her voice appeared to come from all around and sounded as though he had surprised her. Maybe she had been working on something else and he had interrupted her.

In seconds, the port window cleared and he could not see much. "Shut off lights in the room, please."

Trish complied, and after a bit his eyes adapted to the low light. He could see the stars in the sky, but the moon's surface was black. With no sun, he could not see much.

Thoughts swirled through his head and each time he closed his eyes he could see the Lan'khamire lunging for him, trying to grab him and pull him down into a sea of darkness. Jacob jolted awake and saw that no one stood in the room. He was alone, injured but safe. He shook his head to clear his mind and then thought of her. He saw her smile and that way she played with her hair when distracted. Remembering her calmed him, and he allowed himself a moment of peace and rest. Where she had gone to, he could only guess, but he would not give up searching for her. He could not. Fighting to keep his eyes open as long as he could, he closed them for a few seconds and then drifted off into a deep sleep.

Purchase *Faith: The Jovian Gate Chronicles* (book 1) at:
http://hyperurl.co/xxpr10

ABOUT THE AUTHOR

Ron Vitale is a fantasy and science fiction author. He has a Master's degree in English Literature from Villanova University where he studied the works of Alice Walker and Margaret Atwood, interpreting their novels with a psychological Jungian approach by showing how the central female protagonists in their novels use storytelling as a means to heal themselves from trauma. He lives in a small town outside of Philadelphia, Pennsylvania.

In the fall of 2008, he published his fantasy novel *Dorothea's Song* as an audiobook on Podiobooks and for sale in the Amazon.com Kindle store, and in 2011 he published *Lost*, the first book in the Cinderella's Secret Diaries series, in 2012 the second book in the series, *Stolen*, was published and in 2014 the third book in the series, *Found* was released.

Ron has since published *Awakenings* and *Betrayals*, books 1 and 2, of *The Witch's Coven* series as well as *Faith*, the first book in the *Jovian Gate Chronicles*. He keeps himself busy by writing his blog, and on learning how to be a good father to his kids all while working on his next book.

Learn more at www.ronvitale.com

Made in the USA
San Bernardino,
CA